GOLD DRAGON

A RUN AND HIDE THRILLER

JJ MARSH

PREWETT
BIELMANN

Published by Prewett Bielmann Ltd.
All enquiries to admin@jjmarshauthor.com

First printing, 2021
eBook Edition:
ISBN 978-3-906256-15-3

Paperback:
ISBN 978-3-906256-16-0

To Maria Fátima Lima, my dear Portuguese amiga

1

The least Hong Kong could have done to welcome Olivia after travelling over three continents via five airports was to bring out the sun. Instead, weather and light levels were exactly as she had left them in northern Brazil: relentless, dispiriting rain and miserable darkness.

"Kwun Chung Street in Tsim Sha Tsui," she told the taxi driver, making an effort to sound in control despite her jet lag.

"Chungking Mansions?"

"Not in a million years, mate."

"Sorry?"

"Nothing," she muttered and gave him the piece of paper with the address to clear up any ambiguity. "Kwun Chung Street, number 7. Please."

"OK." He handed back the paper and lurched into the traffic. Olivia was transfixed by the lights. Everywhere was colour, blurred by watery windows, but bright and alive and buzzing with energy. She'd reached that phase beyond tired, where delirium was waiting in the wings. So many people, so much traffic, a total disconnection from the time of day, she had the impression she'd landed on an alien planet with no idea what was going on.

The cabbie's radio was playing something frantic and incomprehensible, a suitable soundtrack to her state of mind. She could not think about the past or the future, neither distant nor recent, merely focusing her attention on the immediate present. She needed a safe place to hide and sleep or she would collapse from exhaustion. Of the four flights, she'd only booked First Class on one intercontinental. Brasilia to Addis Ababa was a twelve-hour stretch and her full-length seat was comfortable and quiet. The fact her brain refused to rest was certainly not the fault of the solicitous air crew. A five-hour gritty-eyed layover in the Ethiopian capital persuaded her to splash out on an upgrade on the next leg. She would sleep until Bangkok, even if that meant consuming free champagne until she passed out.

Now she was hungover, disoriented and if she never saw another airport in her life, she could die happy. Endlessly changing electronic billboards assaulted her eyeballs and the synthetic wafts from the scented palm tree over the driver's mirror gave her a headache. She was about to burst into tears when the constantly lane-changing, braking and rapid accelerations came to a halt.

"Kwun Chung, number 7."

She paid him in US dollars with a tip and a silent prayer she would never suffer his driving again. Just in case, she waited till the cab had driven away before crossing the street to her actual destination – The Lucky Bee Residences. She lugged her backpack into the three-star hotel, checked in on a fake passport and paid for three nights in advance. Then she took a shower, drank half a litre of bottled water, secured her room and embraced oblivion for fourteen hours straight.

When she did regain consciousness, it seemed impossible anyone could sleep through such a racket. Traffic, horns, music, shouting from the street below and the rooms above, along with the on-off clatter of the air-conditioning unit outside her window came as such a contrast to her quiet shack on the beach she actually clamped her pillow around her head. The gesture was partly symbolic. As so often when her conscious mind was at rest, her subconscious was busy connecting random associations and images into a wildly incomprehensible narrative.

Flashes of her dreams returned, open to interpretation if she could only recall the detail. Fish? Yes, there'd been a brightly coloured fish with long iridescent blue stripes. He was trying to show her the way. He darted around her legs, glinting with promise, leading her deeper underwater, as eager and helpful as Nemo. She dived, trusting her neon guide, only to encounter a welter of black, suckered tentacles intent on grasping vulnerable prey. When she opened her mouth to scream, salt water rushed into her lungs.

She threw off the pillow and sat up in bed, taking deep breaths. The worst thing about such dreams was waking up before seeing what happened in the end. She told herself not to be ridiculous. Why the hell would she voluntarily replay such nightmares when the symbolism was clear? With a grunt, she collapsed backwards onto the mattress. The temptation was to curl under the bedclothes, block out the world and find peace. No such luck. She had a job to do. The question was, where to start?

Her stomach replied. *With breakfast, that's where.*

She swung her legs out of bed and took in her surroundings for the first time. The carpet was an industrial beige, with so many stains and bald patches they almost created a pattern. The bedside cabinet was taped shut and one glance at its broken hinges explained why. How this place merited three stars, she had no idea. In her exhaustion yesterday, she hadn't taken in the state of the bathroom, but now that she did, she opted to wear flip-flops. Three nights in this shit-hole? She washed her face and sighed. She had no choice.

The second she stepped onto the Kowloon street, she marvelled at how she'd thought the noise was bad from inside. The assault on all her senses was relentless. Humid air mixed with diesel fumes entered her lungs, limp and lacking in oxygen. People swarmed along the pavements at such a terrifying pace Olivia was amazed they didn't cannon into one another. Everyone was shouting, mostly into their mobile phones. The scent of food was everywhere, fragrant, spicy, burnt, meaty and confusing. Cars and trucks jostled for position on the road, while pushbikes and mopeds ducked and weaved through the smallest of gaps, many carrying ridiculous loads.

She pressed herself into the doorway and acclimatised to the chaos until she was able to gather her courage and step out into the Hong Kong sunshine. In seconds she was damp with sweat and craving her air-conditioned room. Street food stalls were ubiquitous and she browsed by looking at the pictures and checking the English description. Offal kebabs and deep-fried pig's guts did not appeal, but Cheung Fun sounded like ... fun. Rice noodle sheets rolled up like pasta with a choice of sauce. She ate a paper plateful with peanut and sesame topping, leaning on a stand-up table and watching the world go by. Braver now, she oriented herself with the map she had memorised on the plane. She turned right, heading towards the sea. Her need for water or greenery was a physical desire. Ducking through crowds, scarcely able to understand the ceaseless blast of advertising placards and desperate for some clean air, she cleaved to the walls until she came across the entrance to Kowloon Park.

It truly was an oasis, with a lake of flamingos, pavilions, fountains, lawns and views across the harbour to ease a troubled mind. The skyscrapers surrounding the verdant sanctuary reminded her of New York's Central Park, a curated wilderness in an urban jungle. Beneath canopies of palm trees and away from the hectic conurbation, she began to relax. Snakes or spiders waiting to drop on one's head were less likely here in this manicured forest than her little corner of Brazilian jungle. *Her jungle?* Olivia meandered along the paths, soothed by tai chi practitioners and painters, and charmed by the sound of birdsong from the aviary. She reached a viewing point and stared out across the harbour at Hong Kong Island. It seemed a long way away. As did her mission to seek a man who, like her, had been trained how to hide.

Is that where you are, Thanh? Or are you here, on the mainland, maybe even watching me from that bamboo thicket by the swimming pool?

She bought some green tea from a vendor on a bike and sat on a bench to make a plan. Koi carp swam in circles around the pool by her feet, triggering memories of her dream. She shook the thought away, still hypnotised by the patterns and movements of the fish. Her jet-lagged disorientation made thinking muddy and slow.

Think in stages, she reminded herself. *To go to Britain, you must be sure they won't arrest you at the border. To be sure you won't be taken into custody, you need to come to an arrangement with the Metropolitan Police. Even opening a dialogue is risky, which is why you have to find Thanh Ngo. To find Thanh ...*

That was where she stumbled. Somewhere in this crazy conglomeration was a man who did not want to be found. It would take every element of her ingenuity to locate him and only then could she begin to apologise. In the unlikely event he forgave her for what she had done, perhaps he would help. She reversed roles and imagined the situation the other way around. Had he cut and run, leaving her to fend for herself, could she forgive him?

To focus her mind, she repeated her sister's name. Katie.

Katie. Katie. The sister she had abandoned without a word, leaving her to care for their father alone. It was for the best, Olivia had told herself then and believed it still. Katie knew nothing, so could not be compromised. Now things had changed.

The hit man sent to kill Olivia failed in his mission, but hit his mark in a different sense. Her nemesis wanted the hired killer to deliver a message: *Tell her I've taken care of her sister.* What did that mean? They knew she couldn't just pick up the phone and check Katie was unharmed. She would have to return to the British Isles, come hell or high water. The only way to be sure neither her sister nor her father had suffered from the fallout of her own career was to go there and see for herself. They knew that. So did she. A voice in her head was whispering, *it's a trap! Don't do it!*

She answered aloud. "I'm not that stupid."

For the thousandth time, she asked herself what she was doing. Was there another way of seeing her family instead of flying to the Far East in the faint hope of begging a favour? Deep inside, she knew there must be. But since discovering Thanh was alive, she was consumed by the urge to see him. If he helped her return to Britain without fear of capture, he no longer considered her desertion an act of extreme selfishness. Then, perhaps, she could come to terms with her decision, let go of the guilt and exonerate herself. She constructed a haiku aimed at concentrating her will.

Find a betrayed man
Beg forgiveness and seek help
Defend those you love

A stall outside the swimming-pool was selling tea eggs. Olivia bought one and walked towards the water. The shell came away in pieces, leaving the egg white marbled with purple veins. It looked like something from the imagination of H.R. Giger. Olivia discarded the dyed shell in a bin and carried her patterned egg in her palm as she approached the expanse of water between Kowloon and the spectacle of Victoria Harbour. With minimal interest, she walked past shopping malls and exclusive hotels all the way down to the Avenue of Stars, where film celebrities were honoured with plaques and a wide promenade offered seating, shade and an admirable view.

She looked at the marbled egg in her hand and the island across the bay. Her chances of finding him were on a par with her hurling it over the water and hoping to hit land. Instead, she bit into it and swallowed. No matter how slim the chances, she had to try.

The Avenue of Stars was a good place to sit and think. For a start it was cooler and quieter by the harbour, enabling her to attune to her environment. Vine-covered structures in the shape of whale tails worked as sunshades, and the presence of water always helped calm her agitated mind. She sat on a bench and gave her mind and body permission to just be, letting thoughts come and go without direction.

Ferries chugged back and forth across the sea, loaded with passengers. A classic Chinese junk sailed majestically out to the horizon, probably for the tourists. Joggers ran along the promenade, sweating and panting. In this heat, they must be crazy. A light sparked in her subconscious but the second she trained her attention on the idea, it retreated into the shadows. She leaned back and looked up at the sky, with Bruce Springsteen on her mind. A jet crossed her vision, dragging its vapour trail and triggering unpleasant memories of her marathon journey from South America to East Asia. Endless hours of waiting, sitting, desperate for the clock to speed up so she could move on.

Then it clicked. The Bruce Springsteen connection.

When they used to work together, the hardest thing for

Thanh was sitting still. The man had the energy of a puppy, bouncing and bounding and pacing wherever there was enough room. Constrained by a police surveillance van, he fidgeted as if he had a flea. Once released, he had to move. Long-distance running, city marathons, moorland scrambles, anything where he pushed his physicality to its limits. A couple of times she'd joined him but it wasn't a happy experience for either runner. Olivia's jogs were not the companionable kind. She used the forward motion and pumping of her limbs to clear her mind. Another person tempering his speed to suit hers or chatting about their caseload had the opposite effect. Thanh was fitter and faster, with differing objectives. He was indeed 'Born to Run'.

The insight made her sit up and look around. There was every possibility Thanh Ngo was one of these men pounding the paving stones in front of her.

She hid. Thanh ran.

That sparked the first concrete thought of how to locate him. She walked back to the park entrance and read the billboards she didn't remember registering on the way in. The Hong Kong Marathon was due to take place at the end of October, by which time she'd be long gone. The cut-off date for registration was 1 September. She wasn't exactly sure of today's date after the time zone confusion but September must be two or three days away. If she could get into that website, Olivia was convinced she would find the Vietnamese ex-detective she'd left behind.

So to the next pressing issue – money, how to get some and where to keep it. On a Brazilian beach, it was easy to live off-grid and survive with little cash. Hong Kong was different. Besides, she also wanted to arrive with a full war chest in Europe. To get her hands on cash was one thing, storing it another. Opening a bank account was something she'd avoided since fleeing for her life. Each country had varying application procedures before letting you into the system, with most requiring a passport and a picture of her face. That was something to avoid at all costs.

Moving around under the radar while utilising modern technology was the only solution. She would store her cash as cryptocurrency in a digital wallet. And in order to keep the wallet completely anonymous, she would get the necessary software from the darknet. That tiny corner of the deep web, where one remained as traceable as a ghost, was notorious for unsavoury, illegal activities. Although its original purpose was to enable journalists or activists to report on stories and evade governmental censorship, alternative uses soon became prevalent. None of those appealed to Olivia, who simply needed financial muscle which was neither tracked nor searchable like the conventional web. Once established, she could use the cryptocurrency to pay for information, employ hackers, or convert the digital cash into hard currency.

On the walk back to her digs, she stopped in various different shops and bought three USB sticks. One she'd use to hold a miniature operating system that connected to the web and ran the digital wallet. Wherever she was in the world, she could insert that little box of tricks into any computer and boot into its RAM. Then she was free to surf all corners of the net and pay in cryptocurrency, without leaving a single trace once that computer was rebooted. The other two sticks would hold nothing more than her private keys and recovery keys to restore the digital wallet on any other device. Those were her back-up for the underground stash. If she lost these, she lost everything.

Everything? In other words, just under $1,000. It was all the money she had managed to bring with her and after paying for the taxi and her ratty little room, she was down to $800. Access to funds was becoming urgent. The most frustrating element was the knowledge that she had a handsome stockpile in a UK bank account but no means of reaching it. Once again, she wondered if clearing out her secret Channel Islands account to buy five flights was had been her wisest move. She rolled her shoulders. Olivia Jones was and always had been resourceful. She would find a way. Just as soon as she had found Thanh.

Olivia's attitude to a problem was a kind of philosophy. Start with the easy option but load the big guns. Prepare her digital wallet and then see how to fill it. But first, she had a go at hacking the marathon website itself. The database of registered runners was publicly available through her little laptop but personal details were blocked by a firewall.

She worked with what she had, trawling through 4,000 names. And that was just the standard marathon. Would Thanh enter the Elite race? Probably not, as it would leave him more exposed. She knew his face as well as she knew her sister's but had to take into account the cosmetic surgery factor. When a detective got a new identity, they went the whole nine yards. She checked 500 runners at a time, took a break and checked other websites to see if any IP address was watching the same stories as her. Tiring, eye-punishing work exhausted her and she lay down to rest, convinced the clamour from the street would keep her awake, but jet lag had other ideas.

Three hours later she awoke, thirsty, ravenous and her mind full of images: a pool in the jungle where she swims, basking in the sunlight through the trees, floating on her back and gazing at the infinitely blue sky. Beneath her, shimmering sands, glittering like a gilded mosaic. Her head dips underwater so only her nose and mouth break the surface. A man in uniform is shouting. She cannot hear his words and his image is fuzzy due to the water in her eyes. She dives and flicks her legs like a mermaid. In a few strokes, she is at the shore.

When her ears leave the water for the steamy air, his voice is still barking harsh words and she longs to sink lower to drown him out. He has a weapon, a trident, and points it at the pool. Whatever language he speaks is unfamiliar but she understands his demand via his actions. She must get out. There is danger in the water. She emerges, dripping and bereft. A fish out of water, yearning for the comfort of her warm, fresh, natural habitat. He stares into the pool, his eyes murderous, then jabs his weapon.

In a seismic reflex, the sandy bed shifts, twists and thrashes, mixing sand with red blood and black effluent. A huge fish, the size of a canoe, roils and writhes, expelling fluids Olivia knows are toxic. She watches, horrified, as the man kills the poisonous fish with stab after stab of his trident. Tears flow down her dream-face as she understands that all this time, she's been swimming peacefully in its golden pool.

The only response to such a subconscious sideswipe was a large cup of coffee. She used two of the little pods but gave the revolting processed milk a miss. The caffeine did its work, chasing nightmares out of her mind and emphasising the urgency of the present.

Find a betrayed man
Beg forgiveness and seek help
Defend those you love

Olivia checked her computer once again, casting her gaze over the names of every male runner, noting every single one of interest in a spreadsheet. Another spark flashed in the darkness, only to evade her gaze. Just like a damned cockroach. It drove her crazy when something just ducked out of sight, never to return if she sought it. Instead, she had to let it be and employ patience.

Her stomach gurgled, so she dressed and went in search of

a restaurant. Tonight, she wanted rice, fish, Tsingtao beer and prawn toast, ideally with no hassle. She got most of what she wanted.

A table for one in a bright, noisy diner. The place was only half full but incredibly loud. She attracted no attention from anyone, including the waiters, and had to physically accost someone before she managed to order Chinese beer, shrimp wontons in broth and silver fish fried rice. Families conversed in around large circular tables, using chopsticks like beaks to pluck items from the Lazy Susan in the middle. Several couples sat in window booths, heads inclined to one another, presumably to whisper sweet nothings over the din. Olivia could think of more romantic venues for a first date.

Brash as the ambience might be, the food was completely delicious. She ate like a wolfhound. Her eyes lusted after the sticky noodles on a woman's plate at an adjoining table but after a hefty belch, she accepted the fact it was dangerous to overdo it. She called for the bill and for want of something better to do, read the menu again.

Peking duck. Which was actually duck, unlike the Bombay version. Maybe duck sounded more appetising then Bombay lizardfish. There it was again, that little flash of subliminal connection just out of reach. She paid and headed out to her hotel. It took fewer than five minutes before a sleazy guy approached, asking if she needed company. She told him to go away. He stepped to one side but began following her the moment she walked on. She took a deep breath. Flash her knife and frighten him off? A touch too strong, perhaps. Ignore him and wait till he made a grab then throw him to the ground? Was he really worth the effort? She could hail a cab to take her half a kilometre down the road, but why should she?

She whirled on her heels and raised her hands, not as fists, but in a martial arts stance. He stopped, his voice wheedling in English.

"Just a drink, no need to be aggressive, come on, I'm trying to be your friend."

"No!" she shouted. "Leave me alone. I don't need a friend like you. No means NO!" She took a pace towards him. The expression on his face said she was more trouble than she was worth. He slouched off, flinging disparaging comments over his shoulder in Cantonese. She glared at him until he shuffled into a currency exchange shop.

Maybe it was like cold-calling. If one in a hundred took the bait, ninety-nine rejections were merited the effort of harassing a stranger. Olivia bought some juice for the morning and returned to The Lucky Bee Residences. Outside the entrance stood a group of drag queens, smoking and arguing in a mixture of Cantonese and English. Olivia slowed to admire their finery and flawless make-up. If only Fátima were here.

The spark flickered again as she walked past them and finally she made the connection. Bombay duck. Thanh's slight, lean physique. Cosmetic surgery. What if Thanh was living as a woman? She went upstairs to her grotty little room and started on the database all over again.

2

The likeliest route to locating her quarry was online, that much was obvious. But the itch to go outside, wander the streets and trust her sixth sense, which twitched like a water diviner when something deserved attention, dragged her out of the hotel and into the melee. Curiosity in this complicated place – an ex-British colony, now administered by the Chinese – certainly played a part, as did the need to get away from her screen and stretch her legs. She tuned into her environment, taking comfort from the ubiquitous electronic billboards stating day, time, temperature and today's humidity levels: Saturday 30 August, 09.23, 28°C and 77%. It was almost like they knew she needed the reassurance. 'Yes, you're here and yes, it's hot.'

28 degrees felt like a sauna on these moist and bustling streets. If she was in Brazil, she'd be running along an empty beach, planning a breakfast of fresh açai with coffee, breathing clean sea air, soothed by a view of the ocean.

You are forbidden to think about Brazil. Dreams are out of your control, but in your waking moments, stay focused.

Olivia walked to the MTR station and at the last moment

changed her mind. The thought of going underground into a metal tube with hordes of other sweaty people was a step too far. Taxis if necessary, but all other forms of public transport frankly terrified her. Ridiculous as it was, she needed to be able to run away from trouble. Once again, she was drawn to the water and the sight of Hong Kong Island with its wheel, skyline and distant peaks. The choice of ferries was bewildering but the most obvious and direct route was the Star Ferry. Someone hoping to stay out of sight might opt for a legion of other destinations, from the smaller islands to mainland China and Macau.

Thanh Ngo, she acknowledged, could be anywhere else than central Hong Kong Island. If he'd crossed the border into China, she might as well give up.

The thought depressed her. But her eternal optimist breathed into her ear. *One of the most effective concealment strategies is hiding in plain sight.* She had to stick to the plan.

Find a betrayed man
Beg forgiveness and seek help
Defend those you love

She bought her ticket and boarded the ferry, keeping to the deck, away from other people. The breeze lifted what was left of her hair and she yanked her baseball cap down over her eyes, her gaze absorbed by the churning water. With her grey hoodie, sunglasses, canvas shorts and trainers, she looked like every other wide-eyed backpacker. The ferry docked at Pier 7 and Olivia followed the signs in the direction of Central Market, gawping up at the skyscrapers dominating the harbour. The crowds, the impossibly tall buildings and sheer scale of the place buffeted her senses until she found a tram stop to sit and catch her breath. How could one feel any more significant than an ant in such a city?

Despite her trepidation regarding exotic animals for sale, the market looked more like a clean, bright and colourful mall, so Olivia tried her luck. Food stalls, tea houses, specialist patisseries, oil vendors and spice merchants lined the broad walkways, all well-lit and shiny. It could have been Borough Market in South London but for the number of Southeast Asian outlets. At eleven o'clock, eateries were already preparing for the lunchtime crowd. Olivia's stomach had no idea what time of day it was and simply squalled when it needed feeding. Right now, it was having a full-on tantrum.

She ordered a *bánh mì* from a Vietnamese stall. It was a chunk of French stick stuffed with pickles, chicken, coriander, chilli and some kind of fish paste. It ticked all the boxes and more besides. Her choice of cuisine was partly in homage to the man she sought but mostly because it tasted fantastic. She ate at the bar, watching shoppers and eavesdropping on any conversations she could understand, most of which involved expats and revolved around international schools. She covered her mouth for an enormous yawn and her radar twitched. She was being watched.

It took under a minute to spot the guy in the fedora browsing the cookie bags and glancing in her direction. Her heart leapt into her mouth. Same height, same wiry shape, same fidgety movements – Olivia could not believe it. She might be jet-lagged and suffering from cultural adjustment but she refused to be credulous. To come in search of Thanh Ngo only for him to find her first? It wouldn't surprise her and yet she remained wary. She wiped her fingers and left the Ho Chi Minh bar to explore the rest of the market.

He followed, as she knew he would, but she gave no indication she had seen him. Once he went ahead and she thought it was a false alarm until she saw him sniffing a lotus flower. He was on her tail. Triumphant, she walked twice around the market, bought some joss sticks to alleviate the stench of damp in her hotel room and left the mall to sit under some trees. The risk of him running off was negligible as he'd already allowed himself to be seen. She waited, wishing she'd brought some water, wondering how long this would take.

"Are you looking for work, pretty lady?"

She twisted in her seat to see the same man leaning up against a tree. What she could see of his face was scarred and the brim of his fedora covered his eyes, but there was no doubt he was much younger than her ex-colleague.

Her disappointment made her voice sharper than necessary. "No. Please stop following me."

"Hey, that's not very sociable. You look like you could use a friend." He took a vape pen from his breast pocket and flashed a nicotine-yellow smile. "My name's Jimmy and I know this island like my back yard."

Olivia got up and shrugged on her rucksack. "Good for you. Bye now."

"Hold on, pretty lady. I know what you're thinking. 'This guy's hitting on me', right? Wrong. I'm a married man with two daughters. I respect women. I want to help. That's all. Backpackers like you are always looking for work. I know places where you can earn good money. Behind the bar, acting as a nanny, secretarial temping or exotic dancing, depends on your skills. I can open a lot of doors. My name's Jimmy and you are ...?"

"Not stupid. Now piss off." She walked along the street, heading for the ferry, with the sudden conviction this trip was a waste of time.

"British, huh? I love your accent. Wait a minute, OK? You caught my eye because you've got it all. Great figure, no-nonsense attitude and a lovely face. Listen to me, princess, you could earn good money. Nothing dodgy, trust me. Let Jimmy introduce you to some of his satisfied clients. They'll all tell you the same thing: Jimmy has the connections. I'm a head-hunter, a recruitment specialist and I can spot potential. Hey, come on, give me a break."

Olivia stopped but did not turn around. She spoke through clenched teeth. "You give me a break, sunshine. Quit hustling or I'll have you arrested for harassment. And I never trust a man who refers to himself in the third person. One more time, Jimmy, in case you didn't get the message. Fuck. Off."

"OK, I get it. I'll leave you alone. But I'm gonna tell you something for free. You're in the wrong place. This is not where you need to be." He sucked his teeth. "Tigers and Dragons? Locked in an eternal battle neither will win."

"What the hell are you talking about? If this is some ancient wisdom based on sod-all, I'd rather discuss pole-dancing. Please just leave me alone." Olivia half turned, her face screwed into a scowl.

Jimmy the wannabe-charmer puffed on his vaper, a sardonic chuckle coming from the side of his mouth. "She hiss and she spit and she got claws! Easy, Tiger Lady. You are looking for something, I don't know what, but you won't find it here. You know what Kowloon means in Cantonese?"

She didn't reply but held her ground.

"Nine dragons. One of you against nine of them? Odds not in your favour. Growl, swish your stripey tail and bare those teeth all you want. Not gonna work. Nothing for you here."

She'd heard it all before, from every esoteric angle: 'I can sense your aura', 'Tell me, are you a Water Sign?', 'Your cards signify great danger', 'Wow, our compatibility is off the chart!'

"Bye, Jimmy, have a nice day." With a cold glance over her shoulder, she left the non-savant dragging on his e-cigarette and scanning the street for his next mark.

Antsy and unsettled, she considered his words. *You are looking for something, I don't know what, but you won't find it here. Odds not in your favour.* She dismissed her discomfort, putting it down to the stupidity of assuming a wiry Asian man must be Thanh. She should know better than to make naïve assumptions. A tram approached, its destination emblazoned on the front:

Causeway Bay. Forgetting her promise regarding public transport, she jumped on with no idea why other than the name sounded romantic.

Romantic? It was about as charming as the shopping channel. Ads everywhere, massive commercial centres and sprawling malls, while screens flicked between skincare products and TV shows, all overshadowed by leaning towers blocking out the light. Homesickness and the comparison with her previous life hit her hard. That quiet little beach where everyone knew her name versus urban anonymity filled with predators – it was a dystopian nightmare she couldn't wait to leave.

The North Point ferry would take her across the bay and she could grab another taxi to the hotel. Then she must get back to work. Her radar was picking up nothing more than sleazebags. If this was a washout, why had she come? To think that rather than waiting and sweating on a steel seat at a ferry port, she could be lying in a cool white room beside a Brazilian detective who kissed her hair as if she was an angel.

Stop it!

She punched herself in the thigh, startling two young women sitting on the same row of ferry port seats. Her apologetic smile failed to convince them she was not dangerous and they moved off to sit somewhere else. *Just do what you have to do and go.* It was self-indulgent to wallow in the pain of loss and she could ill afford the emotional energy. Had she not forbidden herself to think about Gil Maduro?

Find a betrayed man
Beg forgiveness and seek help
Defend those you love

Thanh was not here, and in her gut she knew she was wasting her time. Time to dig deep. No one left footprints on concrete pavements, but digital marks were harder to erase.

Think like an agent, she muttered as she boarded the North Point ferry to Hung Hom. *Because he is and so are you.*

Lucky Bee Residences made her feel anything other than a lucky b. She considered taking the laptop to a co-working space or even a café, anywhere but her dank, noisy room. Only the risks of being observed or hassled by more of Jimmy's kind made her stay put. She lit one of the joss sticks, reminding her of a different time and place, then opened her computer.

Needle, haystack. The task ahead of her seemed impossibly daunting, so she broke it down into manageable chunks. Firstly, she searched in the obvious places, the same ones she always checked whenever she had access to the Internet. When feasible, she noted IP addresses and locations. The job would have been much easier with the kind of security clearance which had enabled Gil Maduro to track Thanh as far as Hong Kong. She released a breath through her teeth, exasperated with herself. Was she really that moony, love-struck female who could think of nothing else but her lover?

"Ex-lover," she said aloud. "Get on with the job."

The first tiny pulse came a few seconds before she was about to take a break and go out in search of food. She was browsing a blog written by a lawyer, where he expressed his opinion on who should take legal responsibility for undercover police work. It was exactly the kind of piece that fascinated her. Ergo, it would attract Thanh. With little hope of uncovering anything useful, she managed to hack into the dashboard of the blog. From there, she could see statistics: how many views, comments and the source of the readership. As it was written by a British lawyer, it came as no surprise to see the majority of views were from the UK. A few in Germany, some in the US and one in Macau. Her antennae twitched. Only that morning, she'd passed the ferry stop to Macau.

She searched the lawyer's blog for any related articles and found two pieces of interest. One on chains of command and another on the individual's right to hide one's identity in pursuit of criminal activity. Both had been viewed by a reader in Macau. She noted the address and sourced it to an Internet café on the island of Coloane. Then she cross-checked all the runners competing in the Hong Kong marathon who regis-tered their home addresses as Macau. Thirty-seven in total, narrowed to nine in the right sex and age bracket. She pored over their details and started with the three living on Coloane. A brief search on social media soon showed none of the three was anything like her ex-colleague. Hunger pangs were gnawing but she was so close, no way dared she stop now.

Two more from the old part of Macau could also be dismissed as having completely different ethnic backgrounds and another from Taipa was two metres tall. Cosmetic surgery maybe, but growing half a metre was unlikely. Three left and only one with no online presence whatsoever. Olivia stared at the mystery figure's home address, her stomach fizzing with excitement.

"That you, Thanh? You'll never guess who's coming to visit."

3

Macau. The more Olivia researched, the more her eyes boggled. A Portuguese colony now under Chinese control, with a gambling licence attracting $36 billion per year, the peninsula was known as Las Vegas of the East. Her heart rate increased as she realised this was an opportunity spelt out in large flashing lights.

As a Portuguese speaker, she could establish herself as a local in order to stalk her quarry. Some disguise would be required, naturally, but Olivia had considerable experience in achieving anonymity. Secondly, the heart-pounding potential of using her other line of expertise made her get up and walk around the room, casting her mind wide, looking for the catch.

Undercover detectives were consummate actors, liars and shape-shifters once inside the organisation they wanted to infiltrate. The conundrum was *how* to get inside. In London, which felt like a lifetime ago, the criminal gang's bosses kept family close and only employed trusted males to run their businesses. Police had no hope of placing an unknown female anywhere close to the heart of the rats' nest. There was a sole exception – the casino.

Olivia's managers used her natural assets and taught her some acquired ones. Young and attractive, she might draw attention if seen more than once. Three weeks under the tuition of a top international croupier, she learned how to deal cards, calculate losses or wins and maintain an unassailable exterior. Two intense days with her handler resulted in a fully developed legend, or back story. If anyone asked questions, she had all the answers. Olivia passed her interview with ease. One month later, she assumed her role as a junior croupier in a casino favoured by some of the most brutal thugs known to Europol. It didn't take long before the invitations, tips, personalised gifts and outright leering began. She rebuffed them all, quoting company policy – no fraternising with clientele. That lasted almost a month. Until she hooked the one she wanted.

In the same way a horse might balk at a fence, her mind refused to go any further. *Recollections are like the clutter in the junk drawer. You can't pull out one without disturbing the rest.* She dragged herself back to the present, aware she was standing directly in front of the air-conditioner, staring vacantly at the opposite side of the street. Below, wheeling a stall selling street food, a woman was yelling. "Esther's best egg rolls. Fresh and tasty. Come and get 'em. Esther's best egg rolls!" Olivia's neck and back were cold and goosepimply, and a fresh egg roll sounded exactly what she needed. She grabbed her rucksack and ran downstairs. Food would help her focus.

Esther was at least sixty years old and a consummate pro. Her patter was honed to perfection. She convinced Olivia to buy a vegetarian and meat version, just to compare, and kept up a lively multilingual commentary as she fried the rolls for her customers. The smell was mouth-watering. With two warm packages and a tiny tub of duck sauce in her left hand, Olivia returned to her room. She slipped a scarf over her shoulders, sat at her wobbly desk and tore into the deep-fried packet of steaming vegetables. Esther wasn't exaggerating – these really were the best egg rolls. The first was so delicious and satisfying it was as if she'd never truly enjoyed food in her life. With the second, she slowed down, dipped it in duck sauce and gave her stomach a chance to recover.

Physical needs gratified, Olivia made a plan. She concentrated on the memories she wanted to retrieve, blocking the associated circumstances from her mind. Whichever side of the table you sat, gambling was a mug's game. She never chanced it, knowing how the allure of the win turned savvy business-people into addicts, both hopeful and hopeless after just a couple of wins and twice as many near misses. *Next time, I'll be lucky.* Fair enough, it had been a few years since she worked the tables, but a sharp brain could be retrained. The rest was muscle memory.

However, there was a catch.

A single European woman, gambling alone and attempting to fleece the Chinese mafia, was hardly taking candy from a baby. She would need to make modest wins from more than one joint in order to keep below the radar, but even pocketing a couple of grand would leave her vulnerable on the streets. Then there was the issue of accommodation. At an honest guess, it would take at least a fortnight to earn a reasonable financial cushion, even if she got lucky. Two weeks at a hotel was unaffordable, so it had to be a short-term rental. Once she had somewhere to stay and a place to store her stuff, she could work her way up to the big money. A little win here and there, dressed as a scruffy backpacker would give her some wiggle room. Step two involved better clothes and maybe a professional haircut before she moved on to the wealthier establishments.

Meanwhile, her main aim remained the same.

Find a betrayed man

Beg forgiveness and seek help
Defend those you love

A swell of confidence rushed through her body. She could do this. But maybe not alone. Working undercover, Olivia always sought an ally. Females were usually easier to bond with because their agendas aligned with hers. True, on more than one occasion she had been let down badly by women she trusted. The question was, when you know nobody, how do you start to find a friend?

By looking for like-minded individuals.

She joined an online expat group and set up a profile using an avatar of Tigger. Thank you, Jimmy-the-Vaper from Hong Kong. It only took a few likes and comments before she gained admin approval to post. She adopted the personality of a wide-eyed Antipodean adventurer, eager to hang out with other party animals and asked for recommendations.

Hey, thanks for approving me! The name's ...

She glanced at the greasy packet by her side.

Esther! Making my way around the world one step at a time from Oz. I wanna see Macau and maybe get to China. Any tips on where I can rent a room for a couple of weeks and the best areas to meet people? TIA!

For the next forty minutes, she researched what she knew of Western gambling etiquette compared to Asia. The most obvious difference was alcohol. In Monaco, London or Vegas, heavy drinking, lavish entertainment and gaming were part of the package. In Macau, gambling was no side dish but a deadly serious main course. Not a problem, she could do sober and serious.

Armed with her vague recollections of the gambling house hierarchies, Olivia outlined a sequence of casinos to visit, intending to alter her appearance on each occasion. Person A wins a couple of hundred here, Person B trousers a thousand there and in two weeks, she might have earned enough to survive another year. A siren howled through the street and she stood up to gaze out of the window. Was this to be her life? Hustling and hiding and making no friends?

She snorted at her self-pity and returned to the screen.

On the forum, she'd received three replies. One from a friendly Australian woman asking where she was from and offering to show her around. Another was a bar owner who encouraged her to stop by for a visit and meet other backpackers. The third interested her the most.

G'day Esther ;) Mike from Canberra here. I'm not currently in Macau – travelling for business – but I rent out my apartment via this site below. It's a great little place and right in the centre of things. It's free till the end of Sept. Hit me up if you're interested.

She explored the link. The apartment looked modern, if a little small, but with terrific views over the harbour. The price was affordable and the reviews positive. Situated on the island of Taipa, it was more or less in the middle of Macau and within spitting distance of all the casinos. She could be installed by tomorrow afternoon. She messaged Mike and offered to rent the place for two weeks. His reply was positive and he sent a long list of chatty instructions about which bars to avoid, where to get the keys from the concierge and the way to achieve optimum water pressure in the shower.

Olivia flicked back and forth between his email and the page on the site. Everything appeared legitimate and she found the building on Google maps right away, precisely where he said it was. Street View showed a colourful neighbourhood filled with restaurants and bars. The site offered a guarantee that her money would only be released by the rental company when she confirmed she had the keys. It was exactly what she was looking for. She transferred the money and once she had her confirmation, took the laptop downstairs to use the residents' printer.

Later that night she lay in bed going over her plans, and made herself a promise. Earn some money, get an assurance from Thanh, then leave this place and never, ever gamble again. She crossed herself and promised, pulling the cover up to her neck.

I'm coming for you, Macau.

4

If Hong Kong had come as a shock to the system, Macau was an all-out assault on every single sense. Even the ferry crossing acted as a warning, the sea turning quite abruptly from layers of blue to a watery coffee colour. It made her think of The Meeting of the Waters in Manaus, a natural phenomenon and tourist attraction. However, this was not the blending of two mighty South American rivers to form the Amazon but a mixture of Pearl River mud and industrial pollution encountering the South China Sea.

The skyline ahead was simply jaw-dropping. The boat sailed beneath Ponte da Amizade, its Portuguese name bringing both comfort and a twinge of sadness. Olivia took in the incredible contrast. On one side, lavish, extravagant gambling venues and entertainment complexes glittered like a Disneyland for adults. On the other, Old Macau. At this distance, skyscrapers and tenement buildings packed into a tiny space under grumbling grey sky looked like wasps' nests. The image was not reassuring.

She disembarked at Doca dos Pescadores, heaved her rucksack onto her shoulders and braced herself for the most densely populated city on earth. The air was several degrees hotter than Kowloon and somehow greasier. While planning her route in her air-conditioned Tsim Sha Tsui hotel room, she thought she might walk the kilometre or so to the Chinese border, simply out of curiosity. The heat and crowds of tourists on the street soon put paid to that idea. Instead she spent fifteen minutes waiting for a cab and soon realised queuing politely was not going to get her anywhere. People cut in front, shoved her out of the way and barged other customers to grab every vehicle first.

Olivia left the taxi stand and went into the street. An oncoming black vehicle with a white roof similar to a police car had a sign on the roof stating TAXI. She stepped into its path and held up her palm with all the élan of an Italian traffic cop.

The driver slammed on the anchors and she was in the back seat before he finished cursing. She instructed him to drive around the old part of the city to see the sights then take her to Taipa. There was no denying the touch of smugness she felt when picturing the apartment she'd booked as the taxi wove its way through cramped grey blocks with views of the stained concrete.

The driver's disgruntlement lifted as he saw the chance of a decent fare.

"Tourist?" he asked, turning off his radio.

"No."

"Working here, yeah? In the casinos?"

"No."

"Where you come from?"

"A country where we tip quiet drivers."

He switched the radio back on.

Macau made no sense at all. As if a normal city had been squeezed by giant hands until it erupted upwards, the place was gloomy, with precious little daylight visible beyond dizzying towers. Their window bars, cables and satellite dishes with occasional lines of washing interspersed with streaks of black mould made her think of cages. Both thought and sight were profoundly depressing. Lining the narrow streets were stalls with rusting corrugated roofs, restaurants with kitsch cartoon characters painted on the walls and construction sites surrounded by bamboo scaffolding. To Olivia, the place was utter chaos and she puzzled over how what she had read the evening before. *Pre-pandemic, Macau's gambling industry brought in $36 billion whereas Las Vegas earned $6 billion.*

Really? So where does all the money go?

The answer came less than half an hour later as they crossed the bridge. Once two distinct islands, Coloane and Taipa were now joined thanks to a land reclamation project known as Cotai. The newly created real estate had become home to lavish, enormous casinos – Venice, Paris, London, Lisbon and other themes recreated on a small scale – with hotels, entertainment venues and a golf club. Yet nothing about these edifices could be called modest. Extraordinary pleasure palaces dominated the landscape, glamorous, luxurious and implausible. On a tiny peninsula of not-quite thirty square kilo-metres, at least 20% was occupied by the biggest casinos in the world. The contrast between old and new stunned Olivia. She knew gambling contributed at least three-quarters of the region's GDP, but to see these huge temples to chance and luck in person robbed her of speech. The taxi driver kept glancing in the mirror, ready and waiting to answer her questions. She kept her mouth shut. Because he would never be able to answer the most obvious question of all. How the hell is this place possible?

He turned away from the airport road opposite the Wynn Palace and past the lake until he swerved into a space on Rua da Ponte Negra. She paid him, with the promised tip, and walked another block along the crowded pedestrianised alleyway that was Rua do Cunha. Smells of roasting chicken, frying spices and perfumed rice emanated from every other doorway. Olivia's stomach responded like a Pavlovian dog but she shut it down. Exploring the area must wait. First she had to find her accommodation.

The address was exactly where the website had promised but its status was far from what was represented online. The place looked practically derelict. Doors shuttered, trash piled up in the doorway and at least three windows broken, this was not the property she'd seen online. She steeled herself for disappointment and the gut-wrenching realisation she'd dropped a chunk of cash on a scam. Passers-by bumped and brushed her as she fumbled for the email printout and its detailed instructions on how to get into her rental. INSERT UNIQUE CODE FOR SAFE, RECEIVE KEYS. The code didn't work. She tried three times but the key safe displayed the word ERROR. Ringing all of the bells of the other apartments got zero reaction. No surprise, the place was clearly abandoned and the photos of that pretty apartment online were probably scooped from some authentic rental agency. Sweat collected on her spine, sticking her T-shirt and rucksack to her back. The heat, stress and hopeless situation forced tears into her eyes. In the extensive history of all her crap decisions, this was one of the most pathetic.

She sat on the stoop and accepted the fact she'd been shafted. No room, no aircon, nowhere to get out of this crazy melee and two weeks' worth of money thrown down the drain. Self-pity overwhelmed her as she watched the uncaring faces of busy shoppers as they strolled the streets. In that moment, Macau became a malevolent force, casually cruel and without compassion. No one even noticed the foreign woman squatting on the steps. Why would anyone want to live in a place like this? It had an air of crushing relentless poverty mocked by the huge symbols of obscene wealth visible from the grim streets.

Every impulse urged her to return to Hong Kong and relative safety. Reconnaissance missions could be achieved via ferry. She slugged the last sip of water from her bottle with the refrain from The Doors song 'People Are Strange' playing in her ears.

A voice, sharp and nasal, interrupted. "What are you doing? Who are you looking for? No one lives in this building."

Olivia turned to see a beautifully made-up face framed by long black hair. The tall woman was wearing a cream linen dress accessorised by gold drop earrings. How something as fresh and elegant could appear on such a steaming, grubby street beggared belief.

The woman waved her silvery manicured fingernails like a shoal of fish. "Hello? Do you speak English? I said no one lives there. That building is condemned."

"Yes, I speak English. Seems I've been scammed. I booked an apartment online at this address but ... well, more fool me. Do you know who owns this place?"

"No! Why would I? Guess it's a criminal gang who take in gullible travellers like yourself."

The woman lit a cigarette, her eyes taking in Olivia's appearance, her contempt visible. She took a half-step away and the flare of her nostrils expressed revulsion. "Backpackers' hostels are mostly in the old town. Are you Australian?"

Interesting. The rental guy had riffed on the fellow Aussie approach. How unusual that this woman should turn up at exactly the time she had planned to collect her keys. She kept up the charade. "British, actually. I'm not a backpacker and I'm looking for something here in Taipa. You might know of a cheap hotel in the area if you're local."

"Who said I'm local? There's nothing here for people like you. Why Taipa?"

This female's rude, snappish attitude rubbed Olivia up the wrong way. "I don't believe that's any of your business. Have a nice day." She shouldered her pack and moved past the supercilious cow.

"Wait a minute. I might be able to help. Somewhere to stay, a place to lay your head, sure. Always willing to help a sister. You look like you could use a cold drink. Follow me." She beckoned with one platinum talon.

Olivia weighed up the situation and pretended to give in. Not one iota of this glamorous woman's interest in helping a 'sister' rang true, but Olivia had her own agenda. She followed her through the throng to a wrought-iron gate, guarded by a chunk of a man in an army vest. He perked up on seeing the woman in white, stood upright and offered a grin. He was missing half his teeth.

They exchanged some words, none of which Olivia understood, and the gate opened onto a hotel terrace shaded by broad parasols, bamboo furniture and dozens of plant pots sprouting tropical greenery. The effect was soothing and due to the fans rotating in the corners, distinctly cooler than on the city streets. They sat at a table near the French windows. Sound of cutlery and crockery and muted chat indicated a dining-room lay beyond the white gauzy curtains. The clientele on the terrace, mostly female and well dressed, gave the two arrivals an expert once-over. It was fair to say Olivia impressed no one.

Her companion attracted a waiter's attention with a snap of her fingers. Before he could approach the table, she performed a rapid mime, involving slapping her clavicle, holding up two fingers and pointing at Olivia. The guy seemed to understand and went through the curtains into the dining-room.

"This is The Humming-Bird Salon, Much loved by ladies who lunch. They make a marvellous Mai Tai." Her elegant fingers extracted a cigarette from a black package and offered it to Olivia.

"I don't, thanks."

She flicked open a Zippo and lit up. "My name is Yoyo. Who are you and what are you doing here?"

Not expecting to mix with strangers, Olivia hadn't worked out a cover story so stuck to her half-baked expat persona. "My name is Esther. I'm a poet, travelling the world looking for inspiration. Nice to meet you, Yoyo." She didn't offer her hand seeing as the glamorous woman was overtly keeping her distance.

"Poet? That's a first. How long are you staying? Why on earth choose Macau?"

"Just out of curiosity. I spent a couple of days in Hong Kong and heard Macau was special, so booked an apartment for two weeks. The idea was to find some part-time work, teaching or bartending, but now my accommodation is screwed, I think I'll head back on the next ferry."

"Special is one word for it." Yoyo's expression changed from slightly disgusted to warmly welcoming. "You're looking for work? Oh, girl, earning money won't be a problem, believe me. Thank you, Manfred. You can put that on my tab."

The waiter placed two long glasses decorated with mint, lime peel and a slice of pineapple on the table, along with a bowl of nuts. He bowed and retreated inside.

Yoyo took a long draught of her cocktail without smudging her lipstick. "Best breakfast in the world. Here's the deal, Esther. I can help you, so long as you're a little bit flexible. My neighbour's apartment is empty. While she's away, you can stay at her place. As for getting work, I have some contacts."

Olivia took a cautious sip of her multi-coloured drink. It was ice-cold, fruity and incredibly delicious. Also extremely potent for a dehydrated woman who hadn't eaten for hours.

"Wow, this really is a marvellous Mai Tai. Thank you. And thanks for the offer of assistance. Just so we're on the same page, I'm talking about casual bar work or maybe some English teaching."

Yoyo wasn't listening. Instead she was waving and blowing kisses at two other women coming through the gate. Both were lean as a wiener and carrying bags half their weight. They joined another table with much squealing and air-kissing, but turned to make heart shapes with their hands at Yoyo.

She responded in kind, her knuckles under her chin, smiling with affection. Then she turned to Olivia. "Look at those bitches," she hissed with a fake smile. "The second I get a chain bag, they run out and get a cheap, nasty copy. I gotta run some errands right now. Take this card and go to that address. It's just up the street. Tell the caretaker I sent you and she'll give you the key to the apartment."

Olivia accepted the card, her brain scrambling to catch up. "Hang on, I'm not sure what's going on here or if I can even afford your friend's apartment."

Yoyo got to her feet and drained her drink in several gulps. "Like I said, the apartment is empty. Come over to my place at five, we'll have a chat and work something out. I'm right at the end of the corridor." She swung a chunky bag over her shoulder and waggled her silverfish fingers. "Welcome to Macau."

Olivia watched her go and remained in place for another ten minutes, drinking her Mai Tai and considering her options. 'Yoyo', if that was her name, clearly presumed she was stupid. In some ways, she was right. Stupid foreigner lured in by a fake website and some pretty pictures of a nice apartment. Yet the sudden appearance of a Samaritan at a traveller's lowest ebb smelt off. Olivia added all the elements together and deduced Yoyo herself or with an accomplice made a habit of renting a non-existent apartment to unsuspecting foreigners and 'rescuing' them when it turned sour.

The question was why? Attentive surveillance around The

Humming-Bird Salon provided more clues. These women, and almost all were women, dressed in haute couture, carried statement handbags and wore shoes that would pay for a normal person's yearly mortgage. Their faces were smooth with make-up that seemed airbrushed. Where did the money come from?

A waiter asked if she would like anything else. His words were polite but his intonation and facial expression told her nothing would make him happier than her absence. She picked up her pack and left via the wrought-iron gate.

Here's the deal, Esther. I can help you, so long as you're a little bit flexible. Prostitution was the obvious answer. If Yoyo and her friends recruited young women and dragged them into the sex trade, they could turn a tidy profit. Olivia was ten years too old for that kind of pimping. So what was their game if not THE game? Only one way to find out.

The address was on the same street, just a few hundred metres from the derelict place where she had first arrived. Olivia stood opposite to make an assessment. In the time she waited, she saw an elderly man heave a bag of shopping up the steps, two mothers manoeuvre buggies onto the street, and a group of teenagers congregate, waiting for another to emerge and bump fists. It certainly didn't look like a sex slave farm but her instinct urged caution. She crossed the street and pressed the buzzer. The caretaker was a tiny woman with a fierce expression. Before granting access to the complex, she recited a stern lecture in English about house rules. No drugs, no parties, no men or women staying overnight and definitely no babies. Olivia swore she would follow them all, wondering where someone would acquire a baby at short notice. Finally she took the lift to the third floor, knife in hand, growing tenser by the minute.

The apartment was minuscule, merely a single room with a

slice cut off for a galley-style kitchen and a bathroom so dinky it could have fitted into a spaceship. A slither of balcony, the size of a bath mat, boasted a view over a rusting junkyard. Small, certainly, but reasonably secure. The door had an inside chain preventing anyone with a key from barging in and a bolt at knee-level. Good signs. She checked the bathroom, kitchen and bed for cleanliness, connected her laptop to the Wi-Fi and drank the rest of her water. The air-con worked so the room was cool and most importantly, Olivia was one block away from the man she suspected was Thanh. One block away. One step closer.

While lying on the narrow bed, she focused on the cash situation. This trip had already cost triple her usual monthly budget in Praia do Pesqueiro and after losing two weeks' rent to a dodgy agency, funds were running dangerously low. Another reason she should return to Britain and claim a pension. But that couldn't happen until she found Thanh.

Find a betrayed man
Beg forgiveness and seek help
Defend those you love

She needed to get into a minor casino and make some pin money. Only then could she style herself as a woman of means and step into the world of Cotai. It was highly likely Yoyo could get her onto the circuit but all she'd seen so far were red flags. Yoyo was out for her own ends. Olivia would have to play the naïf in public with a cynical private perspective. Play the player, which was a very risky game. Another yawn forced its way out of her jaw and she curled into the foetal position and closed her eyes, yearning to let go and relax.

The doorbell rang. Instantly, Olivia was on her feet, knife in hand and ready for trouble. She glanced at her watch, in sudden alarm that she'd forgotten the time. It was only quarter to three. A woman stood on her doorstep, but it was not the glamorous Yoyo. This lady was a very different prospect, half the size, twice the age and dressed in a cleaner's apron. She held a thin plastic bag.

"Hello?"

"*Você é inglesa?*" the lady croaked.

Olivia switched to Portuguese. "*Sim, mas nós podemos falar português.* (Yes, but we can speak Portuguese). I'm English and my name is Esther."

"Esther? Like me!"

"Your name is Esther?" Olivia exclaimed.

The woman's face changed. "No, my name is Nivea."

"Nivea. Like the face cream?"

"My parents didn't name me after a beauty product," said the woman, an expression of irritation crossing her face.

This conversation, Olivia decided, was not going well.

"Pleased to meet you, Nivea. How can I help?"

"I live next door, with my sister. We're quiet people."

"I understand. I'm a quiet person too. I promise not to cause trouble."

The woman looked up the corridor towards a recessed door. "Not everyone on this floor is quiet. I bring you something. We welcome guests. Some are grateful, some not. But it is our way." She held up the plastic bag.

Olivia took it and looked inside. A carton of juice, a bottle of water, a pot of Tiger Balm and two *pasteis de nata*. It was one of the most welcome gifts she could imagine. "I'm very grateful. For a foreigner, Macau is a friendly place. Thank you very much indeed. I wish you and your sister good luck and a happy future."

"We wish you the same. Don't trust everyone who smiles." With that, she held up both hands as if holding some kind of imaginary chalice and closed her eyes.

Olivia had no idea how to respond so chose to do nothing but stand there holding the bag.

Eventually, Nivea's lids flickered open. "You have the

energy of a tiger. My sister would know instantly, but I feel sure. An Earth Tiger, born in 88. This is a sign of great fortune." She smiled, turned away and unlocked her own door.

Twice someone had called her a tiger and in quite differing circumstances, Olivia was confused, yet uplifted by a second random show of hospitality. She scoffed one of the pastries, drank the juice and swallowed half the water, surprised by how hungry she was. Something was missing and it was more than memories of Viviane's padaria at the beach. She craved coffee. Unreliable concentration was 100% due to caffeine withdrawal symptoms. She packed her smallest backpack with the essentials and went downstairs into the street to get a double espresso and something approximating Esther's egg rolls.

Appetite satisfied and thirst assuaged, she acknowledged she had judged the place too harshly on its appearances. At street level, the atmosphere was lively and open, filled with colour and a fascinating mix of nationalities. She wandered the length of Rua do Cunha, absorbing the constant variety of foods, dress sense, volume of conversation and general acceptance of anyone and everything. It was a far cry from her Brazilian beach and very different to Hong Kong, but something about this quirky city tugged at her imagination.

On return to her box room, one look in the mirror confirmed she was not looking her best; red, sweaty face, stained clothes and hair the colour of straw. She took a shower and dragged out some of her least creased clothing to hang on the back of the door. There was no wardrobe. In fact, there was nothing at all in this 'apartment' to show anyone lived here. Every cupboard was empty and the only things in the way of kitchenware were a couple of chipped mugs, some heavy-duty wine glasses and a random selection of mismatched plates with some unhealthy looking chopsticks. She binned them and made a note to buy some basic cutlery. Then she got to work.

Between now and cocktail hour, she needed to study her route and make a stalking plan. The street where she believed Thanh was living lay around a twenty-minute walk from her own accommodation. She searched all around the address for public places where she could legitimately hang out and observe the building's inhabitants. It wasn't going to be easy. His block was smaller than hers but it still had over thirty individual apartments. She couldn't get too close for fear of being recognised while still getting close enough to identify the man as Thanh Ngo. She worked out four different ways of getting to his tower block from her own, earmarked cafés and restaurants where she could wait and watch, and also noted a slot machine alley just a little way up the street. That was where to earn some small change. It was all looking very promising.

At five to five, she slipped on a dip-dyed cheesecloth dress the colour of sunset, spritzed one of the sample perfumes she'd grabbed from who-knows-which airport's Duty-Free and added a slick of Vaseline to her lips. No jewellery, a pair of well-worn espadrilles and she was ready to join her neighbour to explore employment options. Her contribution to the event was a bottle of warm sparkling wine because the fridge seemed to be only a few degrees cooler than the room.

As she dressed, she wondered how Nivea and her sister managed to inhabit a room the size of hers. It was too small for one person. How two could cope was impossible to imagine.

She rang the bell at five on the dot and waited, open-minded yet cautious. Yoyo opened the door, speaking into her phone, but beckoned Olivia inside. She was a vision in silver, wearing an off-the-shoulder sheath with peep-toe sandals. The apartment made Olivia catch her breath. Corner units were obviously three times larger than every other living space on their floor. This apartment had a living-area, an actual kitchen and a messy bedroom. Everything was magnolia, taupe and cream, a blank canvas for the star performer. Only one chair upholstered in deep crimson red stood out like an angry mouth in a pale face.

The view was still over an abandoned shipyard, but the balcony stretched all around the windows, adding light and offering a way to escape the claustrophobia. Olivia came into the room and waited for Yoyo to finish her phone call. She placed the wine bottle on the table and pretended not to listen, as if she could understand a single word of the conversation. She had no idea if Yoyo was speaking Cantonese or Mandarin.

Finally, with a few sharp sounds, her host rang off. "Hello, Esther-the-Poet, you're right on time." She waved at the sofa. "Have a seat and I'll get the drinks."

"Thanks for inviting me. I brought you something." Olivia handed her the bottle.

Yoyo eyed the bottle and raised her eyebrows. Her forehead didn't move. "Why don't you keep that for yourself, honey, and I'll make us a lychee martini. It's symbolic of beauty and well-being. Help yourself to nuts or prawn crackers." She shimmered into the kitchen, her bracelets tinkling.

Olivia did not take offence. She put the warm wine back into her rucksack and sat on the red chair, wondering if it would swallow her whole. The artworks on the walls were an eclectic mix of oil paintings of Chinese junks and 1950s movie posters of Cary Grant trimmed with fairy lights. Even so, after one glance at the bedroom, the living room and kitchen appeared relatively Spartan. Yoyo's bed was invisible under piles of clothes, most glinting with sequins, shoes lay scattered all over the floor and mirrors reflected a theatre-style dressing-table littered with make-up.

"Oh my God!" Yoyo gasped.

Olivia tensed. "What's the matter?"

"Are you blind? Esther, you can't sit there. Look at the

colours! Clashing nightmare. Sorry, you have to move. Sit on the sofa, the cream one." Yoyo was actually shielding her eyes.

With a testy sigh, Olivia changed places, beginning to lose patience with this ridiculous person. "Is that better?"

Yoyo tilted her hand like a visor and exhaled as if she just escaped some dreadful aesthetic disaster. "So much better. Here, your cocktail. I added a slice of lychee because it's visually pleasing, don't you think? A friend of mine is a bartender at The Four Seasons and he says presentation is at least 50% of the enjoyment. To your good health and prosperity!"

"I wish the same for you." Olivia took a sip. The drink was sweet and potent, like alcoholic syrup. Olivia would have preferred warm sparkling wine or a glass of cold water. "Thanks for such an elegant cocktail. It goes with your dress."

"Yeah, I know. That phone call? Another friend of mine. He's looking for English-speaking women to work at his club. Maybe I can get you an interview."

Olivia stiffened. Why only English-speaking *women*? As if she couldn't guess. "That's a generous offer. But I'm only here for two weeks, so I was hoping to get something casual, cash in hand."

"You can do better than that. A couple of months working in one of his clubs and you'll be a very rich lady. No more of this hippy stuff." She pointed up and down Olivia's dress, shaking her head. "I'll have to bring out the big guns, but hey, it could be fun. You seen *Miss Congeniality*?"

By this time, the sickly drink and judgemental attitude had put paid to anything like neighbourly spirit. This woman was a con artist and Olivia decided to push the point, just to see how hard Yoyo would cling on. "Not my scene, sorry." She got to her feet and picked up her backpack. "Thanks for the cocktail. I'll pack my stuff and find a hotel."

"Sit down and don't be hysterical. At this interview, you won't get through the door looking like that. But I can fix you up. Hair, nails, some face work and I can loan you some of my clothes until you get your own. You're too tall. Not a problem. I'm one metre eighty and I make plenty. Nothing we can do about our height, girl, but the rest of it, game on! We're gonna transform a rough backpacker into an elegant beauty. Then you'll earn more than you can spend. Everybody happy!"

Olivia sat, her expression innocent and her brain suspicious. "Why would you do that for a total stranger? What's in it for you?"

"Commission, girl!" Yoyo threw her drink down her throat. "I like a challenge and challenges don't come much bigger. When did you last shave your pits?"

All Olivia's instincts told her to walk. The rudeness, her blunt recruitment technique and personal comments pissed her off, even though she'd abandoned vanity a lifetime ago. Added to that, Olivia had long since rejected any kind of role which involved appeasing male egos. All things considered, this was a thanks-but-no-thanks scenario. The only element that appealed was the makeover and a way into the gambling dens.

Not once in her life had she described herself as glamorous until she started work as a croupier. The effort of maintaining shiny hair, glossy nails, fake tan and epilated skin was the dullest part of the job. Yoyo didn't know it but the *Miss Congeniality* reference hit home. If her colleagues wouldn't recognise her in full slap, sequinned dresses and a glamorous hairdo, that suited her purposes. She could take advantage of the beauty parlour and go along with the idea of an 'interview'. Because she wasn't anywhere near as stupid this predator thought.

She pushed away her drink. "Lychee martinis are too strong for me. I'll stick to wine. Now tell me what you have in mind."

Yoyo smoothed her fingers down her right earring. "Martinis are an acquired taste and let's face it, you got a lot of taste to acquire."

"Where grooming's concerned, perhaps you're right. But when it comes to drink, I know what I like."

"Girl, this is gonna be one steep learning curve."

That, my friend, is a moot point.

They agreed on a schedule. Yoyo had to leave for work at 20.00 and in the meantime Olivia had permission to use her bathroom, razors, loofahs and body products. Tomorrow afternoon, because Yoyo never rose before midday, they would tackle the hair, make-up and clothes. That fitted neatly into Olivia's plan. Tonight, she would don her camouflage greens and greys with a baseball cap and stake out the street where she believed Thanh was hiding. She would play the hippie backpacker tomorrow, earning a few dollars from the fruit machines in her Tequila Sunrise dress. Then having undergone her makeover, she'd stop by for a (not-lychee) martini in one of the bars near his house. Maybe Yoyo would come too. In the unlikely event he noted her as a person of interest, he'd never connect the beautiful woman having a drink with a friend as the same individual.

Lounging in Yoyo's tub was a luxury. While she bathed, Yoyo conducted constant conversations via mobile with giggles and flirtatious tones. Olivia shaved her legs and let conditioner soak into her neglected scalp, aware it was unwise to relax. No such thing as a free bath. But she couldn't deny how glorious it felt to pamper her skin, her toes, her hair. A voice in her head warned her against softening up. She replied in a whisper. *Only on the outside.*

5

Never one to place faith in horoscopes, Olivia had
been unable to resist checking her Chinese zodiac
sign last night. She typed in her birth date, drinking a
can of Snow beer, her cynical shield already activated against
sentimentality. A strange shiver brushed over her skin when she
saw that someone born in February 1988 was classed as an
Earth Tiger. She read the typical characteristics, ready to sneer.
*An Earth Tiger is a loyal friend, generous in terms of worldly goods and
time. This makes them an attractive prospect as ally, colleague and lover.
Tigers are deep thinkers and as a result, bring fresh approaches to problem-
solving. Courageous, strong-willed and potentially domineering, a Tiger can
be too self-sufficient, leaving a big cat's heart rather lonely.*

That last line, to her embarrassment, provoked tears.

When she awoke, she chose not to recall her lurid dreams and
got dressed in a hurry. Shorts, a nondescript top and her baseball cap offered enough anonymity to get a feel for the area as
she and her tiger feet pounded the streets. A lot of people ran
in the hour after sunrise, before the humidity made it impos-

sible to breathe. It turned out that running was exactly what her body needed, giving her mind some time off.

She went the long way round, trying one of the routes she'd committed to memory. In just over forty minutes, she was hot, panting and staring up at the scruffy balconies where she suspected Thanh had gone to ground. She maintained her speed until the end of the street, then bent over, hands on her knees. The perimeter wall meant the garden, courtyard or parking lot was not visible from this angle. Neither was the ground floor. With a sideways tilt of her head, she could see several of the building's occupants, either hanging out washing, smoking or tipping some liquid onto the soil below.

Olivia's next step would be to check the names on the door-bells, but not until she had completed her disguise. If Thanh got the faintest clue she was in Macau looking for him, he'd disappear into the ether like ... like Olivia Jones.

On the journey back to her tiny excuse for a room, she walked rather than ran. The day was already hot and moist, and the streets were getting crowded. She saw a juice bar and stopped to sit in the shade with a glass of orange and ginger. Her bare arms soon began to itch and tell-tale little spots appeared. She hadn't heard or felt any mosquitoes but they'd left their mark. She pressed the cool glass against her skin, trying to soothe the irritation.

"Tiger balm," said the girl behind the counter. "Makes the itching go away."

Olivia stared for a second and remembered her manners. "Thank you. Good tip."

So that was why Nivea had included a jar in her welcome present. It reminded her to purchase some kind of reciproca-tion. "Excuse me? Do you know where the nearest convenience store is?"

"Yeah. Mr Lee's. Down there, turn left and it's at the end. Be careful and always check your change."

"I will. Thanks." Olivia slurped down the remainder of her juice, dropped a tip into the ceramic cat on the counter and followed the girl's instructions. Mr Lee's was one of those places where there seemed to be no order or system to the arrangement of goods. It was also ridiculously cramped. She walked around it once before deciding she'd made a foolish move. If Thanh was living in this neighbourhood, he might come around the next corner any second. She felt the disapproving stare of the man behind the till, presumably the eponymous Mr Lee.

"What d'you want, lady?"

"Just browsing."

"Browsers not welcome. Get out."

"I'm sorry?"

"You heard me. Get out or else." He pointed a finger at her face.

Shaken but determined not to show it, she stalked out of the crappy little store, resisting the urge to flip him the bird.

A few doors down from her apartment block, an ornate entrance caught her attention – the Cunha Bazaar. Curious, she wandered inside, hoping here it was acceptable to browse. Quite the treasure trove, the building was a showcase for local artists and creators, with everything from teas to T-shirts on its three floors. No surface went undecorated from tiles to roof and the whole concept had a carefully curated feel to it. She bought a caddy of tea and some panda coasters, aching to buy a watercolour card to send to Gil Maduro. She imagined his face when he opened the envelope in Soure's police station. But that was not going to happen. Unless she wanted to put a target on his back as well as her own.

At the apartment block, she rapped on Nivea's door and handed over the gifts. The woman's delight was disproportionate and she clenched Olivia's hand, her eyes misty. "You are a good girl, Esther. My sister was just saying this week is going to be auspicious for me due to the position of the sun. She is never wrong. Thank you, *menina*, and may the fates protect you throughout your stay. Have a good afternoon."

Olivia took a cool shower, applied Tiger Balm to her bites and made some noodles for a late breakfast, marvelling at how quickly Macau had got under her skin.

Rua do Cunha was at the heart of Old Taipa, a tangle of lanes and squares wedged into the space between the Olympic stadia to the west and the Natural Park to the east. Overshadowed, if not dwarfed by, the high-rise housing developments to the north and casinos to the south, the place had an energy all its own. Olivia's not-by-choice temporary accommodation might have been the result of bad luck rather than good judgement, but she'd landed herself in the thick of things and rather liked it. A flea market gave way to a colourful riot of vibrant eateries and reminders of Macanese heritage. Wedged between a motorcycle repair shop and a nail bar, a Buddhist temple provided an unexpected haven of peace amongst the hectic mesh of alleys. An incense stick shaped like a beehive emitted a pungent scent, alternately overpowering or combining with the melange of cooking smells. On another broad boulevard towards the harbour, a neoclassical Catholic church overlooked landscaped gardens with a haughty air. Restaurants, food stalls, cafés, bars and hawkers vied for attention, selling Cantonese, Thai, Portuguese, French, Vietnamese, Italian and Goan cuisines, with bakeries and coffee shops on every corner. Olivia gave up on comprehending this cultural hotchpotch and simply soaked it all in.

Daylight was almost entirely absent due to awnings, porches or extended air-con units, and electric cables dangled everywhere, looping along walls or above people's heads. The place was oddly uneven, with a bright fresh mural on a wall next to a rusted shutter surrounded by peeling paint. A pack of stray dogs wandered between people's legs, picking up scraps and helping themselves to the shrine offerings outside people's homes. None would win a dog show, but they all appeared well fed and docile. She kept a respectful distance and wondered if any of them, given a bath, would come up white.

Her dalliance at the local gambling arcade was a partial success. She had a simple technique with a one-armed bandit. It was based on the rhythm method, i.e. pull out early. Just like the form of contraception, it only worked if the participants stuck to their word and did not lose their heads in the heat of the moment. Olivia won enough to eat for the rest of the week and moved on, leaving the big jackpot for another player. The manager came over with her congratulations and offered a free turn on one of the newer machines. Olivia demurred, resisted the insistent pressure and when the woman snarled, "I always hate Brits. I prefer Germans," Olivia chose to leave without changing her silver.

The coins weighed her down, but she'd rather find another exchange joint than tangle with that pushy old hag. She found more arcades and used her money wisely. Five or six barely noticeable wins were sufficient for her to move up a level and avoid shark-like managers. She exchanged her coins into notes, observing the cut taken by the cashier and said nothing. The new girl had no intention of making a scene. She folded the cash into her money belt and went shopping for a hat.

On the second reconnaissance mission to the building she planned to stake out, she took the direct route. Rua do Cunha into Rua dos Clerigos and after meandering past the art gallery, into the tapas bar for a potentially long wait. She ordered a bottle of beer and sat with the menu in front of her, wide-brimmed hat pulled low, sunglasses covering her eyes, watching the blue door of no. 29 opposite. Midday came and went, barely noticeable amid the illumination emitted by neon signs and street lights. The first people to emerge from the stained and shabby building across the street were two teenagers, heading out with their skateboards.

Olivia ordered an *empanada*, green beans and a slice of tortilla, her nerves tempered by confidence. Her skin was clean and soft, her body fragrant and her scarecrow hair mostly hidden by the enormous straw hat. All she had to do was to project a tourist's curiosity in her environment and repel any unwanted advances. On the other side of the road, a woman with a pushchair stopped outside the doorway of no. 29, unloaded her shopping and child, then took everything inside. The blinds on the ground floor came down. Of the apartment windows she could see, eight out of fifteen had blocked out the sun by means of blinds or awnings. In order to check the rest, she'd have to weave her way through the narrow alleyways to the street that ran along the back of the block. For now she chose to sit and eat, listening to snatches of passing conversation.

Many people spoke English in a range of accents, some chatted in Portuguese, while the majority communicated in either Cantonese or Mandarin. A Spanish couple asked if she would watch their bags while they went inside to see what dishes looked good. The atmosphere was convivial and cosmopolitan, and the food impressive. Olivia got chatting to the Spaniards, silently admiring their courage at ordering *gambas a la plancha*. Seafood was a risk she wasn't yet ready to take after witnessing the river pollution. They were comparing notes on Hong Kong when something triggered Olivia's awareness.

A man was bouncing along the street on the balls of his feet, his cap worn low over his eyes. He carried a thin plastic grocery bag. Olivia noted the name with a jolt: Mr Lee's

Convenience Store. He paused to speak to an elderly woman who laughed at whatever he said, and continued his stroll, straight past the blue door and up the street.

How many times would she freeze at the sight of a lithe Asian male only to be disappointed? She released a breath and tuned into her companions. "Sorry, what were you saying? Happy Valley? No, I've never been. I know nothing about horse racing."

She paid the bill and left her companions to their coffees, wishing them all the best for the rest of their tour. Within ten seconds, she'd forgotten their names. She sauntered down the street and took the first right, hoping to come out at the rear of the building with a blue door. This passageway was barely big enough for a moped to pass and not as well populated as Rua dos Clerigos. It didn't feel safe.

She located the block she was looking for and saw the majority of windows showed signs of occupancy. On one balcony, a man was playing a guitar. From another window came the sound of children squealing and laughing. In the apartment above, someone was shaking a rug.

At the end of the passage, male voices approached and Olivia retraced her paces. She'd done enough scouting for one day. Now to undergo her own transformation.

6

"There's nothing I can do with these," said Yoyo, examining Olivia's fingers. "What you been doing to get hands like this, girl? Working as a lumberjack? False nails are the only option but even that is like putting a band-aid on a stab wound."

"I don't want to wear false nails," said Olivia, uncomfortable under the plastic shower cap adding heat to her hair dye.

Yoyo pouted. They'd already got off to a bad start when Olivia refused to have her picture taken. Yoyo insisted it was essential to have a before and after, but Olivia would not consent to her image being used anywhere. Now the nails dispute. This makeover was not going at all well.

Olivia made an attempt at being helpful, "How about gloves?"

"Gloves?" Yoyo scoffed. "What kind of woman wears ... whoa, wait a minute. You got good muscle tone in your arms, yeah? OMG, I just got the best idea! Wait right there."

As if Olivia could do anything else, her feet in a bowl of soapy water and hair dye mixing with sweat at her temples. She breathed, trying to calm her agitation, and recalled the reason she was doing this. Yoyo thought she was trying to take advantage but Olivia was taking advantage of the advantage-taker. *Be sweet.* She thought of Nivea and her open joy at receiving a small present. *Be nice. Remember the auspicious position of the sun.*

Yoyo whooped. "This is so great, I can't even! Would you take a look at this?" She waved something horrible in Olivia's face. It looked like a cross between a dead guinea-pig and the mess dragged out of a blocked shower drain. "Don't worry, I have highlighters for the fringe." She took in Olivia's alarmed expression. "Hairpiece, girl! You seen *Breakfast at Tiffany's,* yeah?"

Olivia was still staring at the toupee on the table. "I'm not sure I understand."

"Holly Golightly! I got it all worked out. Gloves, cigarette holder, dress and shoes. I'm missing pearls and a tiara but I WhatsApped the boys and they'll raid their wardrobes before coming over. Feet out now."

"Boys? Who is coming over and what are you talking about?"

"Two drag queens I hang out with once in a while. Lennie's a hairdresser and no one on this planet does make-up better than Jackson. Come on and dry your hooves."

The men turned up while Yoyo was painting Olivia's toenails. Both were tall and strikingly good looking. The room seemed very small with them in it. Lennie, lean, graceful and a natural performer, brought a bagful of clothes and enormous enthusiasm. The other guy, Jackson, wore a duster coat and moved from pose to pose as if he was a model for Cartier-Bresson. After kissing Yoyo, they turned their attention to her.

Yoyo introduced her with a flourish. "Your challenge today is Aussie backpacker Esther."

Like a mummy wrapped up in a bathrobe with her hair under a conditioning wrap and her face smothered with a moisturising mask, Olivia was unable to protest her nationality or engage in small talk but gave them a welcoming wave. Each gave her a quick smile as if encountering a small child and proceeded to discuss her as if she wasn't present. Lennie kept up a constant monologue, peppering his observations with jokes and excerpts of new stage material. Jackson said very little, either smoking on the balcony or studying Olivia's face. At least he carried a professional make-up kit.

Finally the pedicure was finished and Lennie unrolled his hairdressing kit.

"So, what are we doing today?" he asked Yoyo.

"Esther, go rinse your hair while I give instructions to the boys."

She did as she was told, trying to be grateful but wishing she could sneak out and escape. As she opened the bathroom door, they all turned to stare. It was like lining up to be picked for a team at netball practice. Jackson's voice purred around the room and she identified a faint Parisian accent.

"The bone structure, the physique, the skin tone and the features are all there. We could create two icons in one."

"Yes, we have all the raw material to create a fabulous diva or three. I'm thinking Bond girls or maybe something Fellini?"

"Lennie, would you ever *tais-toi* for one minute and listen to me?"

It took nearly three hours of clipping, snipping, painting, contouring, prodding, pulling and tweaking before Olivia was allowed to look at the result.

The woman in the mirror was a total stranger. Sable-black hair swept into a loose bun with a feathery gold-highlighted fringe sat atop a sculptured face with alabaster skin, huge dark eyes and matte pink lips. Around her neck, a six-string of pearls and in her ears, marquise-cut faux diamonds. Her pale shoulders stood out above the long satin gloves and sleeveless dress.

Lennie whipped out his phone. Olivia was still speechless, so when Yoyo yelled, "No pictures! I told you. It's against her religion," her throat swelled with gratitude.

Lennie twisted his head in incredulity like a cartoon character but replaced his phone in his jeans. Olivia got to her feet and walked gingerly around the room in the strappy heels. She posed in front of Yoyo's bedroom mirror, awestruck at her own image. *One day, Gil Maduro, I will to walk into a room looking like this and your jaw is going to hit the floor.*

"It's unbelievable," she whispered. "How did you ..."

Jackson guided her to the chair. "That was only part one, *chérie*. Holly, meet Sally."

Another twenty minutes of 'open your eyes', 'look up', 'smile', 'say oh', 'lean left', 'to me' with Lennie fussing over her hair and Yoyo working on her nails, they transformed Olivia from gamine girl-about-town to a cartoon doll. The first thing image to cross her mind on seeing her sleek black cap of hair, false eyelashes, green nail varnish and blue eye-shadow was the panda coasters she'd bought for Nivea. Then Lennie placed a bowler hat at a jaunty angle and Liza Minelli burst onto the stage of her imagination, high-kicking and singing 'Mein Herr'.

Yoyo held out a tasselled shift dress and a pair of black patent Mary Janes. "This is your day wear. Try it on."

Neither man moved, waiting for her to change. Olivia realised she was nothing more than a mannequin to them, to be painted, dressed and admired as an artwork. Modesty was pointless. She shrugged off her long black sheath, exposing her washed-out knickers and bra, then slipped on the 1920s frock and buckled up the shoes.

"I do declare that's a wrap," said Jackson in a Truman Capote drawl, as Lennie and Yoyo high-fived. "*Mes amies,* I need a drink before dinner."

"Please, let me buy you all a cocktail," said Olivia. "It's not enough to thank you for what you did today, but when I'm earning, I'll pay you all back. Right now, I'd like to take my new persona onto the streets and celebrate with something frivolous."

Yoyo clapped her hands like an excitable child. "Yes! Cocktails at Carmen Miranda!"

Lennie whooped and started singing in an excellent alto, "She's simply La Est, Esther than all the rest!" and even Jackson laughed. Olivia was touched. It was the same song she used to belt out as a student, a lifetime ago. The men packed away all their paraphernalia, Yoyo and Lennie chattered and giggled all the way downstairs with Jackson and Olivia in their wake. He smiled and allowed her to go first, but made no casual chit-chat until they reached the ground floor.

"I can help you," he said, without making eye contact.

"You already have," said Olivia, regretting her words the second they left her mouth. *Listen, ask questions, then speak.*

He held open the door. "After you."

"Thank you. I really appreciate what you did today. When you say you can 'help me', you mean more than turning this pig's ear into a silk purse?"

He walked up the street, his face impassive. Olivia's attention was on passers-by, convinced people would stop and stare and potentially burst into laughter. Yet no one seemed to notice her outlandish costume or painted face. Part of her was disappointed.

Jackson spoke. "I mean in a practical sense. What we did today was a bit of fun. You don't have to work the clubs. It's possible to earn good money and stay safe, Esther. Meet me at Lord Stow's tomorrow at midday. I'll give you some tips."

"About make-up?"

"That too. *Et voilà.* The infamous Carmen Miranda Cocktail Bar, the ruin of many a young buck. A Long Island Iced

Tea for me, *s'il te plaît*. I'm going to stay outside and smoke a cigarette."

They stayed only half an hour and when Olivia could get a word in edgeways between Lennie and Yoyo's self-compliments, she thanked each of them with true sincerity. They all exchanged air-kisses, then Lennie and Jackson left to go to work. Yoyo refused a second cocktail, claiming she too had to prepare for the evening.

She patted Olivia's cheek. "You turned out a whole lot better than I thought. Next, we gonna prepare for your interview. See you tomorrow, lady. Two o'clock, OK?" She slid off the stool and swished through the beaded curtains onto the street.

The bar was not exactly air-conditioned, other than a large fan revolving overhead to keep the air circulating. It was pleasant and airy, and she was tempted by another Mai Tai. But food and work must take priority. She walked to Rua dos Clerigos, catching sight of her reflection in shop windows and staring in disbelief. Eventually she found the blue building. She retreated to the other side of the street and once again ordered some tapas. In this disguise, even the Spanish couple she had met would walk straight past her.

She ate some Pisto Manchego very slowly, dipping bread into the oily vegetables, glad Jackson couldn't see the mess she was making of her lipstick. While drinking a coffee, she saw a man leave the blue door, his bouncing gait familiar. She threw some money on the table and took off in pursuit. It was incredibly difficult to keep the guy in sight through the crowded streets, as he frequently dodged sideways into an alley or stopped at a shop.

The cocktail and glass of red wine with her meal had warmed her head to the extent she considered catching up and confronting him face to face. If it was indeed him. Then she remembered what Thanh was capable of and changed her mind. Watching and waiting for the right moment would suffice for now. *Then what, Olivia? What next? What would Holly do? What would Sally do? Save their own arses, just like Olivia Jones.* She turned around and headed for home.

Her mantra was clear and simple.

Find a betrayed man
Beg forgiveness and seek help
Defend those you love

The problem was between the lines. It seemed as if she'd found the betrayed man, so how to beg forgiveness and seek help? Her options were frustratingly limited. Were she to confront Thanh on the street, he would likely bolt. Turning up at his apartment was far too dangerous. Like her, he'd been trained to attack, disable or even kill an opponent, and he had greater strength on his side. She had to approach him like a wild animal, leaving his escape route clear and posing no threat. Only then could she initiate a conversation. Whether he would listen was anyone's guess. Personally, she had her doubts.

In her claustrophobic little room, she lay on her bed, cleansed, showered and moisturised, staring at the ceiling and trying to think logically. He was training for the marathon. He couldn't run far on the streets of Taipa so must have an alternative. Perhaps the same place he visited the Internet café to check on websites of interest – Coloane. The southernmost part of Macau was the least built-up, comprising hills, beaches, golf courses and natural parks. Olivia logged on and perused the various trails. None were ideal when preparing for a city marathon, as the whole island was only around eight square kilometres. One track looked like a possibility: Trilho de Coloane. This was a rough trail with some steep inclines and no concrete. Just over eight kilometres, which was a long way off marathon distance but Thanh probably ran it more than once.

She studied the bus routes and prepared for an early rise to catch the first departure. She'd need to wake earlier still to apply all the make-up, but if Thanh took the same bus, it was imperative she was well disguised. Plans firm, she ran down to the street to buy some water and some fast food. The door opened as she hit the ground floor and a man wearing sunglasses entered the main door. She stood aside to let him pass and he gave her a critical stare. She ignored it and brushed past into the noisy early evening action. The wonderful thing about fast food here was that you could eat well and quickly at a street stall, in a cheap air-conditioned restaurant or grab a bamboo bowl of something fragrant and take it home. She chose the latter as she'd left her Tiger Balm upstairs.

With a bottle of Tsingtao beer and a portion of African chicken with rice, she made herself comfortable at the end of her bed and continued her research. She had only just begun eating when someone knocked at the door.

Yoyo stood there in a coral dress with black gauze shawl.

"Hi, you off out to work?"

"Esther, change of plan, yeah? You come round my place on Wednesday, two o'clock, we get ready and your interview is at three." Her eyes looked puffy as if she just woken up.

"Wednesday? I don't even know what this job is! How can I prepare for an interview when I have plans for the next few days?"

"Screw your plans. This is way more important. Wednesday at two, not a minute before. You hear me, girl? What the hell is that stink? You brought street food in here? Gross."

She pranced off along the corridor and Olivia saw the man who'd entered the building waiting by the stairwell. He grunted a question and Yoyo nodded, while they both stared at Olivia. He took Yoyo's arm to escort her downstairs, still wearing his sunglasses. Olivia closed her door and locked it.

7

At half past five the next morning, Olivia was attempting to recreate the Minelli mask of the previous day. It was a ham-fisted attempt, but changed her natural look to something so unlike herself she was satisfied. She dressed in the shift and instead of the Mary Janes, a pair of black running shoes she'd bought in the market. With her rucksack on, she was less *Cabaret* than quirky, but she walked out into the dawn to catch the bus as if the whole ensemble was intentional.

It was a popular time of the day, clearly, as there was barely a free seat on the Coloane bus. At least a third of the passengers were dozing, while others listened to music or talked in murmurs. Four, maybe five were dressed in running gear and once again, Olivia's theatrical maquillage raised barely an eyebrow. Thanh was not aboard, that much was clear. But there were many ways to travel to Coloane. It was possible he'd run through the streets before beginning the trail. Her intention was to place herself at a shady point on the route, pretending to sketch the sea. She was fully prepared with insect repellent, sketchbook and her trusty Tiger Balm.

The plan was to watch and wait until she had to return for her meeting with Jackson, which piqued her interest. If she wasn't lucky today, she would stalk her quarry again tomorrow morning before her assignation with Yoyo and the casino interview. She was not particularly enthused about either.

She got off at Pai Van Park and took off up the trail as if she knew where she was going. It was a delicious change from the rest of Macau, with birdsong, lush greenery, butterflies and cool morning air. None of the signs to the panda park, eco-garden, temples and shopping outlets were of any interest and she walked higher to take in the views of the sea. The place calmed her and she relaxed into nature's embrace. It was early enough to avoid all the picnicking families and day-trippers from the gambling strip. Just her, a couple of locals meditating above the ocean or in front of temples, and the occasional grunting jogger. When she reached a suitable shady spot to sit and sketch, she sat on a bench, drank some water and took in the bay. Now all she had to do was wait. She was practised at waiting. She was also familiar with the frustration of a waste of time.

All morning she checked every runner and got nothing more than a whole bunch of disappointment. Twice someone tried to chat her up and she had to be quite aggressive in her brush-offs before they left her alone. As the heat increased, the runners grew fewer and Olivia had to accept the fact she'd taken a long shot and missed. She packed up her stuff and walked down the trail to catch the bus back to Taipa. A knot of people were already waiting at the stop. In blazing sunshine, her shades were insufficient. No wonder so many locals wore straw hats. Olivia waited under the roof of a garage until the bus arrived, mildly irritated by her pointless morning.

Instead of showing off her new look at a small casino and adding to her stash of dollars, she'd achieved nothing more than a nature outing. Time to focus on what mattered – money.

The return journey took longer largely due to traffic. By the time Olivia got back to Rua do Cunha, it was ten to twelve and she didn't have time to change or touch up her make-up before meeting Jackson. She went directly to the Lord Stow bakery. He was already standing at a table outside with two takeaway coffees and a nata.

"A must in Macau," he said, pushing the plate towards her.

She joined him with a smile, choosing not to share how these little custard tarts had been a part of her life for decades. "It looks lovely."

"So do you." He lit a cigarette.

Olivia picked up on the compliment and tried to decipher the meaning behind it.

"Thanks. A poor imitation of what you achieved yesterday, but ..."

He interrupted. "Esther, has Yoyo given you an interview date yet?"

"Tomorrow. Three o'clock. But I still don't know what role I'm applying for." She bit into the tart, impressed by the pastry and warm, sweet filling. Viviane would approve.

Jackson shook his head, pressing his fingertips to his brow bone.

"Something wrong?" asked Olivia.

"You can't go. Don't let her bully you into this."

Olivia swallowed her pastry. "Jackson, what aren't you telling me?"

"Are you really a poet?" His eyes were intense.

She cleared her throat. "I'm trying to be."

"I read Rimbaud every single day. I learned French just to read the originals."

Olivia looked into his eyes, trying to get a handle on the guy. The moody attitude, the smoking, the drag act, the French accent and contrast to his verbally incontinent friend; it didn't make sense. "Learned French? I thought you ... OK, level with me. What's going on here?"

He stubbed out his cigarette and blew smoke from his nostrils. "Not here. Let's go to my place. It's only a short walk and at least we can't be overheard. I'll carry the coffees."

Under normal circumstances, she would avoid going to a strange man's apartment on second meeting. Yet Jackson had painted her face, assisted in her disguise, seen her tatty underwear and given no hint of any nefarious intentions whatsoever. Still, rules were rules.

She hurried after him, attempting to wrest back control. "Jackson, hey, listen, I don't make a habit of going back to guys' rooms, no matter how much I like them."

He didn't turn around, still stalking ahead, his duster coat undulating in his wake. "It's not a room, Esther. It's an aesthetically soothing garden with a water feature, bonsai trees, lotus flowers and wind chimes. No fish left as the shitty feral cats killed them, *malheureusement*. Zobi used to defend the place but since he died, *bof*! My landlady lives downstairs and tends it every morning before she goes to work. In the afternoons, it's all mine. Did you ever read Verlaine's 'Green'? To me, this space personifies the sentiment. Nature as solace, as apology, as benediction. Daily, I honour my good fortune." He swanned into an alleyway between a supermarket and tea shop. "This way, *ma petite minou*."

Lost for words, Olivia trod in his footsteps to emerge at another wrought-iron gate. Beyond looked like paradise. Mossy mounds, a blaze of flowers, ornate trees and a miniature fountain spilling into a pond combined to seduce a person into paradise. She left the gate ajar and saw Jackson sitting on a black wooden bench resting on two round stones. He waved a hand at the spot at the other end of the bench and placed the coffees between them.

"My sanctuary. Without this haven of tranquillity, life would be insufferable."

A Japanese maple rustled in the breeze and shaded them from the sun's ferocity.

Olivia appreciated the relaxing effect of the lovingly tended garden yet dared not drop her guard. "It's divine. Your very own Garden of Eden. This is where you'd prefer to discuss what's going on with Yoyo?"

Jackson closed his eyes and lifted his face to the sun.

Olivia waited, sipping at her coffee and keeping him in her peripheral vision. She couldn't work him out. Some of his behaviourisms made her think he was gay, yet in other lights, he came across as predatory. Better to maintain her guard.

He finally exhaled, lit a cigarette and sipped at his coffee. "When I first came to Macau from Canada, I shared an apartment with a dancer. We both wanted to work in the entertainment business. We used to do the routine, you know?" He adopted a German accent. "Money makes ze vorld go arount."

"Was she also Canadian?" Olivia asked, her voice soft. There was a story coming, she could sense it.

"No, Caz was British, like you. Funny and friendly and exceptionally pretty. We were best buds. I guess I was a little in love with her. Then someone recruited her, got her a job at one of the casinos as a chorus line dancer. We celebrated her luck." He took a long drag and exhaled a thin stream of smoke upwards.

"So she got what she wanted?"

"Good question. Did she get what she wanted? I don't know. Caz got sucked in by a friend. Can't recall her name but it doesn't matter. That girl said she could help Caz get a foot on the next rung of the ladder, a bigger role, the usual bullshit. Then the job description changed to include more hostess work. Her clients were generous. She was always coming home with jewellery, a new purse, or perfumes and other trinkets. I didn't like it, or the hours she kept. We hardly saw each other and didn't talk much."

"Which casino?"

He gave her a respectful nod. "Another good question, Nancy Drew, and one I asked several times. I never found out because Caz never gave me a direct answer. Apparently, she was working for a consortium. Next stage, she had to bring more girls into said consortium. If she didn't recruit at least one a month, she was punished. Those guys used to turn up at our apartment at nine in the morning to threaten her."

"Nine o'clock?"

"When you work until four am and don't get to bed until five, nine o'clock is the middle of the night."

"Of course. Sorry. Please, go on."

Jackson lit another cigarette off the butt of the last. "After I got into the drag circuit, we started working similar hours. I was up early and in bed late but it was nothing like the pressure on Caz. She started preying on tourists, young girls who knew no better. I called her out, saying she'd lost her moral compass. She yelled and accused me of not having a moral compass to lose. One night I got in from doing my show and she'd gone. All her stuff ... poof!" He made a starburst with his fingers.

"Did you ask at her workplace?"

Jackson gave her a deadpan stare. "Even if I'd known which one it was, do I look dumb enough to tangle with the Chinese mafia? No, thanks. Don't go to that interview, Esther. Just don't. Yoyo is looking after her own interests. You're collateral damage. When those guys get their hooks in, you belong to them and you'll never escape."

Olivia drank her coffee and considered his earnest appeal. How bad could an interview be? She could only guess the answer to that. In her plans, the interview barely featured. It was just another source of information. Her main priority was to squirrel away some money and find a way of speaking to

Thanh. If today and tomorrow went well, she could take the ferry to Hong Kong and a flight to Britain by the weekend, far from this snake pit.

"Jackson, why are you telling me all this?"

"You remind me of her. Caz, I mean, not Yoyo." He stood up and gave her a distant Alfred Camus stare over his shoulder. "I'm getting warm. Shall we go inside for a cool drink? I have some sauvignon blanc in the fridge. We must restrict ourselves to one glass each as I'm teaching this afternoon."

Almost unconsciously she patted her pocket, reassuring herself the knife was still there. "Sure. I could do with the loo, actually. Teaching? Is it English as a Foreign Language?"

A set of wooden steps to the side of the house led to the first floor apartment. "God, no. Those snotty bastards weren't interested in me. Can't blame them. I know more about fishnet stockings than I do about fronted adverbials. Come on in. The bathroom's down there, first door on the left. I'll pour the wine."

Olivia knew perfectly well where the bathroom was. She had studied the layout of this building with great attention to detail. This was the apartment on the fake website which had taken her cash and given her a false address. She waited for a moment, watching Jackson to see if he reacted to her recognition, but he had his head in the fridge, humming 'Don't Cry for Me, Argentina'.

Wary, she opened the bathroom door and locked it behind her. It was the same flat, she was sure. The abstract artwork, the futon style sofa and green scatter cushions, she recalled them all with absolute clarity. While sitting on the toilet, she reached for the window. It opened onto the alleyway towards the garden. The living-room windows overlooked the delightful Japanese garden, meaning the bedroom must have a view of Rua do Cunha itself. Where were the spectacular sweeps of ocean she'd seen online?

Explanations: Jackson and Yoyo were working together to fool backpackers and funnel them into the mincing machine of casino big business. But why his confidential plea just now? Scammer's regret on meeting the victim?

Or, Yoyo was running the scam alone in order to recruit women for her employers and Jackson was nothing more than an associate. But how had she obtained images of Jackson's flat?

One thing was certain, she couldn't trust either of these people and she had other things to worry about. She flushed, washed her hands and emerged with extreme caution. Music was playing, some angelic choral piece she didn't recognise.

"Zumba," said a voice as she returned to the living room. Jackson was lounging on a folded futon against the far wall under a feathery-leaved plant. He indicated her glass on the other side of a glass-topped coffee table with bound bamboo legs. "You asked if I was a TEFL teacher. No, yours truly is a dance teacher by day and entertainer by night. My drag act persona is called Mia Culpa and one of the hottest tickets in town. *Santé*."

Olivia raised her glass. "*Santé*. Oh, would you have any ice cubes? I know it's a shame to water down good wine, but the heat, you know?"

"*Bien sûr*. What civilised home would be without ice cubes? And mine are made with mineral water, so you need have no fear." He sauntered into the kitchen and the second his head disappeared behind the refrigerator door, Olivia switched their glasses.

"No wonder you're in such good shape. Zumba's pretty high intensity, right?"

"Both day and night jobs are high-energy," he replied, offering a ceramic bowl with two ice cubes and a tiny pair of steel tongs. "As for my figure, I never drink beer or eat pastry, surviving on cigarettes and soup and French wine. I make an exception for the occasional cocktail, ideally made with fresh fruit from this little slice of Paradise. My mornings are pure indulgence. I wake late and read poetry while drinking strong coffee and dreaming of Europe."

Olivia studied him as he sipped his wine. He'd removed his duster coat and wore a rough cream linen shirt over tight knee-length Lycra shorts, as if he was about to either leap to his feet and start fencing or man the Parisian barricades. In her eyes, he had a carapace of pride and pretension around a vulnerable soul. But, she reminded herself, he was a performer, a grafter and a master of disguise. She swirled the ice cubes around her glass and tasted.

"I'd say a chilled sauvignon blanc on a summer's day with a view of that garden is quite a luxury. You're lucky to find such a fantastic space." She scrutinised his face for any twinge of guilt. "Have you really never visited Europe?"

He lifted his chin as the voices from the portable speaker rose to a crescendo, his expression beatific. "This piece!" he whispered. "It's Fauré, 'Requiem: In Paradisum'. No finer bliss to elevate the soul." The voices melted into silence and he rested his gaze on Olivia. "No, I have never been to Europe. Isn't that the cruellest? I perform in Venice, Paris and Lisbon every other weekend, my nose rubbed in crude facsimiles, still yearning for the canals, boulevards and trams of the real thing. One day." He looked at his watch. "L'Est, I must change, *parce que le temps* ... no, don't stress. You sit and finish your wine and we'll walk down together." He emptied his glass and with a sad smile, went into the bathroom. "The closest I got to actual French people was three days in Hong Kong's French quarter. It was a birthday treat from Yoyo. That was when Zobi was still alive ..."

"Zobi?" Olivia picked up her glass and moved to the bookcase.

"Zobi la Mouche. I rescued a street-fighting cat from a

pack of dogs and nursed him back to health. He was a tiger, a warrior and a loyal soldier. He patrolled this garden like a park-keeper and our fish, birds and butterflies appreciated him. He was a hero and I miss him every day." He walked down the hallway and Olivia scrutinised the bookcase, ears alert for his return.

On Jackson's shelves stood a classic selection of French literature, or English novels about France: *L'Étranger'. Nausea. Les Miserables. Germinal. Eugenie Grandet. Suite Française. Le Grande Meaulnes. Candide.* Three books by George Sand, including one called *Jacques.*

"What a lovely present! Who looked after Zobi while you were in Hong Kong?" Olivia called over the sound of the taps, already suspecting the answer.

"He didn't need much looking after. Street cat, as I said. My landlady kept an eye on him and Yoyo came round once a day to feed the little guy. He's buried under the maple tree, right where we had our coffee. He always made me think of a different poet: William Blake. 'Tyger, tyger, burning bright', you know the one?" Jackson emerged in the same Lycra shorts, a racer-back grey vest and black trainers. "God, I can't tell you how much I've missed discussing poetry with someone of a like mind. Leave the glass by the sink and let's get out of here. I have Body Pump at three."

Olivia shucked on her rucksack and followed him out. Halfway down the stairs, he stopped and gave her an appraising look.

"Sally Bowles is a good disguise, but your Holly Golightly was uncanny. You could pass for a Parisienne. Those gloves! Come, *chérie, le monde nous n'attend pas.*"

She descended the wooden steps with one last glance at the bench where a tiger was buried.

8

oney makes the world go around. Much as she hated the idea, Olivia couldn't argue with that. In this city, obscene amounts of cash changed hands and she planned to siphon some of it into her own pocket. The first thing was to set a target and once that amount was safely in her possession, quit cold. Otherwise, Jackson was right – she'd never escape. The chances of her getting away were lean enough as it was and she dared not put a foot wrong.

A million dollars was a nice round figure, but overly ambitious. All that was necessary was a substantial cushion to support her father and sister, plus enough left over for her to live a modest life for the next decade. Would 500K suffice? It was a safer aim than a million. The minute her winnings totalled seven figures, heads would turn in her direction, cameras would swivel and a discreet sedan containing two to four men would likely follow her wherever she went. No, as she couldn't trust anyone in this place, she had to win small but often. Only when she was guaranteed a clear passage from here to London could she roll the dice for a big win.

She showered off her morning and changed into a nondescript pair of green trousers and a cheesecloth shirt. The lowest rung in one of the bigger places was the way to gather seed cash and hang on to it. She took a taxi to the Gold Dragon and joined hundreds of people gambling electronically against a massive dealer screen. For such a hub of feverish activity, it was peculiarly quiet. Everyone's focus was on their own monitor and their personal hands of electronic cards, plus those the dealer placed on the stadium-sized screen in the centre of the room. Heads bobbed up and down like pigeons, hardly anyone spoke and the atmosphere reminded Olivia of the days she used to take her grandmother to bingo games. All cheer and chatter and camaraderie until the caller began.

'Rise and shine, twenty-nine!'

'Stairway to Heaven, sixty-seven!'

From that moment on, ruthless concentration and vicious hisses indicated it was every woman, or occasional man, for themselves. When someone called 'House!' you could see a flicker of naked loathing behind the bifocals until the smiles and applause began. And then the complaints about how close they had come. *The near miss. It will drag you back every single time.*

Where this room differed was the total lack of interaction and resolute silence. No one cheered, commiserated or compared losing hands but moved grimly on to the next game. Olivia registered her fake details, took her seat and got to work. Role-playing here was not a question of standing out, but blending in with all the other faces.

Her technique was exactly as simple as when playing the fruit machines. Win a little, then stop. Win a little, then stop. The stopping was how she remained in control. No one who has ever fallen under the thrall of gambling is stupid. Quite the opposite. Gamblers are smart, understand their games and bet with all their experience. The reason they will never win is because the system's experience is greater. The odds cannot be beaten. The punter can.

She lost two games, won three and stopped, walking out with $12,000. That would suffice as tomorrow's ante, where she planned to hit six figures at a neighbouring casino. Only when she had a realistic kitty could she enter the bigger games. Even so, twelve grand was a lot to carry in one's backpack. Olivia took an indirect route to her apartment, waiting in doorways, doubling back and finally hailing a taxi to tour the island before the driver deposited her at the lower end of Rua do Cunha.

Once in her ridiculously tiny apartment, she sat on the bed to think. This was not a safe place. Whether Yoyo and Jackson were working together or Yoyo had used photos of Jackson's apartment without his knowledge was immaterial. She had been ripped off and 'rescued', only to be recruited as casino fodder. Now that she had some hard cash, she could pack her belongings and relocate to a hotel room where Yoyo wouldn't find her. Alternatively, she could play her so-called friend at her own game. Why not find out as much as she could about working the casinos and use it to her own advantage? One question remained – how great were the risks?

She opted to stay on but trust no one and decided against hiding the cash in her room. For a start, there was literally nowhere to put it. Instead, she changed into her combats, tucked the money into an interior pocket of her smaller rucksack and headed out onto the streets. Her to-do list was only partially ticked off. Money was useful but her number one reason for being in Macau was to track down a man. Time was running out and she couldn't wait forever. One more attempt and if he didn't show, she'd have to smoke him out.

To her surprise, when she arrived at Thanh's street she found it had transformed into a street market. Closed to vehicles today, it was stuffed with colourful stalls selling vegetables, flip-flops, straw hats, incense sticks and live chickens. For blending in with the crowd purposes, it was ideal. It was also the optimum pick-pocketing scenario and she was carrying a lot of dosh. She swung her rucksack around to wear it on the front, like a pregnancy pad and waded into the melee. Unlike everyone else in the narrow aisles, her attention was not on the contents of the stalls. She was watching people, scanning faces and trying to keep her distance amid the throng of bodies. After zigzagging from one side of the street to the other, she found herself outside the building where she suspected Thanh lived. This time she walked straight up to the front door and read the names on the bells. No Thanh Ngo, naturally but a Timothy Yee on the ground floor at the rear. A pulse of excitement fizzed somewhere in her stomach. It was him, she knew it.

She turned away, looking up the street for somewhere she could eat, when she sensed someone watching her. Her instinct warned her of danger and she spotted a young man moving in her direction. He glanced to the right and nodded. Another man in a grey shirt was sidling along the pavement, the pair of them approaching in a pincer movement. She reacted immediately, scanning the market for a likely ally. A tall guy with blond curls in a UCLA sweatshirt was examining some hand-carved ornaments. He would do.

"John! Over here!" she called, waving a hand in the air. With a broad smile, she made her way purposefully towards the American.

"Sorry I wandered off!" she gushed and, dropping her voice, added, "Two men are following me. Do you mind if I latch on to you for a minute?"

The guy looked startled, but took it in his stride. "Sure. Anything to help a woman in trouble. Which one do you like best?" His accent was Scandinavian, possibly Swedish, and he showed her two wooden snakes, one painted green and the other black.

"The green cobra is pretty, but the black mamba is more menacing," she replied.

"I like menacing," he said, and held out a note to the stall-holder. "I'll take this one, but I'm not paying five dollars." He argued over the price for a few minutes and finally shelled out another note. Olivia estimated he'd paid two dollars for his menacing mamba. Pretty good haggling.

He smiled down at her with sea-green eyes. "Bargain. That's going on eBay for at least fifty bucks. Are your stalkers still in pursuit?"

Olivia surveyed the aisles and the spot outside the blue building where she'd been standing. The man in the grey shirt and his accomplice were nowhere in sight. "I can't see them anywhere. Maybe they picked a different target. Thanks for your help."

"You're welcome. I like occasional unexpected company. Would you like to have a drink with me?"

"As a matter of fact, I would."

Morten was not Swedish but Norwegian and working his way around the world. Olivia bought the beers and spent a pleasant hour hearing about his adventures. Her curiosity about his success in financing himself via blockchain transactions emboldened her to take a chance.

"I get the whole cryptocurrency thing, technically," she said, as they ordered a second round. "But how could someone convert hard currency, and I'm not talking small change, into digital assets? Surely in a place like this, a lot of money comes from the physical world ... how to pass it to the digital realm?"

"It's possible. You just need to pinpoint the P2P exchanges."

"P2P? What's that and how does it work?"

"Person to person." An awkward expression crossed his face. "For a woman on her own, it's not a great idea. Look, Esther, even I try to avoid this kind of interaction."

"Even you?" She gave him an arch look.

"I'm not mansplaining. I'm two metres tall and can handle myself. But I don't seek confrontation. Cash to crypto facilities are filled with men who want to fight me."

"Why? Because they see you as a challenge? Or do they think you're filthy rich?"

"How would I know their motivations? I suspect most of them have mother issues. How much money do you want to turn into cryptocurrency? For the price of a pizza, I'll show you some places."

Olivia studied his broad, comfortable smile and ocean-coloured eyes. He inspired trust. "Lady Luck was kind to me today. Ten grand up. I suppose you'll want wine with your dinner?"

"To these guys, 10K is nothing more than small change. This is going to be easy. Let's do business before we eat. That way you can relax and enjoy your food. Yes, of course I want red wine. Only a barbarian would eat a pizza without."

It was a smart decision. Morten escorted her to an odd-smelling shop where she explained her requirements to a short man in a three-piece suit, who was smoking a peculiar cheroot. Ten thousand dollars was evidently a minor amount for him and his organisation. With Morten at her shoulder, she handed over a bundle of notes along with the QR code of her digital wallet address. Shortly after he generated a transaction on his PC, it appeared on her laptop. After another ten to twenty minutes there were enough confirmations in the blockchain so that the balance was unlocked and freely available to her. She bowed her thanks and allowed Morten to escort her outside. His height and reassuring hand on the small of her back boosted her confidence. The bouncers at the door stayed frozen in position, their movements limited to following the departing clients with their eyes.

Olivia sauntered onto the muggy street, elated by her newly

acquired skill. "You deserve a huge pizza with a bottle of Valpolicella! Let's eat, drink and celebrate, my Scandinavian saviour!"

La Dolce Vita offered a cool interior, some exceptional tiling and the smell of roasting garlic. None of the pizze on the chalk board had conventional names such as Margarita, Napoli or Quattro Formaggi, because each was named after a famous Italian actress.

Olivia chose the Anna Magnini, with tomato, basil, anchovy and black olives. No cheese. Morten chose the Ornella Muti, with creamy mozzarella, scallops, truffles, mascarpone and a side dish of caviar. It was the most expensive and extravagant dish on the menu, a fact which amused Olivia enormously. They ordered a bottle of Barbera d'Asti and talked until the restaurant staff politely but firmly kicked them out. She could have spent all night listening to this quiet, charming adventurer and knew his stories would stay with her a long time.

She refused a coffee and a nightcap as she had to be up early, but was sorry to leave his company. He walked her home and made a half-hearted pass. Her refusal came as a surprise to neither of them and he accepted with gallant grace. She wished him luck with the rest of his trip and said goodnight.

The world could do with more men like Morten Lund, she decided, and trudged upstairs to remove her clown mask of make-up.

—————

I f at first you don't succeed, make improvements to your strategy and try harder. Olivia was not ready to give up on the hope of catching Thanh while he ran. But today she would try a different technique. Once again, she took the bus south and found a quiet spot to sketch, visible to passing joggers. The surroundings lifted her spirits and she soaked in the views of the sea which she failed to transfer to her sketchbook. Fresh air and greenery was all very well, but that was not the aim of the excursion. At ten-thirty, she closed her pad and considered an alternative plan. If she couldn't engineer an encounter in the outdoors, giving him every opportunity to get away, she would have to take the chance of confronting him at home. It was ten times more fraught with danger, both personal physical risk and the real possibility he would bolt. But she had no choice.

The heat built as she retraced her steps down the trail to the bus stop, and mosquito bites itched on her neck. She crossed the road to the petrol station, where she bought some cold water and waited in the shade until the bus arrived.

She was about to emerge and take her place in the queue when a familiar figure disembarked. She froze. Thanh was wearing running shorts and a white T-shirt, with a pair of well-worn trainers. He scanned the area and set off in the direction of the trail. His gaze had skipped over her but that meant nothing. Thanh was a pro and would give no indication that he'd registered something of interest.

Olivia knew that if he had the slightest suspicion she was anything else than an innocent bus passenger, he would be watching. So she joined the line of people and boarded the bus, taking a seat on the same side as the trail. Like everyone else, she looked out of the window. Unlike everyone else, she was searching for someone. Just as the bus pulled away from the stop, she saw a flash of white bouncing up the path between the trees. It made sense. He wanted to run at the hottest time of the day to build his endurance and tolerance. She glanced at the cheap watch she'd picked up in Kowloon. Eleven-fifteen. *See you tomorrow, Thanh.*

Yoyo was barely recognisable when she opened her apartment. Free of make-up and wearing a Hello Kitty nightshirt, she looked around sixteen years old. She let Olivia in and checked the corridor before closing and locking the door. She flapped a hand in the direction of the kitchen.

"Make the coffee, I have to shower."

Olivia shoved a capsule into the machine and waited, checking her appearance. Jackson had stalked off without giving her any facial contouring tips, but maybe his advice had been the most useful of all. In the time between leaving Lord Stow's bakery and knocking on Yoyo's door, she'd packed all her belongings into her rucksack, including two fake passports. She knocked on Nivea's door and asked if she would keep her belongings safe. The older woman was only too happy to oblige, although she did have a lot of questions. The best way to deflect those was for Olivia to look over each shoulder and press a finger to her lips. She returned to her own cubbyhole with a promise to return sometime after eight. Then she stashed make-up, money, perfume and a passport into her handbag. If the mafia snatched any one of her identities, she was prepared to let go of Ann Sheldon.

Yoyo came out of the bathroom in a cloud of powerful scent. "God, what a night! I got home at five-thirty and let me tell you, I feel like shit." Yoyo did not look like shit. Her gleaming hair was twisted into a clip, her make-up was subtle and she wore a cheongsam with dainty shoes. Beside her, Olivia felt like a painted clown.

"You smell nice," she ventured.

"Nice? I smell like the classiest babe in town. This is an exclusive Clive Christian, a gift from a regular client. 'Chasing the Dragon Hypnotic'. Isn't it fabulous?"

"Fabulous," agreed Olivia, pushing an espresso cup across the counter.

Yoyo waved it under her nose and downed it in one. "The secret to this perfume is subtlety. In fact, the secret to everything is subtlety."

That was a hint. "Do you think I should take this down a notch?" she asked, circling a finger around her face as Yoyo stuffed a stronger capsule into the machine.

"Take it down a notch? You don't get this at all, do you, girl? Sit down. We're going to redo the *Breakfast at Tiffany's* look. Jackson's the expert but I can at least help with the hairpiece and tiara. Then we take a taxi to the venue. They wanna see evening girl first but maybe one other look. Bring all these *Cabaret* clothes, including shoes and accessories. Don't forget your passport. That's non-negotiable. Do you know what to say?" She tilted Olivia's face to the light and started dabbing away her make-up with a cotton-wool pad.

"How in holy hell would I know what to say if I don't know what job I'm applying for?"

Yoyo took away the pad and stared into Olivia's eyes. "Esther, you're no poet."

"Perhaps not yet. The bigger question here is, are you a friend?"

Yoyo resumed her dabbing in silence until Olivia sighed, wondering how much more punishment her skin would have to take. Yoyo stopped, only to mix cream and foundation in her palm. As she applied it to Olivia's cheeks with a sponge, she spoke. "I'll tell you what to say. Two answers only. They ask you what hours, what skills, what experience, what commitment and you always say the same thing in different words. 'Yes, I can' or 'Not yet but I can learn'. That's all you need. You are like a doll they will shape. Don't frown!"

"Sorry. But I am not ..."

"Stop talking now! You're messing up the face. Pull this off, Esther, and you'll become a society girl with a designer hand-bag, fine jewellery and a lifestyle most people can only dream of. Pass me that eyeliner. You're very sweaty, you know. Have you been outside this morning?"

"Yeah, I went for a walk round Coloane. But I showered when I got home."

Yoyo placed a hand over her eyes. "Girl, you are my worst nightmare. Never mind, let's get your foot in the door and you can hire me as your personal life coach. Sit still and I'll fix the hair with some pins. One more coffee and I guess we're ready. Please do not sweat."

Before they reached the end of the street to grab a taxi, the heat and humidity wrung Olivia like a flannel. Sweating was something she could not control, but thanks to all the water she'd consumed, at least she didn't stink. Her gut sent alarm bells, instructing her to run, even as she ducked into the cab after Yoyo.

The casino was only ten minutes away and the interior of the taxi cooled Olivia's skin to the point where she no longer perspired. Such dramatic changes in temperature could not be healthy, she decided. They left the chaotic streets of cars, trucks, buses and bikes to turn through a pair of pillars and through a colonnade of palm trees, beyond which lay the complex itself. Either side of the four-lane driveway were lush green lawns, artificial lakes complete with ornate pagodas and sculptures of gilded dragons, leaping fish and pouncing tigers. The approach to the main building was like nothing Olivia had ever seen. A covered stained-glass porch to protect patrons from the weather was the size of a football field and shimmered with lights, even in the middle of the afternoon. The driveway morphed from tarmac to mosaic tiles depicting grand images impossible to make out from this angle. Limousines and luxury buses dropped their passengers at the red-carpeted steps, where uniformed door staff waited, ready with a welcoming smile. She and Yoyo entered through a smaller – yet still vast – side entrance

The second they stepped inside the astounding hotel, the temperature dropped. This was air-conditioning on an industrial level. The foyer seemed to reach as far as the horizon. Fountains spouted and leapt in choreographed dances, framed by bamboo plants and lit by underwater colours. Far away to the right were individual reception desks, each with its own spotlight, where accommodating staff attended to guests. A dozen sections with sofas, armchairs and TVs served as a comfortable spots to wait for taxis, buses or in her case, interviewers. The chill was enough to make Olivia arrange her faux-fur wrap over her shoulders. She and Yoyo perched on Queen Anne chairs like statues for fifteen minutes until a young man in a bellhop uniform collected them.

Two men in suits sat behind a green-felted desk in an office and the heavy-set one dismissed Yoyo with a flick of his eyes at the door. She patted Olivia's cheek and walked out of the room.

"Name?"

"Ann Sheldon, nicknamed Esther."

Neither man looked up from his keyboard. One held out his hand.

"Passport."

"Oh, is that absolutely necessary? You see, I hoped to earn a bit of cash on the side, nothing official. I can do bar work, receptionist or even waitressing at a ..."

"Passport."

She took out her British travel document with a photograph of her rich red hair and placed it on the table. The short guy snatched it up and stretched it open. He examined the photograph and compared it to her painted face.

"Chameleon, goes with the territory," she shrugged.

"You work in casinos before? Hostess, cocktail waitress ..."

"Croupier." It was another long shot but she knew the basics. Exactly the same way she managed to get herself involved in organised crime two years ago and the reason she was running for her life. "You got a fresh deck of cards?"

The first man opened a drawer beneath the desk, never taking his eyes from her face. He handed over an unopened pack. She flicked off her wrap and flexed her arms, repeating a reassurance in her head. *These guys are no amateurs, but they're no higher than box men. Floor men at best. Do it right or make a mistake and bedazzle. The effect is the same.*

"Ready, gentlemen?" Her expression was as innocent as Holly Golightly's. *When ripping a person off, at least do it with the sweetest smile.* She twisted the pack so the seal broke and flipped open the cardboard flap as if it were a pack of cigarettes. She spilt the deck into two, tilted the corners towards her and riffled them to interlace, pushing them together. She repeated the process, performed a classic strip cut and fan shuffle before ending with a one-handed cut. Then she took the deck in her left hand and pitched cards across the table as if dealing to six players. The cards flew low, spun horizontally in the air and slid to a halt in front of her imaginary players, not once revealing their value. She was out of practice, wearing gloves and her skin was goosepimply cold, but she dealt like a pro. There was no need for a flourish such as a Russian shuffle which looked flashy but simply bent the cards and added extra air. Next the bigger guy handed her a stack of chips. She set them into neat stacks, measured them into whatever combinations they barked at her and pushed them across the felt.

Every question they asked, she answered in a crisp, clear voice, polite and unruffled. Until they told her to start tomorrow night at the blackjack table on the third-floor casino. She remembered Yoyo's advice. *Yes, I can,* or *I can learn*.

"Tomorrow is fine. What time?"

"21.00 for training. Your shift goes from ten till four on the tables, four till six working the floor."

"Working the floor?"

"Being friendly to clients, having a drink, that kind of thing. Tips are pooled with twenty percent to management. Any questions?"

"What's my rate of pay and can I have my passport back, please?"

"We need it to enter you in our system and run the necessary checks. You'll get it back in due course. Currently the basic rate of pay applies and your interview is over. Congratulations, goodbye."

Yoyo was outside waiting for her, her expression tense. "Are they gonna give you a trial?"

"Looks like it. I start tomorrow. Blackjack."

"Yes! Which floor?"

Olivia pointed to the ceiling. "Third."

"OMG! Third floor on your first night? You must have impressed. Maybe we should split your first week's tips."

"Sure, so long as we split your commission."

"Ha, you're funny. Let's go. This time you can pay the cab fare."

They came out of the front door to see a line of taxis waiting and slid into the first like a pair of divas. Olivia could visualise her future if she stayed. Working all night to entertain the punters, shopping, lunching and having beauty treatments every afternoon, on a constant tight leash from the holder of her passport. She gave a little quiver as she put on her seatbelt. Yoyo was already yattering into her phone.

A Range Rover came to a halt outside the complex and three women emerged in a state of high excitement. Clearly wealthy, they were having their modern-day Macau version of afternoon tea – gambling with the girls. The driver pulled onto the drive, and an urge to run far from this place hit Olivia with the force of a lightning bolt. This artificial island was a sticky, honey-filled trap, draining clients and personnel alike. She had to get out and ideally before tomorrow night when she was due to start work. She needed a plan and some security. Playing alone was too risky; she'd need back-up.

"What time do you start tonight?" she asked Yoyo, who had finished her call but was still bent over her phone screen.

"Ten. Before you ask, the answer's no."

Olivia stiffened. Had she spoken aloud? "No? To what?"

"No, I'm not going to give you another make-up tutorial because I'm dead on my feet and need some sleep before another long night."

"Oh, OK." Olivia played crestfallen. "Do you think if I bought Jackson another cocktail ...?"

"Doubt it. He's one moody son-of-a-bitch. Just don't sweat and use matte powder like I showed you. When you get your first wage packet, you and me are going shopping for all the best products and designer ... STOP HERE!" The driver slammed on the brakes and indicated.

"That would be fun," said Olivia, handing over the fare. "I guess Jackson's working tonight, but where can I find him, just in case?"

Yoyo eased her long legs out of the taxi and gave a little shimmy so her dress fell into place, still thumbing her phone. "Drag queens only perform at weekends. That's when they earn sixty percent of their income and the rest comes from their day jobs. Lennie's a personal trainer and Jackson teaches a dance class. Rumba, Zumba, I don't know." She rolled her eyes. "I mean, why bother? I'd send you his number but you don't have a phone so I can't. The dance place is a few doors up from the bakery. Gotta lunch date now. Luv ya, miss ya, ain't gonna kiss ya!"

She teetered along the pavement to an upscale restaurant, greeting an equally glamorous friend at an outside table. Olivia watched them air kiss and squeal, then hitched her rucksack over her shoulders and headed for Rua do Cunha. The cramped, crowded conditions were oddly reassuring after the vast, chilled spaces of the resort. A sense of familiarity embraced her, along with the smell of pork chops and the relentless heat from every quarter. She walked to the bakery where she had met Jackson and assessed the buildings either side. Sure enough, three doors up, above a mobile phone store was a fitness studio offering dance classes. She checked the street behind her and went in.

Jackson was in front of a wall of mirrors, bouncing from one foot to the other, pushing his hands out as if repulsing a crowd. The rhythm changed and he started waving his hands in the air, followed slavishly by the twenty-odd lean beings, all grinning and rotating their hips. Olivia watched for a minute, trying to equate the HI-NRG motivator with the smoking poetry reader she'd met the day before

The class ended abruptly and with much chatter and buzz, the exercisers left. Olivia sidled into the room, conscious of her less-than-perfect face.

"Jackson, hi, is this a bad time?"

He mopped his forehead with a towel and took her in. "So you went to the interview?"

"Yes, I did and I got the job."

He stalked away and started packing a holdall.

"But I'm not going to accept it because I'm leaving Macau. One more night and another day in this place, then I'm out. The thing is, there's something I need to do first. Can I buy you a drink and explain?"

"What kind of drink?" He didn't turn around.

"How about an absinthe? What else would a pair of poetry-lovers drink?"

He looked over his shoulder with a knowing smile. *"D'accord. On y va."*

She grinned back. "Come on, then, Monsieur."

Olivia wanted somewhere quiet and discreet to show Jackson the pictures. She chose Hotel de Ville, because it was expensive, faux-European and like all classic money-laundering operations, completely empty. They sat on velvet chairs in the smokers' lounge, drinking French 75s and listening to crackling recordings of Charles Trenet and Edith Piaf. Shards of sunshine penetrated the blue curtains, acting as spotlights on the carpet, and Olivia could imagine an orchestra tuning up for the night's show. They spoke in whispers until the barman returned to reception and the football game on his radio.

When the moment was right, Olivia showed him the website, the photographs of his beautiful apartment and the faked views from the windows. The photos clinched it.

The ash from his cigarette burnt so long, a third fell off

onto his sleeve. He dusted it off in an absent gesture, his gaze not leaving on the screen. "Can you expand these images?"

Olivia shook her head. "They're static, fixed at that size on the website. Why would you want to look closer? It's pretty clear to me this is your place. My only question is who took these images?"

Jackson stubbed out his half-smoked Gitane and pointed to a dark shape on the sofa. Olivia had assumed it was a cushion.

"Zobi." His eyes glittered, reflections of green lava lamps in his tears. "Zobi la Mouche never slept anywhere else. That was his throne, overlooking his kingdom. How could anyone take these photos without alarming my cat? He didn't trust strangers."

"So the logical assumption is that the person behind the camera was not a stranger. You told me Yoyo looked after Zobi while you went to Hong Kong as a birthday treat. When is your birthday?" She didn't tell Jackson she had hacked the site and dated the photographs.

"28 February. It was a Tuesday and I had a few drinks after class, nothing special because my trip was all planned for the weekend. On the Thursday, I took the ferry to Hong Kong and spent seventy-two hours in the French Quarter. It was a thrill, hearing the language, ordering in *le français* and pretending I was in Paris. On the other hand I was lonely and missed Zobi. I came back early on Sunday. He was so pleased to see me! I've never seen him so affectionate." He blinked and turned his focus on Olivia. "My reminiscences are not relevant, I'm sorry. My birthday is on February 28."

"Don't ask me how I know but I can tell you all these images were taken on the third of March. When you were in Hong Kong. Only your neighbour and Yoyo had access to this place. Which one is more likely to take advantage of you and of innocent travellers looking for a nice place to stay?"

Jackson reached for a cigarette and stopped himself. "Yoyo

..."

"My thoughts exactly." Olivia closed her laptop with a conclusive click.

"No, I hadn't finished. Yoyo is a hustler, it's true, and I can't blame her with the pressure she's under. But she's also my friend. By taking these pictures, she was just being opportunistic. She didn't mean to hurt me."

Olivia sighed, running her finger around the rim of her cocktail glass. "Maybe. She certainly meant to hurt me and dozens of similar women. Imagine these innocents who think they've found a bargain to discover the whole thing was a mirage and their travelling money has gone up in smoke. Then the thief herself turns up like a Good Samaritan, to pluck them from the frying pan and toss them into the fire. It's efficient, you have to give her that. Yoyo is making a killing, and I don't use that word lightly, at the expense of people like me and let's not forget, you."

He withdrew a cigarette and rolled it between his fingers. Olivia wasn't sure if the pout was a symptom of a sulk, or his usual moody persona.

"You're new here," he said eventually, lighting up. "You don't know how hard it is to scrape a living in this place."

"So get out."

"And go where?" He dropped his French affectation and adopted a harsh American accent. "Can I see your CV, Mr Shaw? Ah, most recent jobs include female impersonator and dance class instructor. What skills do you think you can bring to our organisation?"

They sat in silence, Jackson smoking and drinking, Olivia thinking. Finally, she made a decision.

"You're not on stage tonight, are you?"

He gave a slight shake of his head, still pouting. "One can only see my performances Friday through Sunday. Always leave them hungry for more."

Olivia crossed her eyes. "I have a deal for you, Pepé Le Pew. You and me, we're going to hit the tables tonight and we're going to clean up. Your role, should you choose to accept it, is as my make-up artist, stylist and bodyguard. I have to look completely different but equally fabulous at each casino, plus your presence ensures no harm comes to me or my bankroll. I will pay you a walker's fee with a percentage of my winnings as a tip for a job well done. If I do as well as I expect, you can book a flight to Paris, Marseille or Biarritz and live the dream. Time is precious, so don't waste it sitting in your garden, mourning your cat."

Jackson's brow clouded.

"Ask yourself, what would Zobi do? He was a street cat, right out there in the middle of the action, king of the road. You, in contrast, have your nose pressed up against the window, dreaming of freedom. The door's open, Jackson, all you have to do is walk out." She'd overdone it, she knew that, but maybe some of her words hit home.

"You watch too many American movies." He blew a smoke ring which lingered in the air.

Olivia couldn't help but laugh. "And you read too many French books, *mon brave*. Films and literature are wonderful when we need to escape, but sometimes we need to ..." she stamped her heel rhythmically on the tiles and clicked her fingers every fourth tap, "put down the Netflix ..."

His smile transformed his face. " ... the book or the Zoom,"

"And come out with me to play."

He laughed for the first time since she'd met him. "OK. I accept. I must be mad, but yes, I'm in. I hope I don't regret this."

"You probably will, but think of the stories you'll have to tell in Saint-German des Prés. Shall we go somewhere even more discreet and make a plan?"

"I know just the place."

10

The plan was to sleep before the evening's action. Olivia performed some yoga asanas and meditated for twenty minutes to put herself in the mood, then covered herself with a sheet and hoped for the best. An early morning followed by a late night did not augur well for optimum concentration.

To her amazement, she slept a full three hours and awoke with an energy she hadn't felt since Brazil. She ate some cold noodles while watching videos of some old card hands sharing their knowledge. She learned nothing new but it was like remembering a language she used to speak. With a little immersion, it all came flooding back.

At nine-thirty that night, with one eye pressed to the peephole, Olivia saw Yoyo leave for work. She waited a few minutes and then stepped into the corridor. Inside her backpack were all her belongings, including her genuine passport. She knocked on Nivea's door.

"Esther! You want your things?"

"Good evening, Nivea. No, not yet. I'm going out for a

while but I will return in the next twelve hours. Can you give me one of your panda coasters as a token?"

"The coasters? But they're my sister's favourite!"

"That's exactly why I want to borrow one. If I can't come here in person, I'll send someone else. Don't let anyone have my bag unless he or she returns your coaster. That's our secret signal, *está bem*?"

"*Está bem*. Be careful, *menina*." She handed over one of the cartoon panda discs which Olivia pressed to her heart. With a promise to return sometime after eight tomorrow morning, she said goodbye. The little woman crossed herself and kissed her crucifix.

It was an insurance policy, that was all. On the off chance she was recognised by the eye-in-the-sky at any of the establishments she intended to fleece and they came looking, her tiny room would be vacant. Olivia returned to her own cubbyhole, cleared of all traces of her occupancy. All she required to survive the evening was in her rucksack. And her head.

At ten o'clock, she descended the stairs in her sleeveless black dress and heels, threw back her shoulders and stepped into the night. She trod a careful path through the evening crowds, maintaining an aloof air. No one paid her any attention.

As agreed, Jackson let her into the empty dance studio and she stopped dead. He wore a tuxedo, a white shirt and black tie; his shoes were polished and his face clean shaven. His jawline was impossibly square and his hair slicked close to his skull.

"Good evening, Mr Bond," she smiled. "You look impressive."

"Thank you. I can play rich playboy when the occasion requires. It's a pity you'll never see my drag act. Mia Culpa is not just impressive, she's utterly fabulous. Take a seat in front of the mirror and let's get started."

"The thing is, I need at least half a dozen different looks so that even if casinos share images with one another, I won't be immediately recognisable."

Jackson did not respond, draping different fabrics across her shoulders. Then he opened a little pot, rubbed the tip of his ring finger into a pinkish pomade and told her to smile. He dabbed his finger on the apples of her cheeks, swiped some Vaseline across her lips and stretched the skin of her temple in order to apply a catlike flick to the corner of her eyes.

"Is that it?" Olivia demanded. "I need to look wealthy and glamorous and…"

"… and not trying too hard. This is the base coat. Each new casino we visit, we add layers, jewellery and a new outfit. It's harder to take things off. Instead we start small and get bigger. Are we ready?"

Olivia could see the logic but found it disconcerting that woman in the mirror looked very much like herself. "You tell me. Let's go over the plan again. I know, I know, I just want to be sure I've drummed it in. Who are we and what are we planning?"

Jackson replaced his make-up in his briefcase, and folded dresses, tops and handbags into a side compartment. "We're a giddy young couple on honeymoon trying everything once. You're rich, reckless and lucky, I'm the steady hand. As soon as we win over 100K at any venue, we move on, go to a bar, you change clothes and we hit the next place. The aim is to pocket a million and I get twenty-five percent."

"Twenty-five percent of the winnings and a walker's fee. Don't forget there's a possibility we'll end up out of pocket." No way on earth was that going to happen. "What are our names?"

"Ellie and Joe Jefferson. We're Canadians from Sudbury and only in town till the weekend. Next up, Vietnam!"

"Not bad and you certainly nailed the look." Olivia searched his eyes, hoping for enthusiasm and honesty. "You watch my drinks while I watch the table. I won't touch anything unless it comes into my hand from yours and contains no alcohol. When we're done, we split the cash 75% in my favour. Deal?"

"Deal, on one condition. Can we avoid the place where Yoyo works? She will recognise us for sure and it won't take long before she susses she's lost her commission for this week."

Olivia gave him a dead-eyed glare. "You know she was recruiting me into some shitty pyramid scheme but you still want to shield her? How can you be friends with someone like that? She's no better than the person who screwed up your friend."

"I tried to warn you, remember? I told you not to go to that interview, but you knew best. Hopefully you were at least smart enough to not give up your passport."

Olivia said nothing.

"I hang out with people like Yoyo and Lennie because they're just like me, hustling to get ahead. Don't judge us. Our current problem is that Yoyo thinks she has a new recruit and will wake up tomorrow to find you gone. Maybe her bosses will make the connection to the lucky lady who walked off with a hundred grand. You, me and Yoyo could all get punished."

Olivia stalked around the room, clenching her teeth, until she clarified her thoughts. She took a long steady breath before she spoke. "Jackson, I'm not here to rip anyone off, apart from the casino bosses, that is. All I need is a conversation with a certain person and I can leave. I don't want to be disloyal or betray anyone ..." A voice in her head said '*Again*'. She blocked it out and continued. "You think I've treated Yoyo badly. Seriously? Never mind how she fleeced me of all I had. How much of a bleeding heart are you?"

"How much did you pay for the apartment-that-never-was?" asked Jackson, locking his briefcase.

"One thousand Hong Kong dollars."

Jackson whistled and blew smoke in a stream to the ceiling. "For a smart person, Esther, you can be pretty stupid. I'm not being snarky. You aren't the first and you won't be the last. I see that look on your face. Why don't I stop her? Because I have no right. We all bend the rules. Once in a while I whisper a warning in somcone's ear but they nearly always ignore me. You did. The shiny things are too dazzling."

Olivia's skin contracted. Yoyo had played the game perfectly, reeling her in like a master angler. Time to wriggle off the hook.

"The shiny things are indeed dazzling, but I still have a choice. Listen to me. Tonight I'm going to play my game and I intend to win. That way I gain my freedom to leave. You too, if you want. It's a hit and run, so we have to move fast. Win modestly in several gaming joints, split the profits and we never see each other again. I can't fix Yoyo. She would have enslaved me too and then I'd be preying on the next naïf in the cupboard. My plans are bigger than procuring young girls. Can I trust you, Jackson? With stakes this high, I have to be sure."

"You can trust me. Sorry for being so crass and clumsy." He studied their appearances in the mirror. "Looks like we're ready to hit the town. What say I summon our driver?"

"We have a driver?"

"Sure. One of my Zumba clients. I hired him for the night."

Olivia was half impressed, half concerned. "You think that's safer than taking different cabs?"

"Sure. Vasco wants to be a chauffeur. This way we know who's working for whom."

"Good point. I'll call you Joe and you stick to my alias. Listen, I take your point about Yoyo. We'll skip the place where she works. There are enough casinos in this place for us to play without adding to her woes. Pity, I'd love to have slayed them on the third floor."

. . .

She had to admit it, the guy was good. Born for the part and a damned fine actor, Jackson/Joe tried to dissuade her from spending too much, with a good-natured caution. Giggly and persistent, she took her place at table after table. The role of excitable bride was the least of her concerns, as faking was part of her profession, but she needed to keep a clear head to read the room. Smart dealers, professional players and hundreds of pairs of eyes were observing her every move. Too quick and she'd raise suspicion, too slow and she'd get marked as a professional. She promised herself three games at three tables, confident of two wins unless she decided to show off.

The dealer welcomed her, Jackson stood at her shoulder and the game began. In twenty minutes she'd won $15,000 and knew she could double it, but tapped her toe behind her, brushing Jackson's shin.

He leant forward to whisper at a volume that was audible. "Honey, we oughta move on. There's a whole bunch of other games to try. The night is young, sweetheart!" His accent was impeccable.

"Oh, Joe, this is so much fun! What next? Roulette? We have to play roulette, it's such a classic. What's the one with the dice? I want to do everything! Can we order champagne?"

He caught her chin and planted a kiss on her nose. "Whatever the lady wants."

Damn, he was good.

In the first casino, they spent an hour and forty-five minutes, walking out with $109,000. In the car, Vasco asked no questions other than "Where to?" and Jackson did the talking.

Next stop was a cocktail bar for virgin mojitos and a change of appearance. Olivia paid serious attention to Jackson's guidance before switching clothes and face in the bathroom. Now she was 100% Hollywood, with metallic eye shadow, bright red lips and her Audrey gown replaced by a red dress slit to the thigh. It was too loose at the bust, too tight at the waist and thoroughly uncomfortable.

"Who loaned you this frock, Jessica Rabbit?" she hissed as they walked out to find Vasco's car.

"It's one of Lennie's. He wears falsies. Stuff your bra with tissues if that helps."

"Are you going to look the same in every place?"

"Why not? I'm a bland suit, not a player. Nobody's looking at me."

Two hours later, they cashed in chips worth $180,000, even after tipping the dealer $500. Vasco cruised over the bridge to one of the august gambling houses in Old Macau, pointedly avoiding the rear-view mirror. Olivia managed an awkward manoeuvre in the back seat, slipping on an embellished kaftan and wriggling out of the horrible scarlet dress. Jackson added a bejewelled turban and some glittery paste earrings from his briefcase, wiped her lips clean and added false eyelashes. One glance in the mirror was enough. She looked like a drag queen.

"How the hell am I supposed to play this?" she asked, as Jackson slipped a stack of bangles onto her wrist and perched a pair of severe glasses on her nose.

"You're a wealthy widow and I'm your bodyguard. Say very little and hold your hand over your shoulder every time you want a drink. I'll make sure every glass is no stronger than Red Bull. This is one of the traditional places. Play for longer than an hour and we've outstayed our welcome."

He was right. The second she walked in, the change in atmosphere was palpable. No one smiled or welcomed them or wished them a good evening. Instead, everyone from bouncer to barman bristled with suspicion. She ignored it all, played three hands of poker and left sixty grand lighter. It should have been winnings of double the amount but the man with a goatee beard was a cheat. That was not guesswork, because she knew from experience how to spot the tells. She couldn't be sure if it was a scam run between goatee man and the dealer, or if there was external assistance. What she did know was that she won once and lost twice, the second time with an unbreakable hand.

Jackson was not deterred and suggested another of the original gambling houses to recoup their losses. He swore that to his knowledge it was not run by the Chinese mafia so her disguise could remain the same. The place was clearly a brothel with entertainment, but it allowed bets up to a million in the private rooms. Olivia was not brave enough to go up against professional poker players just yet, opting for the noisier downstairs floor. She was the only woman at the table. Jackson stood behind her, his stance protective.

Once again, she played three hands. On this occasion, she won all three and in a strategic move, handed 10% of her winnings to the dealer. $30,000, 10,000 per game and she recouped her losses from the mafia club. Nevertheless, it was nearing one in the morning and she was at one third of her target of $1 million. Vasco drove them across the bridge as steadily as he could while watching for any kind of tail. Jackson focused on her disguise. False eyelashes off, a beauty spot on and a stunning Versace dress.

"It's going to have to be one of the private rooms," Olivia muttered, turning away so Jackson could zip her up. "Otherwise I can't access the big-money games. Where could I get an invitation? Any ideas?"

There was a long pause until Jackson said, "Yoyo would know."

She grimaced. "Sorry. Not going to happen."

"Listen, Olivia, private rooms require fifty grand just to get admitted. We're out of our league. Let's go to The Venetian and play hard. I'll try what you taught me at the tables and if we can triple what we have, maybe they'll offer us an opportunity. The clock is ticking. Lift your chin, this look needs Loren lips."

Five-card stud took all the skills she had. Observation, arithmetic, confidence and attitude. This time the dress helped. Six players, four men, two women. Olivia took her seat and allowed her instinct to absorb her environment as she tuned out the dealer's instructions. She kept her gaze above the other players' heads, as if she was praying, but picked up the vibrations from everyone at the table.

She won three times, purposely folded early on a strong hand, and on the fifth game cleaned them out. When she left the table after thanking her fellow players, she found Jackson sitting in a chair around ten metres away. He'd watched everything.

She air-kissed his cheek. "How much did you get?"

"Ninety thousand."

"You won 19K already? You're a fast learner."

"I said ninety, not nineteen."

She stopped in her tracks and stared. "In that case, it's time to go home."

"Did we hit the magic number?"

"We hit it and then some. Let's find Vasco and call it a night."

"Excuse me?" An elegant woman with a high bun in house uniform stood at her shoulder. "The hosts would like to include you in one of the private games. Please follow me."

It was three in the morning and Olivia's concentration was shot. But the chance of doubling her money was too tempting. The house understood that only too well. Because the opportunity to regain any losses was equally so. This invitation would not come around again.

Jackson shot her an enquiring glance.

"Sounds like fun, right, Joe?" She dropped her voice. The

giggly honeymooner was gone. They were invited as professionals and would behave accordingly.

"Sure, Ellie. Why not?"

She smiled and took his arm to follow their escort. A man who could act convincingly was worth his weight in gold. A private elevator took them to the revolving restaurant, and their guide used an electronic key to open a smaller lift with velvet benches in case the journey of nine seconds became too wearying for the occupants.

"Do you have my glasses?" she asked Jackson.

He hesitated for a beat and reached inside his briefcase. "Here you go."

The elevator doors opened and Olivia strode out as if she was the guest of honour, her hand in the crook of Jackson's elbow. Downstairs was extravagant and showy in stark contrast to this quiet, subdued atmosphere, where lamps picked out tables of players amid the midnight blue lighting and long glittering bar.

Olivia opted to join a game of Texas Hold 'Em and Jackson went to get drinks. He squeezed her hand and she squeezed back. Community games, in Olivia's opinion, were more challenging, but gave her more freedom to observe her fellow players. Two cards to play against the board. She was seated three away from the dealer's left. The small blind, a distinguished American wearing a Rolex, placed the minimum bet, $50,000. The big blind to the American's left was a young Chinese guy who constantly fiddled with his chips. He doubled the bet. So far, so normal.

Olivia was next and the first to act on something other than convention. Her cards were an eight of spades and an ace of diamonds. The ace had potential. She called, adding a 1K chip to the pot. Cautious, yet unintimidated. The player to her left folded but the handsome woman beside him raised to $200K. Olivia's heart sank. She couldn't afford to lose all they'd gained tonight. Half of their winnings was the max she was prepared to bet. An older balding man with a large moustache called and the final player folded.

Four people remained in the hand. As the dealer set the burn card to the side and spread three across the board, Olivia closed her eyes for a second. She blocked out what was on the table and the cards under her hand and instead sent her awareness around the table. One pulse came from the woman. Excitement, a hawk-like focus. An air of desperation emanated from the chip-fiddling Chinese guy. He had weak cards, she sensed it, but he'd take the risk. Nothing from the American. She opened her eyes to see him staring at the three cards in front of the dealer. A two of hearts, a Jack of diamonds and an eight of clubs. Olivia kept her breathing steady and face impassive. Two eights made a pair. Not the hottest hand in the world but with the ace it was worth a risk.

The American checked. The Chinese guy raised to $300K and she called. The woman immediately raised to $400K. That was Olivia's limit. The next card had to be something exceptional or she'd keep her powder dry for another hand. The dealer flipped the turn and Olivia froze. The ace of hearts. Now things were getting interesting. Two aces and two eights. With two pairs and that Jack of diamonds she had a fighting chance of beating a weaker hand. She screwed her courage to the sticking place and readied herself. The American raised to half a million, his face as impassive as if he was watching a TV show. It was too much for the Chinese man, who folded and ordered a drink. Olivia called, which meant going well over the half a million, but she still had another round to pull out.

The woman, whose nationality Olivia couldn't pinpoint, gave every impression of supreme arrogance. Her tell was the ring. When she felt in possession of strong cards, she twisted her ring back and forth, the way a cat might when gearing up to pounce. Now her fingers were still.

Eventually, she sighed and raised to $600K. Although she was damn sure the old girl was bluffing, Olivia's mouth dried. The stakes were too high. Little bottles of water were at every player's elbow, but Olivia lifted her hand to her shoulder. In an instant, Jackson pressed a glass into it. The liquid was a similar colour to whisky yet effervescent. She took a sip. An energy drink to fill her with caffeine. She did not crack a smile and turned her attention to the American as the dealer discarded the top card and placed the final one, the river, onto the board.

Olivia kept her eyes on the dealer's bald patch for a second. That way, her peripheral vision was able to take in the stiffening in the American's demeanour and catch the intake of breath from the game's observers. She called on all her calm and stillness techniques, then looked at the card. She'd already planned her reaction, fingers to temples and eyes hidden behind her fake specs. Widening pupils would give her away.

The ace of clubs. She stared at it, simultaneously disbelieving, amused and chilled by superstition. Between her cards and those on the board, she had a full house. Two black eights, two black aces. Add to that the ace of hearts and she was holding a winning Dead Man's Hand. Not much could beat that and she sensed it. The story behind the name shivered across her shoulders. Wild Bill Hickok was killed while playing poker in Deadwood – shot in the back by a man named Jack.

Superstition was unlikely to scoop the pot, but a cool head just might. The only question was what the American held. Only if he had four of a kind or a flush could he top this. The odds were remote but she was prepared to meet his bid. Her composure slipped just a moment when he folded. So it was down to her and the dowager. Olivia cast her gaze at the pile of chips beside the jewelled hands, noting the interlaced fingers were not twiddling her platinum ring. It could be a superlative double bluff, but Olivia took another sip of fizzy caffeine and made a judgement call.

She pushed the entire pile of chips into the centre of the table. All in. She didn't say a word.

Everyone's focus switched to the steely-eyed woman whose velvet dress functioned as a display surface for all her jewellery. She matched Olivia's bid, thrusting the same value of chips onto the table. The dealer checked that both women were sure with a flick of his eyes, then nodded to Olivia. She splayed her cards on the baize and sent a frisson through the crowd. The woman stood, her face impassive. She flipped over her cards. Two pairs, sixes and threes. To bet a million bucks on such a hand was inconceivable.

Olivia offered to shake, a gracious winner.

The woman withdrew her hands, with a gentle waggle of her head to indicate her refusal was due to hygiene, not hostility. "You play well. We shall meet again." Her accent was faintly Germanic or Eastern European, Olivia couldn't be sure. "Tomorrow."

"That would be interesting." Olivia kept her poker face intact.

The woman did not even acknowledge her answer and walked over to another table. Olivia collected her chips and tipped the dealer, and Jackson escorted her to the cashier. She insisted he accompany her into the cage, where she had the choice of how to cash in winnings. She refused the option of a bank transfer and insisted on cryptocurrency for at least a third. It caused some consternation, but eventually they sent a transaction to her digital wallet. For the rest, she accepted the offer of a briefcase filled with cash and a security escort to their car. With that amount of loose change, she daren't take any risks. Jackson called Vasco, who was asleep, and had him drive to the hotel entrance. The hostess with the high bun caught up with them in the foyer and handed Olivia an envelope.

"You are cordially invited to the VIP room tomorrow evening. May we send a car?"

"My plans are fluid. I'll make my own way, but thank you."

Olivia tipped the security guy and once they were safely in the car, waved him goodbye.

"Successful night?" asked Vasco, yawning and blinking at the lights.

"Not bad," Olivia answered, still stunned by the turn the last two hours had taken. "It's late. Let's head back to Taipa. Thank you, Vasco." She tilted her head to look at Jackson, sitting beside her like a mannequin. "You still awake?"

"I need a drink and I'm not talking about a Red Bull."

"Me too. You know what, I don't plan to sleep in that vile cupboard tonight. Let's have a drink somewhere and honour our agreement."

"Yeah, sure, whatever. What's the time?"

He was either reeling from their success or had other plans. Olivia needed to play this very carefully.

"Almost six in the morning. Vasco, will you do one last thing for me? You're going to need this panda coaster."

Hotel Lotus Flower was stupidly cheap in comparison to the place they had just left. Olivia booked herself a room, told Jackson to order a bottle of champagne and left instructions with the sleepy clerk to direct the taxi driver upstairs with her bag. She assessed the risks as she hurried up the stairs. Jackson knew exactly how much money she was carrying and if he wanted, he could demand a lot more than 25%. She opened the room, locked the door behind her and flung the briefcase onto the bed. She used the same combination she'd given the cashier, i.e. time and date, took out the correct amount plus another three bundles of notes and placed it all in the bedside drawer. She shoved half the remainder in the safe, changed the combination and tucked the briefcase containing the rest behind the headboard. Then she stuck her flick-knife into her waistband. Trust was a luxury even three million dollars couldn't buy.

Nails rapped lightly on the door. Olivia checked the spyhole and admitted Jackson, still carrying his own briefcase, plus a bottle of Perrier Jouet, an ice bucket and two glasses. That sleepwalking air hung over him and he stood in the middle of the room, looking around for a suitable place to put the champagne.

"On the table is fine, Jackson. Are you OK?"

He set the glasses and bucket on the table. "This can't be real. Did we just walk out of there with ... that much?"

Olivia searched his face. "Yes, we did. Due to a combination of experience, skill and some pretty good luck, we're flush, excuse the pun. Take a seat and I'll open the champagne. I think we have something to celebrate."

"Is there a mini-bar? Because I need another Scotch. I just had one in the bar while I was waiting for the bubbles. It hit the spot and my throat is crying out for another."

She gestured at the cupboard under the TV. "Help yourself. Listen, we had a deal which I intend to uphold. God knows, you deserve it. You've been invaluable this last twelve hours."

A louder knock came at the door. "You guys? I got the bag."

Olivia checked the peep-hole and let Vasco in. With some relief, she took possession of her rucksack. "Thank you so much for doing this. I hope the lady in that apartment wasn't alarmed by you showing up so early."

"Estrela? Nah. Nothing fazes her." He yawned and shook himself. "Anyway, we know each other. I used to drive her to the hospital when her sister was dying. She's a good person."

"Her sister ...?" Olivia's skin cooled.

"Yes. She used to have a younger sister, Nivea. They lived

side by side for years. Nivea in your place, Estrela next door. When Nivea got sick, Estrela hired me on a retainer. Back and forth to the hospital every day until Nivea passed away. Every time she sees me, she wants to settle the bill. I tell her, 'Estrela, you're getting senile, you already paid me in full!' with a big grin. She knows I'm lying and I know she knows. We pretend to make each other feel better. You know something else? She really loves those panda coasters you gave her."

"Estrela," Olivia repeated. It was the Portuguese word for 'star'. She thought back to her first confusing conversation with her neighbour.

"*Você é inglesa?*"

"*Yes, I'm English. My name is Esther.*"

"*Esther? Like me!*"

"*Your name is Esther?*"

"*No, my name is Nivea.*"

"*Nivea. Like the face cream?*"

"*My parents didn't name me after a beauty product.*"

Vasco covered another huge yawn. "Guys, is there anything else or can I go now? It's already morning and I've got a busy day ahead."

Olivia gazed at him, her comprehension of the Macanese people and their city shifting by several degrees. "Vasco, you are the best taxi driver in the world. Here's your fare plus a tip." She handed him three blocks of bills.

He stared at the notes in his hand while Olivia kept an eye on Jackson, who was crouching in front of the mini-bar.

"You're kidding me. I can't take a 150,000 dollars for one night's driving! Are you crazy?"

"Call it an investment in your future. Take it, Vasco, with my thanks. All I ask is for your silence. If anyone asks, you know nothing about who I am or where I came from. A foreign woman asked for a driver and you volunteered. You drove me and my escort around the casinos all night and dropped us at Rua do Cunha. You don't even know my name."

He was shaking his head, still transfixed by the money in his hand. "It's true. I don't know your name."

"Let's keep it that way. Good luck with the taxi business and goodnight." She guided him to the door and closed it behind him.

Jackson was sitting on the end of the bed, a glass of whisky in his hand and his tie loosened. She met his eyes and wished for a second she could see him in drag. There was no doubt in her mind he would be an excellent performer. Right now, his body language displayed exhaustion and incredulity, and very little threat.

She took hold of the champagne cork and twisted the bottle until the satisfying pop released the fizz. Jackson didn't react, still staring into his glass. She rinsed the flutes in case of contamination and poured golden bubbles into each.

"To a successful night," she said, handing him a glass. "You were a superlative assistant and I'm profoundly grateful. *Santé, mon brave*."

"*Santé*," he said, slugging at least half his glass. His eyes squeezed shut and his body tensed as he swallowed. He placed the glass on the table. "All things considered, I think I'm a bourbon kind of guy at heart. Esther, the money you just gave Vasco is life-changing. He can buy a fleet of cabs with that kind of cash. Or do whatever he likes with his life."

"Money makes ze vorld go arount?" she teased.

His brow creased. "You know what? It does. Here, Hong Kong, Canada, wherever. My whole life I've been trying to earn a living and you walk out of a private gambling room with three and a half mil? I can't wrap my head around this. Who are you?"

"If you really want to know, I will answer that question.

Unfortunately that means you leave here with nothing because I will have to kill you."

He tried to smile but it shrivelled into nothing. "You're not joking."

"'Fraid not. Alternatively you mind your own business, take your share and we never see each other again." She pulled the bedside drawer all the way out and took it across to the table, her back against the wall the whole time. "I've done the sums. Twenty-five percent of our winnings combined with the ninety grand you earned comes to $915,000. If you make me a promise, I'll add another 85K as your walker's fee to make it a million."

His face sagged and he threw the contents of his glass into his mouth. "A million dollars."

"Correct. How about a fair swap? You give me all the wigs, dresses and accessories out of your briefcase to make room for large amounts of dollar bills. As for the make-up, I'll get my own. Jackson, pull yourself together and get out of here. Just don't get robbed on the way home, OK?"

He scrambled to his feet as if waking from a dream and opened his briefcase on the bed, tipping all the elements of her disguises onto the duvet. She made no attempt to collect it and simply pointed to the drawer. As if he were afraid each stack of bills would combust, he put them gingerly into his case and closed the clasp.

"Now what?"

She reached into the fridge and tossed him another miniature bottle of Bushmills. "Up to you. My advice would be to lie low for a while. Spend a couple of weeks living it up in Hong Kong, or chill out on Lamma Island. Then take a plane to Italy and catch the Venice Simplon-Orient Express. There's no finer way to discover Europe."

He shook his head in wonder but didn't utter a word.

"Right, I need to get some sleep and you need to put that

money into your bank account as soon as possible. If anyone wants to know what happened tonight, you were hired as my walker. I gambled, you drank whisky and you were bored to tears. After that, you never saw me again. Just another forgettable drifter."

"I don't think I'll ever forget you."

Olivia locked eyes with his and gave one short nod. "Oh, I think with a bit of effort, you just might. Now, about that promise you owe me."

"Sure. Anything."

"Swear on your life you will never gamble again."

He cocked his head like a puppy. "I'm sorry?"

"You will be. Jackson, I've seen it so many times it hurts. You're dazzled by our success. You're also confident and the perfect mark. They believe the same of me. That's why they invited me back tomorrow. I'm allowed one win. Maybe two or even three. But eventually, they will drain me like a carcass with its throat cut. Trying to beat the system is a losing game. Promise you'll forget everything you saw tonight. I mean everything. Because if you don't, one of these days I'll blow into a run-down shithole city, stumble down a backstreet filled with losers and find you in some godawful bar, nursing a glass of bourbon with bloodshot eyes, wondering how it all disappeared. Be smart. Take the money and never get greedy."

He nodded with genuine conviction. "OK. I swear. That was the one and only time. Thank you, Esther. You've changed my life."

"Goodnight, Jackson. Take care."

11

She gave it fifteen minutes. In that time, she wiped off all her make-up, changed into her scruffy combats, wedged the money and disguises into her rucksack and pulled on her saggy black beanie. All the while, she was making a plan. It wouldn't be difficult to grab a lone woman carrying large amounts of dollar bills. The aim was to avoid potential enemies and also those who passed as friends. Anyone could be watching so she must box clever.

Now she had a cash cushion, she had to leave Macau as fast as she was able. One last job to do and that was to speak to Thanh. There was a strong chance he'd listen, especially if she caught him at the end of his run. After that, she had to stash the remaining cash. It would require some ingenuity. Before she could achieve any of those aims, she had to get safely out of the hotel. It wasn't easy to judge the time of day based on daylight, but the sound levels from the street were far more reliable. Engines, breaking bottles, horns, shouting traders, ringtones and the beeping of reversing trucks formed Macau's dawn chorus. Time to go.

Olivia shouldered her pack, palmed her knife and opened

the door. No one was waiting in the corridor. She moved silently towards the stairs, alert for any observers in nearby rooms. Once through the fire door, she stopped to listen, sending her awareness outwards to detect any sign of company. Not a single pulse. She paced down the stairs, with random checks up and down the stairwell. When she reached the ground floor, she stood behind the exit for a full three minutes. Then she strode out and turned away from the signs to reception, heading for the staff areas. In top London hotels where she had done much of her undercover work, it would be impossible to enter the kitchen without a swipe card. Here, the rules were different.

She parked her knife in her pocket and removed her casino pass from the previous night. Every time someone looked askance, she flashed it with a confident smile. Nobody tried to stop her. When she reached a delivery bay where men in overalls were unloading the contents of a seafood truck, she jumped off the platform into a puddle of melting ice, splashing her fatigues with fishy-smelling water. With one more glance over her shoulder, she walked away from the Lotus Flower Hotel.

Tiredness made her eyes itch. Her backpack, heavier than usual, was already weighing hard on her shoulders. She checked the time. Quarter to eight. Three hours before she needed to be in Coloane for her surprise assignation with Thanh. Unless she got some rest, she would be below par and likely to make poor decisions. She walked in the direction of the bus stop, her exhausted mind searching for somewhere safe to sleep. The answer came from her combat trousers.

She stank. She looked like a backpacking traveller with no valuables. First in the queue for the bus, she paid her fare and occupied a corner of the back seat. From there, she watched all the other passengers avoid the whiffy hippie. Satisfied no one was about to ambush her, she dabbed some Tiger Balm under her nose and laid her head on her pack. The wheels on the bus went round and round ...

No one could call it a deep sleep, due to the constant invasions of voices, sudden braking, constant stops and the unpleasant pong of her own clothes, but when consciousness returned, she was at least partially restored. She sat up and checked the digital display above the driver's head. 10.45. She had half an hour for some breakfast and a litre of water before heading up the track to confront Thanh.

Over a bowl of noodles, Olivia's body chose to unleash all the nerves she should have felt the previous evening, adding to her trepidation at meeting her ex-colleague. Her hands shook as she tried to scoop the hot and sour soup into her mouth, attracting concerned glances from fellow diners at the roadside shack who obviously thought she was an alcoholic or something worse. She finished the food, drank her water and crossed the road in search of somewhere shady to get herself under control. The best thing was to meditate, focusing on nothing more than her breathing.

A sandy hollow caught her eye as she ascended the track, shaded by the tree canopy. It was no more than five paces from the main trail, but a place of peace as it housed a small shrine to the gods. Anyone passing by would assume she was praying and let her be. She slipped off her pack, crossed her legs and wedged the rucksack between the small of her back and the curvaceous rocky shelf. Incense hints tickled her nose but the breeze wafted most of it into the sky. Although the air was humid and sticky, Olivia's temperature cooled after a few minutes in the shade. Her breathing calmed and the noise of insects and birds morphed from distraction to natural soundtrack.

She closed her eyes, allowing everything to settle. Her guts, her skin, her concentration and most importantly, her breath. Inhale, exhale. Turn inwards. Minutes ticked by and she gathered herself. Everything she needed was within. Her mind wandered like a restless cat but she brought it back to centre, uniting it with her body. Calm, cool and in control, she rested.

Birdsong and a soft whistle. She jerked awake with a gasp.

Crouching two metres in front of her was a lean man in a white T-shirt. His features were familiar, as if she'd once known his brother.

"All right, OJ?" he rasped.

She blinked at this vision, all senses on full alert.

"Hello, Thanh." Her emotions raced, shock, fear, relief and anger colliding and competing to increase her pulse rate.

They held each other's gaze, the weight of what needed to be said almost crushing.

"I came to say ... I'm sorry," she faltered.

"Bullshit. You came because you want something. Sorry is just wiping the table clean before you ask me. You owe me a whole lot more than sorry." His words were quiet and precise, the way he used to speak before he struck an opponent down. It robbed her of speech. All she could do was nod like a chastened schoolgirl.

"You look well," he observed, his brow shading his eyes.

Every word was a potential misstep. "Thank you. So do you."

"That's the wonder of surgery, you see? Smoothes all the lines and makes you appear ten years younger."

Her mouth was dry and she yearned for her water bottle but didn't dare move a muscle. Thanh's crouch gave him the advantage. "Yeah, and you're obviously in good shape, what with the running ..." she tailed off, terrified of antagonising him. All he needed to do was rush her, stick a knife under her ribs and push her over the ridge and she was finished. Her body might lie in the forest for weeks, maybe months before she was discovered. Perhaps if she offered him a share of the money she'd won? Her conscience caused her to flush with embarrassment. *He would spit in your face.*

"You came here to compliment me on my fitness?" he sneered.

"Thanh, I had to come here in person because ..."

"You know, I wasn't keen on the babushka look you were wearing at the bus stop yesterday, but I appreciate why you used a disguise. That's another advantage of being a woman. Altering your face doesn't have to be permanent."

Olivia looked into his eyes, ignoring the same-but-different frame in which they were set and acknowledging his icy fury. "I couldn't see your face. I recognised your walk."

"Funny that. I recognised yours. Feline, predatory, almost like a big cat but over-confident of her camouflage. Lesson learned for both of us. Masks only hide the face." His tone was even, yet Olivia sensed his rage was about to erupt. "Come on then, what do you want?"

She assessed their situation. He was light, fit and unencumbered by a rucksack holding all his worldly possessions. If he ran now, she'd never find him again. She was as vulnerable as a sacrificial lamb. If he tried to kill her, she'd let him.

"I want," she began, "to apologise." She cleared her throat, trying to clarify her thoughts. The number of times she'd rehearsed this speech in preparation for meeting this man, how was it possible she was scrambling for words? "What I did, absconding without warning and leaving you exposed, was unforgivable."

"But still you want me to forgive you."

In a rush, the horrors of those few days when Olivia chose her own life over his overwhelmed her. Tonight, or whenever she next found sleep, the nightmares would return.

"I had ..."

"If the next words out of your mouth are 'no choice', I'll

cut your fucking throat." Thanh's voice betrayed no anger, only a cold disgust.

"That wasn't what I was going to say. Thanh, I had to make a decision. All I ever did, all you ever did, was to obey orders." She spoke in a rush, recalling the imaginary pleas she had rehearsed as she jogged the streets of Taipa. "Remember our motto? Borrowed from less ethical undercover teams but the principle held true. 'By Any Means Necessary.' You know as well as I do what that means: infiltrate, befriend and even form relationships with our targets, glean intelligence and report to our superiors. Then they moved the goalposts. I knew what they were planning because they pretty much said so. Undercover activity became a dirty secret. When the public finds police tactics unpalatable, the system won't change. Hell, no. Apologies from the top brass, an official inquiry and a sacrifice to appease the crowds. Guess who? A trial at the Old Bailey, all the force's dirty secrets dumped at my door and a five- to ten-year stretch in Holloway. All in order to protect everyone else up the hierarchy, from the DCI to the Commissioner. We've seen it all before with the left-wing infiltrators like the SDS and NPOIU – moles routed by Jack Russell terriers." She warmed to her theme and shook her head. "Not for me. Not after I gave them years of my life, risked torture and death, and even lost my husband in the line of duty. Either I left everything behind, including you, or I'd be the fall guy. Yeah, I had a choice. I saved my own skin. If there was any way I could have warned you, I would have done."

He made a motion as if filing his nails. "Know what this is? The world's smallest violin. That's a politician's apology, OJ, and you know it. Poor you, having to go to court and possibly an open prison for a few years, knowing your name would be all over the papers for at least a week. My heart aches for you, truly. The fact is, when you disappeared into the ether, you left me wide open. The first thing they were going to do was shake out other suspect plants. We've both witnessed their methods. Scenes like those still give me the heebie-jeebies."

Olivia dropped her gaze. "Me too."

"But you chose to abandon me to exactly that fate, purely to save yourself. Now you turn up here to apologise. Excuse my language, but you can go fuck yourself." Finally, a flicker of emotion in those ophidian eyes.

"I'm already fucked. My decision to run and hide means I have to live off-grid with no police protection, no plastic surgery or new identity. I'm on my own. Various members of the network are still out for my blood. On one occasion, they got pretty close. They sent Uncle Jack."

"And you're still here?" Thanh's tone was openly scornful.

"I am, but Uncle Jack is not."

"Nope, not buying that." Thanh narrowed his eyes. "You didn't kill Uncle Jack."

"I didn't, but I swear he's dead. Desperate measures, you know? The network will spend years trying to avenge my betrayal. No one has the authority to call them off. It's different with the police." Her mouth was sticky and her speech thick.

Thanh rolled off his heels and onto his backside. His posture became less of a pouncing cat and more of a campfire storyteller. "A-ha. She finally gets to the point. You want me to clear you with the Met? Are you seriously that naïve? You never used to be this dumb, OJ. Inexperienced, impulsive with a questionable moral code, most definitely, but not stupid. What the hell happened to you?"

She blinked, refusing to let his words hit their mark. "I'm thirsty. I'm going to drink some water." With a gesture to the bottle in her pack, she asked permission with her eyebrows. His shoulders lifted a millimetre.

She tugged the bottle free of its net and unscrewed the cap, aware of his eyes following her every movement. After she slugged several mouthfuls, she wiped her mouth and composed her response.

"Stupid? Yes and no. I've kept myself off the radar until now, so I can't be completely useless. Yeah, I have my weak points, just like everyone else." She replayed his words. "As for my questionable moral code, surely that goes for both of us? We lied and deceived our way into that organisation, pretending to be something we were not, out of a strong sense of right and wrong. We were the good guys."

Thanh barked a bitter laugh, a sound so harsh she recoiled. "A strong sense of right and wrong? You were shagging Milo Vargas, for God's sake! How the hell you can claim the moral high ground after ..."

"A-ha. He finally gets to the point." Her choice of words was a conscious echo. "I knew it. All that sincere back-patting and expressions of admiration from the SOCS guys hid a deep disgust. Funny that Johnny, Mick and even Spike, if I remember correctly, were 'heroes for sleeping with the hairies'. Faking relationships with women in left-wing protest groups earned them the badge of 'deep swimmers'. Whereas the deepest swimmer of all, a woman sleeping with a far more lethal enemy to elicit vital information, is only seen as one kind of pro."

She caught her voice rising and took a moment to master her emotions. "Sorry, Thanh, I interrupted. You asked how I can claim the moral high ground after ...? After what? What were you going to say?"

He didn't meet her eyes.

"Cat got your tongue? OK, this is what I think you were going to say. How can I claim the moral high ground after I willingly got into bed with a violent gangster? Because I was DOING MY JOB. Yes, it was morally suspect and yes, it's now viewed as unethical, but at the time, I had the backing of my superior officers and, I hoped, the rest of the Special Organised Crime Squad. I naïvely thought we were all making sacrifices for the undercover operation, right? Wrong. Even you, my best mate, despised me for what I was doing."

"I didn't despise you." His voice was low, a deliberate contrast to her strident defensiveness. "But I will admit I didn't like it. You were still grieving. To ask a vulnerable person, whatever their sex, to form a fake attachment was worse than manipulative. It was cruel."

A swell of pain threatened to overcome her. Not his fault. He couldn't know that she had closed the door on a particular set of memories.

"You're a liar, Thanh Ngo. You despised me. Your eyes give more away than you think. To be honest, I couldn't care less anymore. When I cut and ran, I had only two regrets. One was abandoning my family. The other was you. I have never forgiven myself for leaving you at the mercy of those vile scumbags and I doubt ever will. Uncle Jack gave me a cryptic message before he died and now it's my top priority to see if my sister and my dad are safe and well. Even to the point of risking arrest until I got wind you were still alive. That chance of reconnecting gave me hope and I had to grab it."

He folded his arms. "Save the schmaltz. What do you want from me?"

"You have contacts. All I'm asking is for you to clear my passage in and out. Especially out. If I get arrested, I'll be stuck in Purgatory for the rest of my life. After everything we've been through, is that too much to ask?"

Thanh got to his feet, his eyes half-lidded. "Sticking by your colleague on an undercover op? Is that too much to ask? Go to hell, OJ, this conversation is over. Hear this. If I ever see you again, it will be the last time." He took off at a steady jog and vanished between the trees.

Olivia sat there for another five minutes, her mind attempting to process his words and berating herself for a clumsy, self-serving speech. Maybe he was right – she was stupid. How was it possible that Thanh, her best buddy, right-hand man and confidant, hated her that much? Not just the chill in his tone and blank refusal to lift a finger to help but also an unmistakeable death threat. She knew he meant it. Her skin quivered in the breeze and the overly familiar sense of dread settled on her shoulders. With a bone-weary sigh, she stood up and stretched. Time to get the hell outta Dodge.

All the way to Hong Kong on the ferry, she battled with the same question – whether to try talking to him again – but she knew it was pointless. Thanh was nothing if not a man of his word. Her only option was to move on without his help, risking arrest and incarceration ad infinitum. In other words, back to square one. The alternative was to abandon her family and go to ground, again. She changed clothes in the ferry toilets, relieved to get out of her fishy combats, then stood on deck, willing the universe to give her a break. The wind blew her hair into her face and the sun beat down on her shoulders. *Face it, kid, the universe doesn't give a shit. Make your own luck.*

Backpack secured, she trudged down the gangway in Kowloon and made a call from a telephone booth to reserve accommodation. It was a convenient moment to check if she'd been followed. No one registered on her radar so she beckoned a taxi and told him to take her to Kowloon Xanadu, right in the middle of an exclusive shopping district and mere streets away from the Lucky Bee Residences. She needed a few hours' sleep and the chance to assume the persona of a well-heeled European jet-setter. From there, it was imperative she convert the remaining money she was carrying into something portable and accessible. A cryptocurrency transfer required some P2P exchange. If only she could have brought Morten along.

Tomorrow, she had to catch a flight to somewhere in

Europe and enter the UK via a less obvious route than Heathrow Airport. Presuming she was willing to stick her head over that parapet. The taxi driver, she suspected, was the same one who'd transported her from the airport, judging by his driving style and nauseating air-freshener. Fortunately, she was no longer jet-lagged and culture-shocked. In fact, it was almost like coming home.

The desk clerk at Xanadu quickly concealed his alarm with a fake smile but obduracy had set in. Olivia summoned all her energy. This was one fight she was not going to lose.

"Good afternoon, madam, how can I help?"

Accent first. Cut-glass upper-class Brit. "Oh, hello." It sounded like *hellayer*. "Can't tell you what a relief it is to get here. Nightmare journey, total nightmare." She rolled her eyes. "The name's Isherwood and I have a reservation for two nights."

He turned his attention to his screen. "I don't appear to have anything under the name of Isherwood, I'm afraid."

"Impossible. My father's PA sent me confirmation twenty minutes ago. I could show you the reservation number if some utter bastard hadn't filched my handbag! A luxury suite, that much I recall. Oh, wait! She probably booked it under my married name. Do you have anything for Isabella Dauncey?"

Doubt crept over his face. While he checked the screen once more, she withdrew a twenty-dollar bill from one of the pockets of her combat trousers and placed it on his console. "I'm in urgent need of the loo, so if we could hurry, I'd be most grateful."

"Dauncey, yes, a Victoria Suite. Can I take your ID and credit card details?"

She gave a bitter laugh. "Someone already did that. When that man mugged me I lost my passport, purse and phone and a damned expensive piece of arm candy. No matter, I'll get replacements sent and I always keep some loose change in my luggage for emergencies. How much is the room? I'll pay in cash."

"Madam, we don't deal in cash and the suite is 500 dollars a night."

She counted out a stack of notes. "So here's a grand. That should cover any extras. Now please may I have my key? If I don't get to a lavatory in the next five minutes, we'll both regret it."

He handed over a card in a mini envelope. "Suite 762 on the seventh floor. Madam, we require every guest to complete a registration form. The porter will carry your bag."

"No, he bally well won't. Send the forms to my room, if you'd be so good. Thanks awfully. Cheerio."

Even though she expected upscale accommodation, the suite came as a wonderful surprise. The size, the light, the view and one more time, the vast, bright space. A lounge with an enormous flat-screen TV opposite a long sofa gave way to a bedroom ten times the size of her little Macau matchbox. Added to that a bathroom with separate toilet and a well-equipped kitchenette, the suite occupied more square metres than the entire sixth floor on Rua do Cunha. In both main rooms, floor-length windows looked out across Victoria Harbour. A weight fell from her shoulders in both a physical and metaphorical sense. She dumped her backpack on the bed and gazed out at Hong Kong Island.

Her mood vacillated. On one hand, she had gained neither Thanh's forgiveness nor assistance. On the other, she'd cleared the air between them, for what it was worth. In addition, she'd earned herself some solid cash and proven she could still play the game. Sitting at the vanity desk, she looked herself in the eye. As she'd made Jackson swear, so she swore to herself. *Never again. There are safer ways of earning a living.* Her priority now was to put the money somewhere accessible and find a way into the UK without attracting any attention. The clock was ticking.

Food, sleep and then action. She picked up the phone and called room service.

While waiting for her meal, she shifted thousands of dollars into the safe, shoved her rucksack under the bed and took a long shower in the marbled bathroom. There was a time when hotel amenities seemed ridiculously decadent. Now she embraced it all. Wrapped in a freshly laundered robe and wearing towelling slippers, she sat at the table to think. Her mental plan became a reality by using her laptop and a piece of hotel notepaper. Hong Kong to Istanbul, the border of Asia and Europe. From there, a flight via Frankfurt to Dublin. A ferry across the Irish Sea to Liverpool and she could rent a car to Dewsbury. Travel on one passport only because she needed another for emergencies. Since her Ann Sheldon identity was in the hands of the Chinese mafia, she had to use her fake IDs wisely.

That wasn't the only thing she had to use wisely.

The bell rang and a deferential young man wheeled in a trolley. A trio of ravioli, a half-bottle of Barbaresco, her registration form and a complimentary fruit bowl for their esteemed guest. She tipped him $20 and wished him a wonderful evening.

As she ate dinner, she focused her mind. No TV, no music and certainly no scrolling the Internet. The stuffed parcels of pasta tickled her taste buds and the wine complemented the lightly oiled tri-colour dish as if they'd grown up together. She ignored the registration paperwork, secure in the knowledge none of the hotel staff would bother her until the following day. As with all plans, the key was to work in stages. First, she had to look the part, shedding all her previous roles. A five-star joint such as this would have designer shops jostling for space and she intended to take full advantage the following morning. Once she looked moneyed, she'd find a way of securing her winnings and head out of town. Hong Kong was risky. Far too many people wanted to know the precise location of Olivia/Ann/Esther.

Meal over, she put out the Do Not Disturb sign, clipped the security lock into place and closed the curtains. Now to catch up on some sleep. Her mind sneered. *As if you'll be able to sleep after the last two days.*

Her body proved her mind wrong. She slept an uninterrupted ten hours and awoke with a fierce appetite. It was nine am and a deluxe hotel must surely cater for every guest's whim. If there was ever a time to indulge herself, it was right now.

She grazed on exotic fruits and drank a pot of coffee while checking the current cryptocurrency rates. She congratulated herself on having established an anonymous way of keeping her money safe yet accessible. When she set it up, it was a just-in-case measure. Now, it was her most useful asset. The problem remained. How to protect just under a million dollars in cash? Buying this amount of cryptocurrency would attract unwanted attention. The answer was clear. Convert some and wear the rest.

She unpacked her rucksack, throwing most of her clothes into the laundry bag for housekeeping to wash, but rinsed her fishy combat trousers herself. The disguises she stuffed into a spare pillowcase in the wardrobe. Then she dressed in Yoyo's Audrey gown, applied her make-up just as Jackson had taught her, stuffed $200,000 into her mini-pack, slipped into heels and unlocked the room to go shopping. The gloves she left behind.

The hotel's ground floor was a plaza. Big-name outlets glittered, inviting wealthy guests to splash out and fit in. Handbags, dresses, jewellery, shoes, luggage, perfumes and high-end timepieces at premium prices offered on a platter for those who could afford them. Olivia channelled her inner Holly Golightly, gazing wistfully at jade earrings, silk scarves and a silver and gold ladies' wristwatch like a child in a sweet shop. It didn't take long before a slightly fey salesman wafted over to stand beside her, his smile fulsome.

"That's a beautiful piece, madam. Would you like to try it on?"

Olivia gasped. "No, no, thank you but no. I'm only window shopping. My husband wants me to write a Christmas list and I don't know where to start. I'm new to all this." She giggled, knowing the Armani-clad assistant would sense an opportunity in the same way a shark scented blood.

"My dear young lady, we all start somewhere. My name is Jason and I've been a personal shopper for many years. I think I can help."

She gazed up at his amber eyes and breathed, "I feel like the luckiest girl in the world!" Good job her shoes covered her toes so no one could see them curling.

Stage one: the uniform. Jason convinced her to buy a new pair of pumps, a jacket, two dresses, one handbag and three items of jewellery. It was all she needed to pass as a wealthy woman with plenty of disposable income. She returned to her room and tried on her disguise. She'd pass. The bracelet and earrings above a well-cut pale grey dress signalled class, and her low-heeled sling-backs were elegant and not too impractical.

Stage two: the grooming. She placed a call to the hotel spa while eating her salad and reading the latest tech/financial news. Manicure, pedicure, facial, depilation, hair treatment, plus cut and colour. She spun the staff a story about volunteering at a panda sanctuary to explain the state of her hands and hair. They smiled politely. At five o'clock, she emerged with a nondescript auburn bob, clear skin and understated beige nails. She called it her 'wallpaper' look – fit in but fade out. Then she went shopping for a second time, this time at a theatrical costumiers and specialist clothing store. Everything was to be delivered to her hotel room.

Stage three: the financial situation. It was ludicrous, unsafe and suspicious to travel with huge numbers of dollars. Instead she needed to split the money three ways. The largest amount she would use to buy cryptocurrency. This would be tricky as she had to move large wads of cash without raising eyebrows. So it had to be via several person-to-person transactions. Another set of USB sticks would allow for different digital wallets to minimise cluster risk. 50K into her luggage – *note to self, buy some luggage* – and spend the rest on items she could resell. Looked as if she'd have to go shopping and with the length of her list, she'd need a car and personal security.

Later that evening, the Xanadu doorman escorted a polished, classy female to her discreet sedan and wished her a pleasant evening. She tucked herself into the rear seat and advised the driver and bodyguard as to their schedule. She emphasised the need for discretion, promising it would be worth their while. They exchanged a glance, but nodded their understanding.

Eight stops to buy cryptocurrency in cash, each more stressful than the last, enabled her to place three-quarters of a million dollars in her digital wallets. All the dealers were intimidating and she was profoundly grateful for the presence of Kai, the human equivalent of a Rottweiler, looming over her shoulder. Finally, she had hidden her stash. Next, to hit the mall and hard. The driver waited outside even though her hotel was less than a block away. Kai followed her in and out of Cartier, Dior, Mulberry, Gucci and Chanel, carrying an increasing number of shopping bags. She made a last stop at a beauty store to purchase three sets of goody bags. Foundation, mascara, bronzer, lipstick and concealer for every kind of look. She handed over another roll of notes and tucked the packages in her tote.

Her bodyguard stepped closer.

"It's OK, Kai, I can carry these. Let's go, I'm done for tonight."

Kai rearranged the bags on his arm, his actions a complete mismatch for his words. "A man is following you. He's not subtle. Look over my left shoulder, but only quickly and continue the talking. Grey hair, aviator glasses, wearing an anti-virus mask and an ugly suit. Do you know him?"

Olivia opened her tote and began rifling through her packages. She raised her head to address Kai and changed her focus. Their stalker was screamingly obvious and Olivia knew at the briefest of glances the man was British.

"He's not familiar at all, but that means nothing. I say we get back to the hotel."

She exited the store with Kai at her shoulder and was surprised to see their shambolic stalker straighten and approach. "Ah, hello, good evening." There was no other way to describe the guy than a shadow of a civil servant.

Olivia took a step backwards whereas Kai moved closer to the crumpled napkin of a human being and dragged his voice from the depth of his lungs. "What do you want, mister?"

"As a matter of fact, I am the harbinger of good news."

Kai lifted one nostril and part of his top lip, summing up his contempt. "Madam?"

"One moment. Good news?" She scanned their surroundings for any back-up he might have brought along. "Please explain."

"Very well, no problem. Shall we walk to your car? Isn't this whole mask option handy? One no longer has to fear lip-readers. In the old days, covert conversations were held behind our hands. Things aren't what they used to be."

"You said you had good news?" repeated Olivia.

"Indeed. Excuse my waffling. I'm charged with delivering a message. Quite simple really but for your ears only. Sorry, I know, terribly old school." He cast a wary glance at Kai.

They stood at the top of the steps. Below, electronic doors admitted a stream of shoppers, and wafts of humid night air were soon chilled into obedience by the mall's relentless air conditioning.

"Give me a second, please, but don't go too far." She didn't use Kai's name. "Leave the bags, thank you."

He placed her purchases by her feet and walked to the opposite side of the stairs, not taking his eyes off her.

"Where the devil did you find such a chap? Looks like a sumo wrestler. Anyhow, the message is this: you may return to Great Britain for no more than a fortnight without fear of official reprisal. The powers that be cannot be held responsible for any further action should you outstay your welcome. All clear? I must get off."

"Who sanctioned this?"

"Seems your ex-colleague is prepared to do you one last favour. Goodbye and I wish you a smooth trip back to Blighty." He started to shamble towards the doors, checking his watch.

"Wait a minute. How can I trust your word?"

He looked around, his expression one of utter bewilderment. "Because, dear girl, I'm British. Have a pleasant evening."

He shuffled down the steps and just before he stepped out into the night, he turned and lifted a hand. "Forgot to say, your time starts once I deliver the message. Or in other words, now. Jolly good luck!"

Kai appeared at her elbow. "Is everything all right?"

"I think so. Kai, I asked you to drop the bags not because I don't trust you but because I wanted you to have your hands free. Same still applies. I'll take these out to the car and you watch my back, OK?"

"OK."

They made it back to the hotel without incident. Olivia gave the driver a lavish tip and once Kai had carried all her bags to the door of her room, she handed him an even more extravagant bonus. For the first time the whole evening, he cracked a smile.

"Thank you. Very kind. Here's my card, in case you need me again."

Olivia took it and placed it in her purse. "You'll be the first person I call if I have any further need for personal security. You're very good at your job. Goodnight, Kai." She didn't mention the fact she'd be leaving the country the following morning, unlikely to return.

All thanks to Thanh Ngo.

12

It all came down to whether she believed the crumpled civil servant. Taking the circuitous route into the country would keep her under the radar, but would take three days. Or she could accept the offer at face value and fly in tomorrow. She opted for something in between. Not a direct flight to London Heathrow and into the jaws of Scotland Yard, but via Amsterdam and a short hop into Manchester. If all ran smoothly, she could be at her sister's place within twenty-four hours.

Time for yet another transformation. The packages she ordered had all arrived promptly and she started with the bump. It took several goes before she managed to attach it correctly. It took even longer to learn how to move as if the foam-filled pouch was an actual pregnancy. The smocked top and elastic-waisted trousers were comfortable enough, despite the eye-watering prices. No matter what the cost of top-drawer 'mumswear', she had to keep up appearances. She also had to leave before the hotel's day shift arrived.

With over $50,000 hidden in two brand-new suitcases, her cryptocurrency cold wallets in her handbag and her purse stuffed with notes, Olivia ordered a hotel car to the airport, checked out of the Xanadu and began another intercontinental journey. She asked the driver to stop at the post office, where she sent packages to two different people in the same Macau tenement block. For Estrela, a silk kimono embroidered with a Chinese dragon reaching for a star. For Yoyo, a Louboutin wallet. As Olivia's grandmother had told her, one should never give an empty purse. Inside was a folded note stating that Yoyo's fraudulent website had been passed on to the cybercrime police. Hopefully that would both pacify and deter her would-be recruiter and save future victims.

The Cathay Pacific flight to Amsterdam boarded on time. As Olivia took her First Class seat, the steward tucked her weekender holdall into the overhead bin, still bearing its price tag. Olivia cringed. What a dead giveaway pointing to a rank amateur. She waited till he'd gone to fetch her a glass of orange juice and on the pretence of retrieving a cashmere wrap, heaved herself up and tore off the tag.

She accepted the juice and refused the little packet of nuts with an air of one accustomed to being waited on. The Dior Lady handbag containing her crypto wallets fitted into the section beneath her armrest. No way was she going to let that out of her sight. She made herself comfortable by closing the divider between the seats and settled in for the next twelve hours.

To her surprise, she slept well and awoke with only the faintest recollection of dreaming about massive beating wings. When the cabin crew undimmed the lights and offered breakfast options, she found she was rested and eager for a cup of tea. The flight touched down at a chilly Schiphol airport ten minutes later than scheduled. Olivia was wide awake and already bracing herself for trouble. On a transfer flight, she wouldn't need to clear immigration, but there was always the security risk. Especially because this time she was travelling under her real name: Olivia Jones. Previously, European airports would have had her name on a watch list as she was sought by the British police. But since Brexit, such cooperation was limited to known terrorist threats and Olivia could traverse Europe unchallenged.

She entered the Netherlands without a hitch, praying her luggage would do likewise. Three hours remained before her flight to Manchester. The executive lounge offered showers, a buffet and quiet areas in which to work. Olivia took advantage of all three. First she booked a car and driver to collect her on arrival while drinking some proper coffee and a superfood smoothie.

Then she hit the showers. She ditched the bump, cleansed herself thoroughly and started from scratch. Her weekend bag contained two changes of clothes, plus a variety of cosmetics and accessories. The impression of casually minted mum-to-be was abandoned for businesslike manager. She wore a dark grey suit with black loafers, exchanged the pink diamond clusters at her ears for simple crystal studs and took off the Rolex, placing it gently in her glasses case at the bottom of her bag. Make-up included a flash of deep red lipstick, understated eyes and a pair of heavy-framed glasses with clear lenses to complete the look. She'd deliberately chosen black luggage so as not to attract attention. She was now a European professional attending a conference in Liver-pool, should anyone ask.

No one did. She cleared immigration at Manchester Airport with only minor delays, collected her suitcases and walked through Nothing To Declare with a purposeful expres-sion. Once through the scattered hopeful relatives and lovers, she spotted a sign with her name on it.

Olivia Jones, Lucky Bee Consultancy

"Good afternoon. I'm Olivia Jones. You're my driver for today?"

"It's only half eleven and my name's Norman. The car's parked just over there. Lemme take yer bags. This way."

She crossed the road in his wake with a glance up at grey, swollen clouds. A light drizzle misted her glasses. Manchester looked bland and leached of colour, but she supposed after Hong Kong and Macau, anywhere but Vegas would pale.

Norman, thankfully, was not a chatty sort, simply guiding the Mercedes along rain-soaked streets and out of the city. It was not yet midday but the streets seemed dull and the people colourless, only wearing navy, black, brown and grey. Tyres hissed along the tarmac and each time the wipers cleared the windscreen, they emitted a groan.

"Dewsbury, in't it?" said Norman, slowing at a red light.

"Yes, please." She rustled for some papers, even though she'd memorised the address. "Heath Hall Conference Centre. How long will it take?"

"Depends on traffic. Hour and a half?"

"That's ideal. Check-in is at two. Is there a mobile phone shop en route?"

He grunted, and Olivia blessed all Yorkshiremen and their taciturn ways.

If she wanted to catch Katie at her practice, the smart thing to do would be to turn up at five-thirty, just as she was due to leave. By then it would be dark and she could move through the shadows without attracting attention. Throughout the journey from Manchester she checked the mirrors regularly, but spotting a tail in grim weather was a near impossibility. In all likelihood, her ex-colleagues at Scotland Yard already knew where she was, where she intended to go and why. Armed with such intelligence, they could pick her up whenever suited them. If it suited them.

Olivia sat in her hotel room, staring out at the dismal afternoon. If the police reneged on their word, she would spend the next five to ten years being processed by the justice system. That was a risk she had to take, but calculated her odds as decent. The most lethal danger was the underground organisation she'd infiltrated on official orders. She was no stranger to governmental double-speak. They promised she could return to the United Kingdom and the police would not touch her. But nothing was stopping them from dropping a word in the right, or in this case, wrong ear. The kingpins might be in jail but the organisation still had people on the streets. Although lower down the food chain, they were still under orders to exact vengeance on anyone who had helped put their bosses behind bars. The more violence they inflicted, the further they could ascend in the hierarchy. She was the fly circling a spider's web. One false move would entrap her.

Fretting in a bland room was not conducive to her mental health when she could be out in the countryside, retracing the steps of her youth. The Blahniks and Choos stayed in their protective bags because Yorkshire required footwear of the sturdier sort. She walked into the town centre, her trusty backpack stuffed with a ridiculous amount of jewellery, cash and two brand-new dumb phones she'd acquired an hour ago. The store had cameras, naturally, but she'd paid in cash and worn her glasses, attracting minimal attention.

The risks of calling Katie directly were still too great. Her father's and sister's communications were definitely under surveillance by more than one party. So if her sibling agreed to speak to her runaway sister, they would have to communicate off-grid. Olivia's palms started to sweat despite the cold, drab afternoon. Of all the terrors she'd faced over the last two years, her family's rage and grief scared her the most. Mild-mannered Katie hardly ever got angry, but when her temper was roused, she was a fire-breathing ferocity.

Something about tramping around the place where she had

spent her childhood, so comforting and familiar, while unable to participate in its delights, was unsettling. She ached to pop into The White Rose pub for a glass of wine and a catch-up with Nicky and Mal. Or stop at the bakery and ask after Mrs Wilkinson's sprawling family. One long sweaty summer she'd done work experience there, bagging tea-cakes and barms, cobs and scufflers for five quid a day, her benefits being a cheese sandwich at lunchtime and a stale loaf to take home to her da.

She stood at the crossroads, acutely aware of what she had lost. Not just her family but her sense of community, her connection to daily life, her roots. This place had shaped her and given her the confidence to pursue her career. That same career had taken everything and endangered the people she loved. In her heart, she knew there was no way back. Little Livvy Jones no longer existed. Pining over the past was a waste of emotional energy. She'd made her choices and if living with them caused her pain, she wasn't the only one.

Dewsbury had changed. While The White Rose pub was still open, it looked a lot shabbier than the picture in her mind. Gone were the flower baskets and outdoor tables. Cigarette butts lay scattered around the doorway and the scent of urine from the passageway caught in her throat. Some lazy gits had always seen the alley as a handy urinal, but Mal used to hose it down daily and he'd even set up a light sensor to shame them into using a conventional toilet. The high street was a bleak sight, with a shocking amount of shops boarded up and graffiti-covered. Not Wilkinsons' bakery, she was relieved to see. On the benches in the pedestrian precinct were fewer old ladies chatting to friends and more drunks arguing over cans of Tennent's Super. She reminded herself it was a chilly grey day in September and her memories were probably rose-tinted.

Street lights came on, forcing her out of the shadows. More than one person gave her a second glance so she turned up her collar and strode up the side streets to the vets' practice. She was too early and would have to stand out in the cold until Katie left, risking recognition from one of the other vets, assistants or clients. No way could she go inside. She skulked around the car park and identified Katie's ageing Volvo estate in under two minutes. It looked exactly the same – muddy spatters from her farm visits, a pile of blankets and wellington boots in the rear and on the dashboard, a packet of Werther's Originals. It must have been the jet lag and cold that caused tears to spring to Olivia's eyes. Someone came out the front door with a cat carrier, and lights flashed as the owner unlocked her SUV.

Olivia melted into the darkness and crept along the row of vehicles towards the lighted windows, hoping to catch a glimpse of her sister. The interior looked warm and friendly, despite its sterile colours. The veterinary assistants wore green scrubs and the walls were painted white with a green frieze at head height. Olivia looked closer and realised what she had assumed to be a representation of ivy or another climbing plant was actually an interweaving of pets' names painted in green letters: Buster, Mrs Miggins, Kiki, Bampot, Hedwig, Lady Chatterley, Rufus, Laddie, Max, Gingernuts, Sheba and Uncle Tom. She smiled, picturing all the creatures and owners who had left their thanks.

A voice caught her attention.

"Mind how you go, Doctor Lane."

"Don't you worry about me, Mr Chaudhry. My father always says I drive like an undertaker." Katie's kindly tones were as warm as a hug, her northern accent unchanged.

"Better safe than sorry. How is your da?"

"I'm off to see him this minute. You look after that little bird and I'll see you next week."

Katie was almost at her car and Olivia cursed under her breath. *Not now, not here, with nosy neighbours and passers-by.* The sound of a mobile trilled into the night. Katie stopped under a street light and answered her phone.

"Y'all right, love?"

She listened for a moment, her face in shadow.

"Yeah, I saw your message but didn't have a minute to reply. Mr Chaudhry and his pigeons again. Course I'll get the coriander and natural yoghurt. Anything else? Because I need to get off to the nursing home and I'm late as it is. Hopefully the Spar on the way home has got some and if not I'll pop by the curry house and ask Iqbal if he can spare some. See you in a bit."

She rang off and Olivia stepped out from under the shadow of a tree.

"Hello, Katie."

Her sister froze in the act of unlocking her car. Her head turned as slowly as an owl's.

"You?"

"Yes, me."

"You. Here. Now. Why?"

"I can explain."

"I doubt that. Get in. We're going to see our dad."

Katie's jaw was clenched so hard, Olivia feared for her molars. She drove out of the practice and through town, turning onto Leeds Road.

"Listen, Katie, I ..."

"Where the fook have you bin?" Katie never swore. This was unprecedented.

"I had no option but to run and hide." Even to herself, Olivia's voice sounded whiny and weak. "The shit was about to hit the fan."

"We thought you were dead, Livvy! We planned a memorial service and everything. When the money came through, that was the first tiny glimmer of hope. Why didn't you say something or at least let us know you were alive? You've got no idea what I imagined."

"I couldn't. Any contact I made with you or Dad would've put you both at risk. My choice was simple: disappear or die. I warned you something like this might happen one day. It's an occupational hazard."

Katie indicated up Borrowdale Road, her eyes blazing. "Worst case scenario, you said. Not going to happen, not in a million years, you said. Then you left. Went up in a puff of smoke." In spite of her rage, she parked the car neatly in a spot near the entrance to Lakeview Residential Care Home. There was no lake or much of a view as far as Olivia knew, but the name sounded nice. Maybe the golf course had a decent pond.

"You have a lot of explaining to do and you can start with our father." Katie unbuckled her seatbelt and reached into the back seat for her handbag.

Olivia caught her arm. "I can't go in with you. Not now."

With an icy reserve, Katie removed Olivia's hand from her elbow. "Your own father, who is barely able to recognise me, hasn't seen his eldest for nearly two years. The least ..."

"Katie, if I come in there with you, all the alarms will go off. You go in on your own and I'll wait here. Say nothing about me, OK?"

"Why did you come if you don't want to see our dad?" Katie's eyes glittered with a combination of tears and temper.

"I want to see him, of course I do. I'll find a way in tomorrow, in disguise, so I can keep everybody safe. Just let me play this my way, will you?"

"As if I've got a choice." She sniffed. "Back in twenty minutes."

"OK, take your time. Shall I walk down to the Co-op and get some coriander and yoghurt for Graham?"

Katie shook her head. "See? Once a spy always a spy. Are you coming to ours for your tea?"

"I'd love that. I really would." Olivia sighed. "But the kids and Graham are going to have a whole bunch of questions I just can't answer. Let's you and me have a quick drink on the way into town and I'll get back to my lodgings. We're going to work out the next steps and find a safe method of communication. Come on, our kid, shake a leg."

It was early doors at The Fox and Hounds and far enough away from Katie's suburban semi-detached in Mirfield that no one would recognise them. Olivia bought herself a large glass of red and her sister a white wine spritzer, soda, not lemonade. She didn't even need to ask. The pub was warm, which came as a relief after the walk to the supermarket and a ten-minute wait in the Volvo. It occurred to her that she hadn't been cold-cold for almost two years. In Brazil, Hong Kong and Macau, she made a lot of effort to stay cool, seeking out air-con, shade and protecting her skin with creams and hats. Half a day in Yorkshire and she was convinced she'd never be warm again.

Katie was on the phone to her husband when Olivia returned to the table at the rear and she ended the call with a very diplomatic sign-off.

"As fast as I can but as long as it takes. Start without me and I'll see you when I see you."

"Did you tell him there was an avian emergency?"

Katie's eyes narrowed. "No, because I'm not in the habit of lying to people I love. I said something has cropped up and I'm running late but it's nowt to worry about. Thanks for the drink."

"My pleasure. Cheers. How was Dad?"

"Cheers. A bit brighter today. He called me by my name, which is a good sign."

"What's his situation?"

Katie looked outraged. "As if you don't know! You're

picking up the bills for his posh ground-floor unit with a view down to the water. I'm sure a full and regular report is included in the eye-watering price."

Tell her I've taken care of your sister.

Olivia massaged her temples, piecing the facts together. Someone was anonymously funding her father's healthcare in an unusually expensive facility. Someone who expected her to turn up, one of these days, and the door would slam shut on her freedom. God knows where that would leave Dad and Katie.

"I don't know his situation and I'm not picking up the bills. Whoever is paying for this is laying a very expensive lure, hoping I'll come skittering out of the forest like Bambi. This is why we couldn't visit him together. Someone will raise the alarm and a blacked-out SUV will come barrelling out of a garage to snatch me and make me regret the day ... sorry, no need to go into details."

Katie's face drained of all its colour. "What do you mean?"

Olivia gave her a deadpan stare. "Do you really want to know?"

"No, I don't."

Neither spoke for a moment, sipping at their drinks.

"Katie, you know what you said earlier? It's not true. I've never been a spy. Nowt more than a common-or-garden copper, me. No access to flashy gadgets or my own Aston Martin or anything that glamorous. Truth is, it was pretty grubby." Thanh's face flashed into her mind.

I didn't despise you. But I will admit I didn't like it.

"So what did you do?" Katie's face had a stubborn set. "I don't want the details, but your average plod doesn't disappear without trace."

Olivia chose her words with care. "I was working under-cover. Things got sticky and I had to do a runner. Some unpleasant people want to track me down and the first place they'll go is to the people I love. Seeing as I no longer have a husband, that's you and Dad."

For the first time, Katie's expression relaxed and Olivia caught a glimpse of her wide-eyed, soft-hearted little sister. "In that case it's too dangerous for you to go into Lakeview. To be honest, Dad might not even recognise you. Even with me, and I see him every day, it's pretty much hit and miss. Why did you come here if not to see him? Especially if it's that dangerous."

Olivia took a large slug of her cabernet sauvignon. "I wanted to know the two of you were managing. Someone sent a message ..." Her voice petered out.

They sat quietly, sipping their drinks and sneaking glances at one another. In two years, they had both changed. Katie had gained some weight, softening her face and filling her clothes. She gave the appearance of being comfortable. Over the last few days, Olivia had stood in front of a lot of mirrors and accepted the fact she was not ageing well. Sun, sea, and a healthy diet had benefitted her body, but damaged her skin. Add to that pollution, late nights and fast food from her sojourn in Hong Kong and Macau, and she was the crab apple to Katie's peachy complexion.

"Are you managing?" she asked, her voice gentle.

Her sister lifted her chin and looked directly into Olivia's eyes. "On the surface. You've no idea of how sleepless nights and endless questions can take its toll. What happened to you, Livvy? Where did you go?" Her brilliant green eyes shone, reflecting the optics behind the bar.

"The less you know the better. But I will say this. I've done nothing wrong. From the start of my career to its godawful ignominious end, I played by the rules. They moved the goal-posts and I found myself on the wrong side of the law. Someone had to take the rap. The writing was on the wall and I can read. It was going to be me, prosecuted and jailed for doing my job to the best of my ability. The really shitty part was that doing my job meant mixing with some well-connected characters. If I was detained at Her Majesty's Pleasure for infiltrating and disbanding a criminal organisation, I wouldn't last long inside. As much chance of survival as a mouse in a cage full of cats. Katie, my bosses were going to throw me under the bus and that weren't fair."

Her sister's sense of justice and honour had always been her North Star, so Olivia's words and accent were judiciously chosen.

"No, that weren't fair. You know what else weren't fair?"

Olivia dropped her chin to her chest, giving Katie the floor, ready to take her punishment. "Go ahead. Shout, scream, hit me or throw your drink in my face. Just one thing. Don't use my name, eh?" She cast a sideways glance around the slowly filling public bar.

"What's not fair is making us grieve twice." Katie's voice was calm and controlled. "You and me, we know only too well what it means to lose a member of the family. After Mum died, we supported each other through that pain and found a way of bearing the grief. Together, we helped Dad through his darkest days. He was getting weaker even before you left, reminiscing about the old days and floating away into the clouds, but he had the pair of us to peg him to the ground. Then the oldest and the one who looked most like her vanished into thin air. It was like losing her all over again. I can see that expression on your face and let me tell you, I'm not being dramatic. He grieved the loss of you as if it was her."

The pain in her voice cut Olivia to the quick and she took a large swallow of wine to quash the swelling in her throat. "I'm sorry. If there had been any other way ..."

Katie interrupted. "And now what? Are you home for good or about to leave us again?"

"I have permission to be in the country for a few days without fear of arrest. I'm reasonably safe from the police, but at as much risk as ever from the others. It's vital I keep it short and hit the road before anyone catches on. But I do want us to be able to communicate while I'm here. That's why I bought us each one of these." She slid the mobile across the table. "It's only got one number programmed and that's mine. No Internet connection, no apps, nothing, and it's only to be used as a secure connection between us."

She took it with little enthusiasm. "Then what?"

Olivia couldn't find a way of prettying up the facts. "Depends. If I want to stay alive, I have to keep off the radar. That's why I'm going to sneak around with my head down until I'm sure it's safe. Then, well, let's see." Making wild promises did no one any favours.

"You've already missed so much, Livvy." Katie's voice was plaintive. "The kids starting school, my operation, Christmas as a family, selling Dad's house, I don't know where to start. Liam remembers you, but only vaguely and Sarah-Jane thinks she does because of all the stories. It's so peculiar, having but not-having a sister."

"Hold up. What operation?"

"Nothing to fret about, it's all fine now. I had a mastectomy and the last scan was clear."

Guilt and empathy crashed over Olivia like a freezing wave. Breast cancer, the same disease that took their mother. "Oh, Katie, that must have been terrifying for you. I'm so, so sorry. I should have been at your side. But you had to go through everything on your own."

Katie shook her head with a touch of irritation. "I was not on my own. Graham held my hand every step of the way. His support is rock-solid, especially when I grieve for my sister. We all miss you but no one quite as much as our da. Will you visit him tomorrow? Promise?"

"Yes. I promise. The thing is, I might not be ... me."

"What?"

"I'll have to go in disguise because whoever is paying for his care is not doing it out of the goodness of their heart. I cannot risk being recognised."

"By whom? No one at Da's care home has ever met you!"

"I don't know. This much I swear – I will visit and spend some time alone with him. If I deem it safe, I'll tell him who I am. You have to let me play this by ear, and alone, OK?"

"Whatever you say." Katie's voice contained a vast weariness.

"Thank you. Hey, here's a thought. What are the chances of you getting a babysitter tomorrow night? Then I could treat you and Graham to a nice meal at The Malthouse. I trust Graham to say nothing to anyone about my popping up out of the blue. The kids though, it's too much to ask to keep me a secret."

"The Malthouse?" Katie traced circles on the table with the condensation from her glass. "You have to book months ahead to get a table there."

"Just sort a babysitter and I'll do the rest. Now, you'd better get home. Graham will be waiting for his coriander." The pub had become considerably more crowded since their arrival and Olivia was eager to leave.

"Yeah. I should go. But you won't disappear again, will you? Where are you staying?"

"Some place in town. Can't recall the name. Drink up, our kid."

Together they walked across the car park to Katie's Volvo.

"My B&B isn't far, so I'll walk from here," Olivia lied. "See you tomorrow?"

Katie opened her arms and wrapped her in an embrace. She hugged so tight Olivia thought she might never let go, and in a way she hoped she wouldn't. They rested their chins on each other's shoulders, too full of things to say to utter a single word.

When Katie finally released her with a watery smile, she said, "I love ya."

"Love ya too. Good night."

Olivia watched the Volvo's tail-lights turn the corner and began the long walk back to Heath Hall. She really did love her sister but didn't trust anyone on earth with the name of her accommodation.

13

The first thing she did when she got back to the hotel was make sure she hadn't been followed. Walking through the town she'd grown up in was a strangely distracting feeling and she wondered if anywhere would feel quite as loaded with emotion. Her mind played a colourful slideshow of memories at every significant location, splitting her concentration and making her vulnerable. She crouched between two plant pots and watched for anyone coming up the drive. Not a soul.

The second thing was to check at reception for any messages. There was one, as she'd known there would be. On the route here, she'd called the hotel herself. Her Cockney accent was out of practice but with the background sound of traffic, it would do. She'd described herself as Olivia's boss, expressed exasperation at not getting hold of Olivia herself and left a message insisting on her restaurant reviews in time for next Sunday's edition of the paper.

Olivia read the handwritten note and groaned. "Ah. The reviews. Oh dear."

The receptionist in her neat Next jacket gave her a kindly smile. "You all right there?"

"Yeah, well, no, not exactly. Matter of fact, I'm in a bit of a pickle. Part of the deal for my coming here for the conference was to write a couple of reviews of top-flight restaurants. I must admit, I hoped my editor would forget so I haven't been answering my phone. Any chance of a table here this evening?"

"Certainly, madam. What time?"

"In half an hour? Just time enough for me to get changed."

"I'll book that for you now. Anything else I can help you with?"

Olivia sighed. "You couldn't do me a favour and advise me on somewhere else to eat tomorrow evening, could you? It's just I have to file two reviews of high-end eateries."

The woman chewed her lip. "There's The Spread Eagle in town or a bit further out, The Malthouse. Both have an excellent reputation. Shall I call and see if I can get you a table for tomorrow?"

"You're very kind. Although I had lunch at The Spread Eagle yesterday, so perhaps The Malthouse would be best. Two of my food-writing colleagues will be with me, so I'd need a table for three." She glanced at the woman's badge and slid ten pounds across the counter. "Can I leave that with you, Valerie?"

"Thank you very much. I'll call them right away." The tenner vanished and with a last glance around the lobby, Olivia returned to her room.

She dressed in an Alexander McQueen trouser suit and took her notebook. The attitude served two purposes. She was working, so company and casual chit-chat were unwelcome. Her clothes spoke of professionalism but stopped short of ostentation. The ensemble coupled with that word in the receptionist's ear pretty much guaranteed good service. She was stalking in the direction of the dining-room when someone called her name. Valerie confirmed a reservation at the exclusive Malthouse for eight o'clock the following evening with a proud smile.

Olivia beamed. "People like you are worth your weight in gold, Valerie."

Over a cheese soufflé with grated truffle, Olivia made notes. Not on the food, that was merely a pretence, but a rough sketch of her plans. Katie's voice seemed to echo from the glass of Castelnau. *Then what? You've already missed so much, Livvy.*

Then what indeed? The pull of her hometown was as sweet as toffee and sticky as a fly-trap. She shook her head at her own sentimentality. At the age of seventeen, she couldn't wait to leave the place, so why now the ache to return?

The answer arrived as the waiter cleared her first course. *Because you can't, that's why.*

"Delicious, thank you," she replied. He was earnest and keen to know which wine she would like with her main course.

"Oh, I hadn't thought about it. What would you recommend with the skate and burnt butter? In that case, a Roero Arneis it is. Could I have a glass of sparkling water? Thank you so much." She made a note with a nod and intended to give the young man an excessive tip. It might compensate for the hopeless scanning of broadsheet restaurant reviews for the next two weekends.

Her thoughts returned to Katie and her father. She had indeed missed so much. Tomorrow night she would listen, ask questions, read between the lines and catch up on all those months of no contact. With a strange sense of the world tilting, Olivia understood Katie's pain. She herself had undergone months of nightmares, a sense of grief and being adrift from everything that rooted her. The difference was that Olivia had chosen that path. Katie had not.

Somewhere in her mind, a long-closed door creaked open and sunshine flooded in. Weekly phone calls with her sister, holiday plans with both their husbands, a surprise treat for their father, birthday parties for the kids, a girls' day out in Manchester and endless apologies. It wasn't just since she'd fled the country that Olivia had missed so much. One in three events got cancelled due to her job. Katie's tone of disappointed resignation was a weight on her conscience. After she joined SDS, Olivia stopped making plans. There was no point because she had no life. Communication between them shrank to the occasional text, usually on the subject of their father's health.

Once, and it stood out in her memory because it was so rare, Katie announced she was coming to London. Olivia tried everything in her power to dissuade her but Katie was adamant they needed to talk. Either Katie came crashing into her world or Olivia must meet her halfway.

"Ms Jones? Would you like to taste the wine?"

Distracted, Olivia shook her head and could barely offer a tight smile when the waiter delivered the fish. She ate and drank without registering anything significant, her mind focused on the past.

Halfway was Birmingham. With every intention of making this another girls' day out, Olivia suggested Harvey Nichols. Katie said no, she didn't want to shop. She booked a quiet Italian restaurant near the station and insisted she was paying. Olivia was late because the taxi got snarled up in roadworks, so the atmosphere was awkward from the beginning. They ordered *bruschetta* and had a minor disagreement over the pronunciation.

"Whatever. Feel smug about your accent if it makes you happy." Katie scowled at the menu. "I suppose if I order spaghetti Bolognese, you'll judge me for being unimaginative."

"Hell, no. We're having a nice meal and eating whatever we want. Maybe I'll have spaghetti too. Always best when wearing a white top so I can leave with an original Jackson Pollock." She grinned and raised her glass.

"I know who Jackson Pollock is, Livvy. Don't patronise me."

In that uncomfortable ambience, twisting spaghetti strands around their forks, Katie broke the news. Their mother had Stage 4 breast cancer and was about to embark on a course of chemotherapy.

"Shit. I had no idea." Olivia allowed her cutlery to rest on her plate.

"Why would you? We've not seen you since Christmas and that was only for twenty-four hours. Mum wants to talk to us, both of us together. Can you come? Nothing is more important, Liv, not now."

Olivia promised. They made arrangements for the following weekend. The very same two days Milo Vargas chose to whisk his girlfriend away for a romantic break in Venice. Risk her cover or upset her sister? She took the low road and had regretted it ever since.

"Was the skate to your taste, madam?"

"Very nice, thank you. I'd rather not have dessert. Would you bring me a glass of champagne and the bill, please?"

Head bent over her notebook, she called on all her resources, refusing to cry a hundred times over one bad decision. Otherwise, she'd spend the rest of her life weeping bitter tears. *What's done is done – now live with it.* She inhaled deeply and assumed her mantle, packing all her grief, regrets and unspoken apologies into a convenient pocket behind her heart. She was an expert packer.

With one last sip of champagne, she left a third in the glass. In Macau, in Brazil and even in London, she would consider that wasteful, but here she had to maintain appearances. Eyes were studying her, she sensed that, but more with expectation than threat. A restaurant critic tasted rather than troughed, sipped rather than slurped and would never wipe the juices from her plate with a slice of seeded bread. Damn shame. That glass of bubbles was seriously good.

Her brain was working on three tracks simultaneously. How to see her father tomorrow morning without being recognised? How to leave Katie with some slight hope of a future reunion? And most pressing of all, where to run next? In the balsamic and oil mixture on her side plate, the outline of Brazil took shape. She'd been happy there, by the sea, surrounded by greenery and wildlife. She clenched her fists in frustration. Maybe one day, but not until she'd got herself out of trouble.

Her waiter, confused by her tucking a fifty-pound note into his hand, evidently thought she required a more personal service. His eyes widened, whether in alarm or delight, she couldn't say. She quickly disabused him.

"Thanks, Ian, but that will be all for this evening. I have another busy day tomorrow. You're an excellent waiter. Good night."

Once back in her room, she shucked off her clothes, brushed her teeth, checked all her belongings were where they should be and left her breakfast order hanging from the door handle. Two more nights of luxury, because the day after tomorrow, she had to run for her life.

It must have been long-forgotten home comforts and warmth of a sisterly embrace which triggered her subconscious. Or perhaps the relief of finding her family safe and sound offered a different kind of release. Maybe something as simple as sleeping on British soil unlocked the sealed memory box in Olivia's mind.

Whatever the catalyst, that night she dreamt of her husband, Salvador Simon.

Sal was the only man who'd ever brought her breakfast in bed. On Sunday mornings, they made love while half asleep, savouring each other like a delicacy long hungered for. She often had the sense they were refilling their reservoirs, absorbing as much of each other as possible to fortify themselves for the week ahead.

He used to lie beside her until she fell into a post-coital nap, then slithered out of the covers and ran downstairs to the kitchen, where his high spirits could not be suppressed. Scrambling eggs, grilling bacon, making coffee, he sang. Opera, rap, disco or Portuguese folk songs, it didn't matter as long as it had energy and passion. Olivia woke gradually, buoyed from the depths of sleep by sounds and scents, luxuriating in the joy of a day off with the man she loved.

They ate in bed, leaving toast crumbs on the sheets and spills of orange juice on the duvet, but who cared? Once the food was devoured, they would satisfy other appetites. Two people whose weekday professions demanded the tightest control threw themselves into abandonment at the weekend. It was one way to remain sane. Because both knew it couldn't last.

His presence, his scent, the weight of his body beside hers was tangible. Sal, her safe harbour. She was home again.

Olivia opened her eyes to a grey Dewsbury Wednesday morning and an empty bed. She peeled her face from the damp pillow, wishing dreams had a remote control so she could close her eyes and pick up where she left off. In the bathroom, she couldn't decide if Sal emerging from her subconscious was a positive or regressive sign. She performed her ablutions and made up her mind to leave getting dressed till later. There was no lithe and lusty man beside her, nor was it a sunny Sunday morning in South London, but she could still enjoy breakfast in bed.

The waitress knocked at exactly the right moment, just before old memories became overwhelming. Olivia took a tray of pastries, fruit and coffee back to her queen-sized bed. If she was going to indulge in memories of Salvador Simon, music was required. A brief scroll through a streaming platform threw up the obvious Mariza and Amália classics, but she dug deeper to find Pedro Abrunhosa, swaying in her sheets and punctuating the lines by thrusting a croissant into the air as she sang along and cried to *Tudo O Que Eu Te Dou* (All I Give You).

When the track ended, she wiped her eyes and ate some raspberries washed down with cooling coffee. All Sal gave her was everything. His passion came from his heart, whether for her, for FC Porto, for his career or that weird little restaurant behind a chip shop in Brixton. She had never encountered such a force of nature. He drew her into his orbit like a powerful magnet and she made no attempt to resist. Their love was built on hope and a belief that if they followed the rules, everything would be fine. They followed the rules. But terrorists did not.

It was a chilly Sunday morning when he got the call. She replayed the same scene, practically bleached from over-exposure, through her mind.

04.03. Darkness in the bedroom, sodium orange leaking under the curtains, the bolt-upright tension at the sound of a mobile phone ringing. He answered, already on his feet.

"Be there in under an hour." He reached for her in the dim light. "Hijack and hostage situation at Heathrow. I gotta go. I'll take the bike."

She was alert and already assessing the situation. "Traffic will be minimal at this time of night. Why not the car?"

"Bike is faster. I'll keep you posted if I'm not back for brunch, OK? I love you." He kissed her and ran.

"I love you too. Be careful." She wasn't even sure if he heard her.

She listened to the sound of him yanking on his jacket and boots downstairs in the hallway, the growl of the BMW bike and his steady progress along the terrace. Once the engine sounds had evaporated into the night, she got up and scoured police and news sites for any information. Blackout. She went to bed, tucking a pillow around her back, convincing herself that when she woke up, the man who was racing across London to deal with a potential terror threat would be downstairs cooking eggs and singing fado.

Lakeview Residential Care Home was situated close to the centre of town, but too far to walk. After her breakfast, Olivia dressed in jeans and a black sweatshirt, took a cab into town and asked the driver to stop outside a charity store. It proved useful. For under forty quid, she bought a headscarf, a coat the colour of mildew, a pair of Hunter wellies in pretty good nick and a tartan canvas shopping trolley. The accessories served as the opposite image to her wealthy restaurant reviewer. She looked like a woman twice her age. Not only that, but her rucksack fitted neatly into the tartan wheelie case. The majority of her luxury goods were sitting in a suitcase with a combination lock behind Heath Hall's reception desk. Depending on how the day went, she might retrieve them and return to her room. Then again, she might not.

An overcast sky leached light and colour from a landscape bordering on wintry, but Olivia added sunglasses, just in case. She opted to walk and took the long way around. It was unlikely a team of security guards with Rottweilers paced the perimeter of the care home, but it made sense to approach the building from the rear. Her father's room, according to Katie, was one of the few that lived up to the facility's name and actually overlooked the lake. Of course it did, as one of the costliest available. Whoever was paying for this was either generous or patient. Somebody had to be biding their time, waiting for her to flutter in. A honey trap? If so, when they caught their butterfly, would the care home turf her dad into the street?

The weather brightened as she lugged her trolley along the shadows of the tree line, careful not to let the wheels fall off the path into the mud. A dozen bay windows dominated the ground floor, six of which were occupied by the canteen and day-room. That left three either side for the highest-paying residents. Olivia opted for the furthest away from the entrance and stomped across the lawn as if heading for the delivery door at the rear. She blessed and cursed the shifting clouds as they shaded her vision or exposed her position.

Each 'unit' as the brochure liked to call them had a small outside area beyond the windows, so 'guests' could sit outside in the fresh air on the rare occasions the weather was fine. It was close to eleven and the weather was changeable, moody and cruel to those susceptible to sudden chills. Behind some French windows, an elderly woman reclined on a daybed, pen in hand, head bent over a newspaper. Olivia smiled. Dad loved crosswords, his atlas and dictionary always to hand. It was perfectly possible this woman and her father were friends, bonding over word puzzles. Yet at the moment, that lady had no company.

A gust of wind shivered through some wind chimes and Olivia speeded up, aiming for the middle room. Its curtains were still drawn. An empty room or had the occupant retired for a mid-morning nap? Patient deceased? Her breath grew shallow – *wait for me, Dad, I'm coming.*

She reached the decking, with a single wrought-iron chair and matching black table sheltered by a wooden overhang. She tiptoed up three wooden steps and tucked her trolley against the wall. Gauzy cream drapes hid the interior but the light of a television stood out amid the blankness. Olivia tried the handle and it opened with ease. Inside, Kenneth Jones was sitting in an armchair, scowling at the screen.

"Not a shred of shame, you duplicitous liar!" he spat at the politician burbling excuses for his latest failure to deliver. "You never had any intention on making good on your promise and more fool us for believing you." He threw a balled-up tissue at the image of a chinless cabinet minister. "Get out of my sight and take your silver spoon with you. Deplorable charlatans, every last one!"

With a busy and professional air, Olivia stepped into the room with a broad, not entirely authentic smile. "Now then, how are we today, Mr Jones? Have you had your brekkie?" She accentuated her northern vowels and kept her sunglasses in place.

"Breakfast? If you can call it that. I had a bacon sandwich and some bilge water they described as coffee. Hold up, who are you? Not another social worker, so help me God."

Olivia laughed with no real mirth and moved around the space as if checking all was in order. En route, she scanned the front door for a lock. There was none. Of course an assisted living space would have no lock. Staff needed to access the room at all times.

"Not exactly a social worker, Mr Jones, but I can tell you I am here on behalf of the council. Do you mind if I sit?" She didn't wait for an answer. "My team and I have the responsibility of assessing all private supportive residences in the area and rating them according to an established set of standards."

Dad's face twisted into an expression of disgust. "Come again?"

Olivia gave another false laugh and jerked her head at the television. "Eh, I sound like 'im, don't I? Sorry. Let me speak plain. My name is Audrey Hardcastle and I'm a civil servant, checking whether these profit-making care homes are more about profit than care. I've got your interests and those of your daughters at heart. Can I have a minute?"

Kenneth Jones had aged since she last kissed his patchily shaven cheek. His hair was thinner and his face bore two thumbprint-like indentations beneath his cheekbones. Her heart and throat filled, and she yearned to throw her arms around him. She was glad of the sunglasses.

He wore pyjamas and a dressing gown, new slippers and a cashmere rug over his knees. Yet his eyes switched from dull disinterest to bright curiosity at the word 'daughters'.

"My girls."

"Nowt like family, is there? They pay your bills, Mr Jones, and my job is to make sure they get value for money. Would you say you're happy here at Lakeview?"

His eyes drooped and the remote fell from his palm into his lap.

"It's alright, but I'd rather be at home."

"With your daughters?"

"No, they've got their own lives to lead." He frowned. "Why did you come through the window? Door not good enough for you?"

Olivia laughed and again and reached for the remote to tune out the farmyard sounds of the House of Commons. "You don't mind, do you? This lot give me earache. I was out there making sure the grounds are in a fit state of repair and took a short cut. How would you rate the standard of care, Mr Jones? Staff, catering, opportunities for residents to interact sort of thing?"

His gaze was on the lake, a faint smile wafting across his face.

"Mr Jones?"

"Is it lunchtime yet?" he asked without turning, his tone placid and his eyes sleepy.

The clock on the television said 11.40. "Not likely, it's only twenty to twelve. So, your opinion of the facilities? Are you happy with the way you're looked after? Do the care workers pass muster?"

His head lifted, like a hound catching a scent. He fixed her with an unblinking stare, a sudden clarity in his expression. "What did you say your name was?"

Olivia took off her sunglasses and dropped the Coronation Street shtick. "My name is Olivia Jones. Hello, Dad."

There was a long pause as his eyes searched her face. "My little Livvy. I miss her so much."

"Dad, I'm right here. I had to go away for a while, but I came back to see you and Katie. I missed you both." She stood up to embrace him, tears flowing as she felt his thin shoulder blades and knobbly spine through his pyjamas.

He held her close, his grip surprisingly strong. "She's in the police, you know. Can't say too much 'cos it's all top secret. Bright as a button, that one, she got her brains from her mother. And her name."

She released him and crouched, holding his hands. "I know. You used some letters from Violet to make Olivia. Just like you used letters from Kenneth to make Katherine. It's me, Dad, I'm Livvy. Different hair, lost some weight and gained a tan but it's me, I swear."

He reached out her, nodding his head in slow motion, his fingers shaky as they touched her face. "Livvy got her brains, her name and her eyes."

A knock came at the door and Olivia sprang away from her father, replacing her sunglasses. Without waiting for a response, a tall woman with sharp eyes entered. She was not wearing a uniform, but jeans and a jumper. Her Lancashire accent was soft. "Right then. Come to fetch you for your lunch, Ken. Toad-in-the-hole today so I hope you're hungry." Her kindly demeanour changed to hostile on seeing Olivia. "Oh, hello, who's this?"

"Hello." Olivia changed her accent to classic RP. "The name's Audrey. We were just about done, so I'll let you get on with your lunch. Toad-in-the-hole! There's a blast from the past."

The care worker's eyes darkened in suspicion. "Mr Jones wasn't due any visitors this morning. His daughter only comes in after he's had his tea. Did you register at reception?"

"No need for that." She shook her head with an easy laugh. "I pop in to see my old bridge partner when my daily constitutional crosses the grounds. No appointments, no expectations and I can't speak for him, but for me it's a pleasure to chew the fat with this silly old bugger. Enjoy your lunch, Ken, and I'll see you next time. Try not to pop your clogs before my next visit, there's a dear. Goodbye and enjoy your Sunday afternoon." She ducked out of the French windows and collected her tartan trolley, aware of the woman watching her.

"Is that Audrey a friend of yours, Ken?" the carer asked, as Olivia waved goodbye.

"Aye, that she is." His voice was not as strong as it used to be, but she caught the conviction in his words. "Bridget's a nice lass. She should come round more often."

She had no idea if it was confusion or cunning but his words served her well. Swallowing her grief, she strode off in the direction of the lake, wishing she could 'come round more often'. The reality of the situation was she'd probably never see him again.

The emotion she'd suppressed for so long would be denied no longer. A sob erupted and once she was out of sight of the care home, she made it to a bench before her knees buckled and she let it all flood out. It took a while.

Nobody bothered Olivia as she grieved for the loss of her father, her mother, her husband, her little sister and even her younger self. She cried until she had nothing left. The biting wind caused her body to stiffen and contract while her head throbbed and her face pulsed hot and swollen. As always, she was prepared. Cool water from her bottle to ease the pain in her throat and a cleansing wipe to remove the streaks of mascara from her cheeks. She was presentable once more and her pain back in its box. Not for the first time did she think how much simpler life could be if she just didn't care. Love was a liability.

She put the water bottle in one coat pocket and scrunched the dirty wet wipe into the other. For a change, she was in no hurry. Her next appointment was dinner with Katie and Graham in around seven hours' time. The forest beckoned and she heeded its call. How many days had she hidden among these trees as a teenager, avoiding people to be alone with her imagination? Forest, jungle or suburban woodland had always provided sanctuary. Trees were where she went to hide.

Despite the ominous roiling skies, she walked for over two hours, tracing old trails through the depleted wood, many paths having overgrown and fallen into disrepair. The trolley, an asset on asphalt, was a hindrance in the woods. Her infallible sense of direction and local knowledge led her out onto a country lane, where she knocked the mud off her wellies and headed towards her hotel.

She'd seen her dad. Her imagination might have been deluding her and then again it might not. For a second there, just for a flash, he'd seen her, recognised her, she was sure. She had said her final goodbye. Raindrops spattered her face, mixing with some tears she'd dredged up from nowhere. She tightened her headscarf, ready to shake off a shower. Her mother's voice echoed in her ears: *you're not made of sugar, you won't melt.*

No, she wasn't made of sugar. She was made of the same Yorkshire stone as the church, the houses and the ground under her feet. Solid and resilient, whatever the weather.

She was on the outskirts of town when the heavens opened.

Water poured from the sky with a viciousness Olivia hadn't seen since Brazil. At least in Praia do Pesqueiro the water was warm. In fewer than five minutes she was sodden, shivering and unable to see. She stumbled past closed shops hoping for a café or even a garage where she could escape the deluge.

A cab splashed to a halt on the opposite side of the street, with a warm and welcome TAXI light illuminated on the roof.

"Need a ride, love?"

Olivia ran across the road. "You're a lifesaver!"

14

"Heath Hall, please."

"Right you are, sunshine." The driver was middle-aged with glasses and an avuncular smile. "Cats and dogs out there, innit?"

"Nightmare! Good job you came along. Look at me! I'm like a drowned rat."

She rustled in her rucksack for a packet of tissues and mopped her face. Her hair was drenched, dripping into her eyes. The rain-soaked charity shop coat weighed her down and had begun to smell of damp dog. At least her feet had stayed dry. Those wellingtons were the real deal. She checked the shopping trolley to make sure her rucksack had suffered no water damage and looked forward to the fluffy towels in her hotel room.

Outside, the cloudburst was easing and Olivia spotted the lights of the sports centre. She did a double take. The driver had gone the wrong way. She shuffled forward and rapped on the glass divider. He did not react. She rapped again as he drove across the Calder River.

"Excuse me! You should have turned left back there, not right. I want to go to Heath Hall. Hello?"

He gave no indication of having heard and realisation dawned. This was a London Hackney cab, something rarely seen on the streets of Dewsbury. The red lights in the door panel indicated she was locked in. This bloke had plucked her off the streets and was taking her into the industrial estate, where no one would be around on a Sunday. Someone somewhere had tipped them off. How come she'd dropped her guard after hardly more than a day in this country?

Her body changed gear into fight mode, pulse pounding, hands sweaty and her mind in overdrive. Every mile they travelled took her farther away from safety. She had to stop him now. She withdrew her knife from the pocket of her rucksack and pressed a few random digits on her phone. He could hear her, she knew that much.

"Police, please. Hello, yes, I'm a single woman in the back of a taxi travelling through Dewsbury. The driver is ignoring my instructions and driving me in the opposite direction to where I want to go. I'm locked in and I genuinely believe he plans to attack me. Number? Hang on." She scanned all the windows for the identifying registration of driver and car to see there was none. The driver's eyes met hers in the rear-view mirror and he drew a thumb across his throat in an aggressive gesture. Not so avuncular after all.

She flipped him the finger and he braked sharply, sending her off the seat and into the foot well. Despite the fact no one was on the end of the line, Olivia kept talking. "Ow! The vehicle has no ID but I can tell you it's a black Hackney cab and we're driving down Mill Street, heading south. The taxi driver has just threatened to kill me. Please help!"

He pulled over with a sudden jerk, leapt out of the driver's seat and yanked open her door. She screamed. "Please don't hurt me! I don't have much money but it's yours, just please don't ..."

He cursed and snatched the phone from her hand, turning to hurl it onto the roof of a discount mattress warehouse. That was all the time she needed.

In a split second, she had flicked open her knife, jumped out of the taxi and pressed the blade to his throat. Her hands were wet and slippery, the ground was uneven and rain lashed her face, but she forced his chin skywards with her forearm.

"Who sent you?" The bloke was a good six-foot and she was on tiptoes. *Don't give him any thinking time. Prove you're serious.* She stuck the point of the blade under his jaw and jabbed. Blood mingled with rainwater as she forced his chin still higher.

"I asked you a question."

His right elbow crashed into her ribs as he tore her knife from his throat. He wrenched her arm with such force she could feel the tendons scream and he tossed her onto the wet pavement like a child's toy. His strength outmatched hers and she sensed from his use of disproportionate violence that he was a man who relished brutality. That answered her question. She knew who he worked for and if she lost this fight, she would lose her life.

Encumbered by the sodden heavy coat, she scrambled backwards, her arm protesting. He squared his stance, his brow lowered like a bull. They stared at each other, both panting, and he wiped blood from his neck. This was no Uncle Jack. The guy was little more than a courier with extra muscle, no obvious weapon and limited intelligence. He'd been sent to collect a package and deliver it alive.

"Drop the knife," he grunted. "I said, drop it."

She did as she was told, tossing her weapon to her right. It skittered across the tarmac and landed in a puddle.

He exhaled in exasperation. "I meant drop it and kick it over 'ere."

"You should have been more specific."

He gave her a death stare and she memorised his features. *99% certain I've never seen him before.* He side-stepped onto the pavement, moving in the direction of the puddle. At every step, he kept his eyes on her. When he reached her beloved knife, the balance of power would change. She had to act fast, a near impossibility while weighed down by wet wool. She raised her hands to shoulder height, preparing to shuck off the manky garment, and shifted the position of her feet to something like a boxer's stance. Her metal water bottle bumped against her leg. It wasn't much of a weapon, but until she accessed her rucksack, it was all she had.

The oldest trick in the book was worth a try, as this meat-head wasn't the sharpest tool in the box. She was about to gasp and look over his shoulder as a distraction when an emergency siren sounded from the town centre and did the job for her. He started and looked over his shoulder. She yanked out the bottle and pitched it with all her might at the side of his head. It hit him on the cheekbone, lower than she'd intended, but the blow was enough to make him stagger and lose his footing. He fell to all fours, still gripping her knife.

She threw off the coat and in two strides, leapt onto his back, flattening him. The sound of his breath escaping his lungs was satisfying but she knew he was already anticipating his next move. *No you don't, sunshine.* She cracked the top of her skull against the back of his head; a move that hurt her more than him but the difference was that she was expecting it.

With blurred vision and a throbbing forehead, she wrested her knife from his grasp, yanked his head up and drew the blade across his throat. The resulting gurgles made her wince. He went limp and she scrambled to her feet, waiting in case she hadn't cut the carotid artery after all. After a full minute of no movement and a steadily spreading pool of blood, she pressed her fingers against the spider tattoo on his neck. Nothing. She rolled the body into the gutter between the cab and the pavement.

With a glance around the deserted estate for observers, she got into the driver's seat and wiped her shaking fingers with her soaked sweatshirt. She got her breath under control and searched for any identification. Seemed it was a genuine London taxi, as all its documents were stuffed into the glove compartment. Of her not-so-cheery cabbie, there was nothing. She closed the door on the rain and thought.

Fact 1: this man had been sent to kidnap her. Fact 2: he picked her up in fewer than two hours after her visit to Lakeview Residential Home. Fact 3: stealing a London cab and driving to Dewsbury took at least four to five hours. Fact 4: the logical conclusion was that someone had betrayed her. Fact 5: she now had a body to dispose of.

The windscreen was steaming up as her body warmth dried her clothes, and the pong the coat had left on her clothes was becoming unbearable. Cold, shaken and probably still under threat, she made up her mind to deal with the situation. She gunned the engine and turned the heater to full blast. Then she surveyed the area for observers or CCTV cameras. No one in sight and the only cameras she could see were trained on the buildings, not on the street. She dragged a baseball cap from her rucksack, got out of the car and walked around the vehicle. Both number plates had been skilfully muddied so as to be unreadable. Handy.

Her assassin wasn't particularly heavy or fat, but he was very wet and very dead. Heaving his body into the back of the cab took an enormous effort. By the time she slammed the door, she was sweaty, soaked and heartily sick of this shit. She drove the taxi into the delivery area of DeepDreamz. The facility backed onto the river, with a neglected path and a picnic table presumably for staff to escape the canteen.

Olivia sat and waited for a few minutes, her eyes widening

as she spotted an array of sack lifters stacked beside the rear doors. Gloomy skies heralded the onset of dusk and the rain petered out. It was now or never. Cap pulled low, she fetched one of the lifters and wheeled it down the slope. It was large and unwieldy, meant to carry mattresses rather than dead taxi drivers, but it would do the job. She laid it flat beside the cab and dragged the body onto the metal frame. In the boot she found a yellow oilskin jacket and a set of jump leads. She slipped on the oilskin and pulled the hood up over her cap. Fluorescent yellow was not exactly unobtrusive, but it would keep her drier and freer than long, wet, malodorous wool. She retrieved the stinking charity coat to cover the body and used the jump leads to lash her would-be kidnapper to his final resting-place. Light was fading as she dragged her load down the muddy path, and without ceremony tipped both the body and heavy metal lifter into the water.

The swollen river carried the bundle a few metres before it sank below the surface. Olivia hurried back to the cab, careful to keep her face downturned for fear of cameras. She sat in the driver's seat, her nose wrinkling at the stench of blood. She'd overstayed her welcome. It was time to make a decision.

Working phone boxes in the Savile Town area were hard to come by. Eventually she found one, directly opposite the police station. She appreciated the irony as she dialled Heath Hall.

"Good afternoon, how can I help?"

"Is that Valerie?"

"Yes, it is. Who's this?"

"Thank heavens I reached you. Olivia Jones here, one of your guests. Work emergency has cropped up and I'm heading back to London. Could you do me a huge favour? A taxi is coming round to collect my suitcases in the next five minutes. Would you get the porter to collect them from my room and leave them outside so the driver can just grab them and go? Time is of the essence. My bill is all taken care of and I've left a little something for you personally."

"That's fine, Ms Jones, I'll see to that immediately. Do I take it you won't be dining at The Malthouse this evening?"

"Oh, shit, I'd completely forgotten. No, I can't. Would you let the restaurant know I've been called away, but my guests will take the table? Thanks so much, I am in your debt."

"I'll inform the manager as soon as I've placed your luggage by the door."

"Outside the door, Valerie, if you don't mind. My driver is in a hurry and will be there in a few minutes."

The woman paused.

Olivia pressed on. "My review of the hotel will mention you by name. Must dash, thanks again!"

She ran back to the cab, her speed nothing out of the ordinary while everyone was trying to avoid the downpour. Before pulling out onto the main road, she made sure the For Hire light was off. The traffic lights changed to red just as she arrived so she used the time to rummage under the seat. Bingo! An umbrella. The stink in the rear was getting worse and would need attention before she began her drive.

True to her word, Valerie had placed the two cases just inside the portico. Olivia threw off the oilskin and used the umbrella to shield her head. She snatched up both cases and shoved them onto the back seat beside her rucksack. Nothing should touch the contaminated floor.

She was ready. She had everything she needed to run away. So why did she drive to The Malthouse and wait in the car park until she saw Katie and Graham emerge from their Volvo?

As they handed their coats to the cloakroom attendant, Olivia shook her head. They were dressed to the nines, Graham in the same suit he'd worn to her and Sal's wedding,

Katie in a long skirt and sequinned top. *Enjoy your meal. Sorry I can't join you but someone just tried to deliver my head on a plate.*

Olivia switched on the ignition, glanced at the fuel gauge and headed for the motorway. At the first service station, she drove into the car wash and used the steam hose on the rear carpet. The foul-smelling water wasn't blood red but dirty rank filth. Even if anyone had noticed the colour, she'd prepared a story about a lady giving birth on the way to hospital. No one was around. After the torrential storm, few people were bothering to wash their cars. Olivia grabbed the chance to clean her wellies and the number plates, and replace all the vehicle's identifying information. A run-in with the traffic police was the last thing she needed.

Cab clean, she filled up with diesel, and parked in front of the refreshments area. With the help of some fresh clothes, trainers and make-up in her rucksack, she transformed a bedraggled wretch into a bland-looking commuter who drew no attention in the brightly-lit toilets. Her filthy clothes went into a car park bin. She bought a salad, two sandwiches, a bottle of water and an espresso then scoffed the lot in the car park. All the time, she was thinking.

One of only two people could have tipped off her enemies and sentenced her to death. One was her ex-boss. The other didn't bear thinking about. She sat in the car park, her rage building to boiling point. The police had exploited her, prepared to throw her to the wolves and pursued her when she went AWOL. Then they sent word she would be safe for two weeks in the UK. From police arrest, perhaps, but not from the Osman-Vargas organisation. Someone, somewhere, let slip her location for a return favour. She should never have trusted the establishment. This kind of betrayal had their fingerprints all over it.

She stuffed her food waste into the litter bin and set off for London. The taxi rolled down the M1 through the night, the

passing lights rhythmic and regular, with frequent signs
advising drivers to take a break: TIREDNESS KILLS.

Olivia wasn't tired. She was burning with vengeful energy
and determined to get answers. If it was her police colleagues,
then what? East or west, north or south, the topography of
Olivia's professional landscape had gone haywire and she no
longer knew where to run or who to trust. But her moral
compass had never been stronger. A fish rots from the head.
When you have questions, start at the top. In the mirror, she
caught sight of her own face, demonic in the red glow of brake
lights. *Ready or not, I'm coming for you, Meredith Reed.*

15

Shaken, tired and sentimental was never going to be the best frame of mind in which to make vital decisions. Olivia entered the outskirts of London at 02.20. She made her way through the city, intent on crossing the river to Kennington. There she would park her stolen cab by the flat she'd shared with Sal and sleep outside the house which held so many memories.

Then exhaustion set in. Her eyes itched and her body begged for sleep. Maudlin memories could wait until she was a bit less knackered. As she was driving through Golders Green, a 24-hour chain hotel caught her attention. She parked the cab at the far end of a superstore car park, took all the documentation from the glove compartment and locked the vehicle. It would be a few days to a week before anyone bothered to investigate an abandoned taxi.

She shouldered her rucksack, wheeled her two cases across the street and dumped the vehicle ID in an open skip. She took a deep breath and prepared to check in, explanations for her bruised head at the ready. She soon saw they were unnecessary. The receptionist couldn't care less where she'd come from or why she had a swelling the size of a duck egg on her forehead. She accepted the completed registration form, scanned her fake passport and handed over a key card.

Olivia paid for two nights, just so she could sleep past the official checkout time of ten. Her next appointment would be late tomorrow afternoon on the other side of Lambeth Bridge. What would happen after that was anyone's guess. The room was basic, clean and secure, which was all she required apart from a hot shower. A three-course meal with a bottle of Merlot in relaxing company would have been nice, but she'd foregone that pleasure. She closed the door on guilty thoughts of Katie and Graham. Fresh sheets and a bottle of water would suffice. She put the Do Not Disturb sign on her door and added the chain for extra safety. Then she got into bed, trying to make sense of the last twenty-four hours. It was hopeless. Her eyes closed but a far-off siren penetrated her ears. It made her grit her teeth. When it faded into silence, her mind offered other sensory memories: her sister's scent as she hugged her tight, that perfectly matched fish and wine on her tongue, her father's fingers brushing her face, the belly-flop of a corpse splashing into the river, stiffness in her shoulders and endless headlights in the darkness as she ran away. How the hell had this become her life?

Monday morning. Or to be completely accurate, Monday afternoon. Olivia woke at 12.15 with far more clarity than when she'd fallen asleep. First priority, food. While she was thinking clearly, she had to make a plan. The bar/café at the hotel looked tired and unappealing, much like herself. One street away, she found a kosher deli and ordered enough food for two people. Eggs Royale on a bagel, shakshuka with pita bread, a superfood smoothie and a pot of coffee. The place was buzzing with the lunchtime crowd, so Olivia sat at a corner table, facing the room so no one could sneak up behind her. She missed this. Lazy mornings just reading the paper and people watching were favourite pastimes when she and Sal were at leisure. She sighed and faced the fact she could not eat the bagel as well as two eggs, asparagus, tomatoes and spinach.

The waiter agreed to put it in a doggy bag with a knowing expression. "Eyes bigger than your belly, yes?"

She couldn't argue.

The weather was warmer and brighter than Dewsbury, so she wandered a while, taking in the Jewish cemetery and trying to suppress memories of Sal. How was it possible she'd kept him out of her mind in Ilha do Marajó, up Rio Negro, through Hong Kong and Macau but the minute she landed in the UK, she could think of no one else but the man she had lost? Sunshine lit a stone seat and she gave up all resistance. If sitting in a graveyard, weeping for her husband who wasn't even buried here was a phase she needed to overcome, so be it. She sat, her gaze skimming the headstones and succumbed to the wave of memories. People crying and blowing their noses was nothing new in a cemetery. A few kind smiles acknowledged her grief but nobody intruded.

That dreadful bloody Sunday, the call had come just after seven, three hours after Sal had rushed off to Heathrow. Olivia was still in bed scrolling the news sites on her laptop, ears cocked for the sound of his bike. His ringtone on her mobile suffused her with warmth. In those days, she'd assigned a different call tone to each of her favourites. When Katie called, her phone trilled Billy Joel's 'Uptown Girl' and set the mood for the conversation ahead. Dad's tune was 'Can't Get Used to Losing You', a title Sal said was far too sentimental, but the voice of Andy Williams relaxed Olivia and reminded her to be gentle with her widowed father. For Sal, she chose 'Protection' by Massive Attack. Those drumbeats and comforting chords instantly offered an embrace, even before she got to the lyrics.

It was 07.19. As she reached for the handset, she calculated he could still be home for brunch. A Florentine omelette, perhaps?

"Hey, you. How did it go?"

"Olivia? This is Mikey. Sorry to be the bearer of bad news. The airport hostage scenario went tits-up and three of the team got injured by an incendiary device. I'm in an ambulance with Sal, because he and Dagmar took the brunt of the impact. We're going to West Middlesex Hospital Trauma Unit. I think you should come."

She swallowed twice before she could speak. "Can I speak to him?"

There was a pause and all she could hear were the sirens. She understood.

"Mikey? Put the phone next to his ear. Even if he can't hear me, I want to say something."

"Sure. Here you go. I'm so sorry."

Machines, urgent voices and the sounds of an engine slowing or accelerating made it impossible to hear a human being breathe. Tears flooded her eyes but she forced out her message.

"Sal, I'm here. I'm right beside you. Heart, body and soul. I'll always be there because I love you. You're so strong, so full of life, a man of integrity and honour and ... let's not forget a crap singer." Her voice broke and she swallowed. "You're a fighter. Keep doing what you do best. I'm here. Stay with me. Please, Sal, stay."

There was no reply. Finally Mikey's voice broke through the background racket. "Going into intensive care. Get here as soon as you can, mate."

The second she saw Mikey's face in the hospital corridor, she knew it was too late. *Nothing we could do*. It was a phrase she heard a lot over the next few weeks. *So sorry, there was nothing more we could do.* A nurse advised her against seeing him but Olivia would not be deterred. In a hideous anteroom, she sat beside her husband's blasted body while medics worked on the next emergency next door. Sal's face was only partially visible under a green sheet and what she could see was speckled with blood. She kissed his cheek and told him she loved him, but her voice sounded like she was speaking underwater.

That was where her recollections ended, as if she'd fallen asleep in the middle of a film and missed what happened next. Later, much later, she learned the facts, piecing everything together from what she'd learned from Mikey and his colleagues, the nursing staff, Sal's boss, plus the news reports.

Sal and Dagmar had been back-up for the anti-terrorist bomb squad, supposedly safely positioned outside the hangar while expert negotiators and explosive disposal teams defused the situation inside. But there was a second bomb, placed underneath a luggage truck, designed to wreak maximum havoc on attending officers. It detonated while Sal and Dagmar were crouching fifteen feet away. Both suffered devastating injuries from the impact. Dagmar was pronounced dead in the ambulance and Sal went into cardiac arrest within minutes of reaching hospital.

Facts were facts, but emotional aftershocks reverberated for months. The funeral, compassionate leave, financial decisions and the vast hole of his absence debilitated her to the point she was barely functioning. That was when Meredith Reed stepped in and offered her a job with the SDS. At the time, Olivia assumed she'd earned her interview on merit. *We're keen to recruit people with clear minds and emotional distance.* In other words, those with no conscience or nothing left to lose.

· · ·

With four hours to go before confronting her ex-boss, Olivia prepared herself, physically and mentally. She called a luxury car hire company to take her to Albert's, an exclusive apartment block two minutes from Lambeth Bridge. The contrast between last night's budget hotel and this high-class accommodation could not have been starker. Bedroom, kitchen and dining area all had views across the Thames all the way down to the Houses of Parliament. Luxury fabrics, exquisite artwork and a bathroom tiled with onyx green marble made her reluctant to leave.

She showered, and dressed all in black with serious knee-length boots. Her make-up was subtly professional if a little heavier over her bruised brow. She added sunglasses as an extra distraction. Goodbye, Ms Minelli, hello, *The Matrix*. The outfit said businesslike but tough and the contents of her rucksack backed her up. Her target might not stop by the watering-hole that evening but it was unlikely. An hour with a gin and gossip was factored into Meredith's day. The only reason she'd miss it would be a political or security crisis and according to the BBC, today was a slow news day.

Olivia registered as a guest, claiming a meeting with a member of the club. She flashed a fake press pass. *Never throw anything away; you never know when it will come in handy.*

"Hello there. My name is Carolyn Moss of the *Evening Standard*. I have a meeting at six o'clock with Dorian Denis, the MP for East Norwood? I know I'm a bit early, force of habit, so I'll just sit at the bar till he arrives. Of course I'll sign in. There you go. Thank you, no, I'd rather keep my rucksack with me. It contains all my work stuff. Cheers." Bulletproof vests, helmets, masks and weaponry were all very well, but nothing protected you like an air of confidence and a belief you belonged.

Olivia strolled into the bar and found herself a stool on the corner, turning neither left nor right. She adopted an American accent and ordered a Negroni while surveying the clientele in the mirror. As usual on a Monday, the place was sparsely populated. If it were Friday, she'd have to elbow her way through the noisy crowds. Tonight, a clutch of civil servants were muttering in a corner, some journos prowled for gossip and the rest of the booths were occupied by key personnel from the Director of Public Prosecutions, Transport for London, Downing Street, the Mayor's office, Scotland Yard, Whitehall advisors and various FTSE 100 board members. In other words, the people who ran the country.

She recognised half of the faces, if not from personal interaction then from the television or radio interviews as they tried to spin and skim. Her toes curled and her instinct was to run from this self-serving cabal. Instead she took a restorative slug of her cocktail. One thing you could count on, the staff knew how to make a Negroni.

The door opened and three people entered: Meredith Reed accompanied by two men in sober suits. Many heads turned and several journalists began whispering like wind through pampas grass. Olivia gave no reaction, concentrating on her cocktail. One of the men came to the bar and ordered three different gins and three different bottles of tonic. Olivia, her expression hidden behind her sunglasses, rolled her eyes.

"So that's a Hendrick's with Fever-Tree cucumber, a Monkey 47 with Schweppes and a No. 3 with Fentiman's. Anything else I can get you?"

"That's all. Put these on my tab." He flashed his card and Olivia noted the lack of please or thank you. Her cursory glance caught his attention and he offered a smile. "Good evening."

Olivia responded with the swiftest of nods and returned to her drink, which offered no more entertainment than orange peel. The guy got the hint and joined his companions in a booth in the corner. Olivia checked him out and noted he was wearing elevator heels.

Across the room Meredith held court, sitting opposite the two men and pressing home a point with emphatic gestures. With only part of her attention, Olivia watched the barman make the gins: one with a curl of cucumber, the second with a slice of orange and the third with the classic wedge of lemon. A waitress took the drinks to their table and placed them on silver coasters.

She glanced at their table and raised a finger to the barman. "Those gins looked pretty cool. Could I get one of those?"

"Sure. Which one would you like?"

She mugged a rabbit-in-the-headlights face. "Umm ... the one with the cucumber? What was in that?"

"Your choice depends on your taste. For example, Hendrick's is a ..."

From the booth with the Met top brass, Meredith Reed toasted her colleagues and took a swig of her drink. Then she picked up her bag and headed for the ladies' toilet.

Now was the time.

Olivia interrupted with an apologetic wince. "Sounds ideal. Let's try that! I gotta go to the bathroom, be right back. Oh, I guess I should ask where it is."

"It's at the rear. You can go left or right and follow the bar all the way around."

Perfect. A woman with a rucksack following Meredith Reed into the bathroom would alert her colleagues. Olivia would try the opposite direction and confront her ex-boss when she came out of the loo.

She tugged her rucksack onto her shoulder and walked purposefully in the direction of the bathroom, aware of the curious stares. Everyone here was somebody and if they didn't yet know who, they'd want to find out.

The bathroom door opened silently and Olivia took in the space. Half a dozen stalls, a bank of sinks, dressing-room-style mirrors and suede-covered stools for patrons' backsides or handbags as they retouched their faces. She checked the cupboard under the sink and found detergents, cloths, sponges, a first-aid kit and a sign saying CLOSED FOR CLEANING. At a crouch she saw a single pair of ankles. Meredith and her ex-protégée were the only people in the room. She hung the sign on the outdoor handle, leaned against the wall and waited for the flush.

Meredith opened the door and tensed the second she saw Olivia in the mirror. Her head snapped around and her hand went to her jacket. Olivia realised the hair, black outfit and sunglasses rendered her unrecognisable. She lifted the shades to reveal her eyes.

"Hello, Meredith. Long time no see."

The senior officer relaxed a touch and came out of the stall. "Olivia Jones. I had a feeling you might appear sooner or later. The new look suits you. How have you been?" She walked to a sink at the end and began washing her hands.

"Up and down. You're looking well. Congrats on the promotion." The comment was barbed and both women knew it. Meredith Reed's new position was thanks to their huge operation to dismantle an almighty alliance of two crime gangs. Olivia and Thanh both played central roles in infiltrating the networks. Now one was on the run and the other had been relocated with a new identity. Unlike their boss, who had been garlanded with awards and elevated in status.

Meredith dried her hands on one of the freshly laundered towels. "Thank you. It's certainly a challenging role. Do you plan to stay in Britain for long?" She looked up at Olivia's reflection in the mirror. Her hair was shorter, more of a crop than her previous shoulder-length swaying grey. With smooth skin and a lean figure, she could pass for forty-five rather than her real age of fifty-four. An Assistant Commissioner surely should have steely-blue eyes, but Meredith's were a chestnut brown.

"No longer than necessary. I have a question."

"I thought you might." Neither woman changed position. Olivia could see both front and back of her former boss, lit by the dressing-room lights and sunken spots. Whereas Olivia was semi-shaded, her rucksack invisible.

"Spit it out, my G&T is getting warm."

"Did you clear my visit, Meredith?"

"Yes, I did." She ran her fingers through her hair and walked towards the door. "For a fortnight and then your protection runs out."

Olivia stepped into her path, glad of the height the heels afforded her. "Who else knows I'm here? You know I'm not talking about National Security. Did you tell any members of a particular gang where to find me?"

To Olivia's surprise, Meredith seemed offended. "I went to considerable lengths to give you a window of two weeks to see your family and arrange your affairs. High-level clearance on a need-to-know basis. The message you should have received is that this is a one-off and no immunity will be offered going forward. Do we understand each other?"

"Less than an hour after I'd seen my father, somebody tried to kidnap me."

With a weary groan, Meredith lifted her chin and met Olivia's eyes. "Clearly he or she did not succeed. Is that incident going to cause me a headache?"

"Out of your jurisdiction, isn't it? How did he know where to find me?"

"Any intelligence on your whereabouts did not come from anyone in the Met, that much I can promise. Look, I wanted to help you, so I cleared your path with the police, an action I already regret."

"Why would you want to help me?"

Meredith gave her a searching look. "Olivia, when everything blew up, my intention was to shield you from harm. But you ran."

"Yeah. I tend to do that when I see bus wheels approaching."

"Taking off like you did meant I couldn't protect you. I wanted to mitigate the fallout, but there's no way of doing that when you simply disappear." Meredith's tone was even and modulated, as if she was giving a sound bite to a reporter.

"Bullshit! Why should I suffer a jail sentence and take the rap for doing my job? The job you asked me to do! You were going to leave me to twist in the wind simply to deflect from your unethical practices."

Meredith fluffed out her hair. "A field agent should present as an ally or sympathetic mind. Resorting to physical intimacy is seen as poor tradecraft."

Her cold quotation of revised policy came as an icy slap in Olivia's face. "My handler actually encouraged pillow talk. Meredith, we operated under the slogan 'By All Means Necessary' for fuck's sake!"

"Not anymore. Old school thinking, now reformed under my oversight."

"Well, good for your current agents. I'm on the run but Thanh got a new identity and police protection. How is that fair?"

Her face pulsed with an emotion Olivia could not decipher. "Not that it did him much good. Thanh Ngo's body washed up under a bridge in Baia de Tai Van two days ago. I'm so sorry."

The blood left Olivia's face. "What? How?"

"I honestly don't know. But if you were able to find him, so did someone else. You're not quite the ghost you think you are, Ms Jones. My advice is to go away, keep your head down and never look back. If you have committed any kind of offence on British soil, I must ask you to leave within a week. To make myself absolutely clear, that's within a week of your permission to travel. By midnight on Wednesday, you should be gone. Goodbye and good luck."

She gazed at Olivia for a few seconds more then stalked off through the bathroom door, tossing the cleaning sign onto the floor at Olivia's feet.

Not Thanh. She had to be lying. Not Thanh. Not now.

16

The return journey to her accommodation at Albert's took ten times as long. Olivia ducked and wove, doubled back and even hopped on a bus for a few stops, using every trick she knew to shake off a tail. When reasonably convinced no one was following her on foot but unable to avoid the constant surveillance of CCTV, she made her way through the discreet porch of the apartment block. She spent fifteen minutes verifying her quarters were secure before pouring herself a stiff gin. Only then did she begin to process Meredith's message. She believed it, or at least most of it. Her ex-boss had not betrayed her location. Whether she was telling the truth about Thanh, she couldn't be sure. She scrolled through Macau news sites with little hope of learning more and was proved right.

Thanh. After all the time she'd beaten herself up for abandoning him and blaming herself for his inevitable death, he had been alive and well. Only when she sought him out for her own selfish purposes did she inadvertently cause his demise. He used his influence to call off the police and paid for that favour with his life. The dull ache of guilt scratched at her throat.

Words so familiar they might have been her own name escaped her in a whisper. "I'm sorry, Thanh, I'm so sorry."

She stared out at the Thames and the Houses of Parliament, breaking down her actions and evaluating the consequences. Risk-taking, loss of life, exposure – was any part of this worthwhile? Who had benefitted from her insistence on seeing her remaining relatives?

Excuses squawked like seagulls but she insisted on focusing her mind and asking the hard questions. She'd hunted down Thanh for a reason. He was the key. Only he had the connections to open the back door for her to get in and out of the UK. And the desperate need to enter the UK was to see her family: her father and sister. If Meredith was telling the truth, Olivia had to face facts.

Only one person in the world knew exactly where she would be yesterday morning.

Katie.

Tell her I've taken care of her sister.

It hit her with the force of a blast and she sat heavily on the sofa, some tonic spilling from her glass over her wrist. On first hearing, she had interpreted those words as a threat. 'Taken care of': a euphemism used with casual cynicism by the underground network she'd infiltrated. It meant the individual in question would cause no further problems. 'Taken care of' could mean anything from gentle intimidation to a brutal beating or dismemberment and disposal of the evidence.

On arrival in Dewsbury, seeing her sister operating as normal and observing the comparative luxury of her father's care home, she began to think the message meant something else. Rather than wreak cruel vengeance, the man for whom she had feigned desire and loyalty might have done the same and looked after her loved ones. It was not beyond the realms of possibility. He was good at playing the long game.

In those slowed-down moments when a hit man trained his

gun on her forehead while she cowered in the upper reaches of the Amazon, he was supposed to deliver a message along with the bullet. His words floated to the surface of her memory.

Our mutual friend paid the price because he's still sweet on you, even after what you did. He wants you dead, of course he does, but that's all. If the others get their hands on you, well, let's not go there.

Long story short, your ex is doing you a favour. His message is this. Wait now, he made me promise to get this right.

Tell her I've taken care of her sister.

It was stupid and naïve to imagine the best of those people. She'd seen what they were capable of and it still haunted her. But not every member of the organisation was a bullying sadistic bastard – the smarter ones were gentle, thoughtful and sweet. Just so they could attack the softest spot. A strong body accompanied by a stubborn mind can take a lot of punishment. That's why the fastest way to gain information or acquiescence is to hurt their loved ones.

Finally, she understood. Katie had indeed been 'taken care of'. In other words – recruited. No need to keep a spy in her father's care home when her own sister was willing to alert the network the moment Olivia popped up. There was no other explanation. Katie had sounded the alarm then turned up at The Malthouse to feign surprise at her sister's no-show. Olivia could almost picture the scene.

"She's not coming, Graham. I shouldn't be disappointed, I know that's what she does, but this time I thought it would be different." A few tears, a restorative sip of wine and on with the tasting menu.

Her squeamish little sibling had overcome her revulsion to violence and blasted a flare into the sky, summoning a professional assassin to kidnap, torture and in all likelihood kill her sister. Blood might be thicker than water but obviously no competition for an intravenous line of credit.

In a fury at her own gullibility, Olivia kicked herself, forgetting she was still wearing the Bottega Veneta boots. Adding injury to insult hurt like hell. She poured another drink, washed the spilt tonic off her arm and with considerable effort, dragged off her footwear.

Katie. The epitome of integrity, the good girl who never got into trouble, who studied hard, got married, had the classic boy/girl combination of two children and served the community so well they had asked her to run for a council seat. Heart-of-Gold Katie, who had changed sides and sold out her own sister. Impossible. But there was no other explanation. Who else had known where she would be and when?

She took a long swig of gin, now too warm, and rejected the sense of victimhood. Her ankle throbbed as painfully as her conscience. Thanh's death was entirely down to her. She was also personally responsible for the taxi driver lying at the bottom of the River Calder, but she couldn't give a shit about him. This was all Katie's fault. If Olivia hadn't panicked about her family's welfare, both men would be alive and she'd be in Brazil, safe in the arms of Gil Maduro.

She recognised the pattern. Three strong drinks always ushered in the same three predictable stages: over-confidence, clumsy lack of self-awareness and sentimentality. Now was not the time to lose control, although the urge to do so sucked her in like quicksand. She emptied the contents of her glass into the sink and made a pot of coffee.

Meredith Reed's advice was solid. *Go away, keep your head down and never look back. By midnight on Wednesday, you should be gone.* Thirty-six hours to escape the butterfly net.

But before she did so, a few things needed fixing. First, she had to collect her husband's bequest. Right now, she had no need of the money, but she was damned if she was leaving it where it was. Sal had insisted on both of them having a private pension in addition to the police benefits. *Because you never know what might happen.* It wasn't the most romantic wedding gift, but he was right. Not in any of her wildest imaginings had she foreseen her current circumstances. The pension belonged to her and she intended to claim it.

Second, there were a couple of people she wanted to see. They wouldn't want to see her so the element of surprise was essential. She already knew which members of the gang had gone down and in which high-security units they were held. Those who interested her were the ones who'd evaded a jail sentence, cut a deal or made a plea bargain. Because they were equally vulnerable and/or vengeful. Their overseers were in jail, but their influence extended far beyond bars. Tomorrow it was time to visit an old mate. Tonight, she planned to order Vietnamese food and cry. Not for herself. For Thanh.

The safety deposit box where Sal had stashed three 500g bars of gold bullion was in a private bank in the Square Mile, just off King William Street. Olivia took an Uber to a restaurant one street away and walked the rest. She had come prepared. Her passport, the original documentation, Sal's will and death certificate plus the unique code for the box itself. She hadn't been here since they'd opened their account and rented the safe, but the same sense of mistrust crept over her as she buzzed the entry phone. She'd mentioned it to Sal, but he assured her loads of his mates used the same bank. She didn't say anything at the time, but in her opinion, some of Sal's mates were not the brightest lights on the Christmas tree.

Once admitted, she showed her paperwork at reception, which took an insufferably long time to process. Then a security guard escorted her to a private room for a consultation with her personal banker.

She didn't need a consultation, she told them. All she wanted was the contents of that box and to close the account. No dice. It was 'standard procedure'. The personal banker was called Kyle and spent a very long time explaining that once she opened the box in front of him, a new access code must be generated which she must keep in a secure place.

"Kyle, can I interrupt? Sorry, but I'm not sure my instructions were clear. I wish to open the box, remove its contents and terminate my agreement with your organisation. I will not require a new access code because I no longer need the account. My husband's wedding present to me was the contents of this box on his death. As you can see from the coroner's certificate in front of you, my husband is deceased. Also, I'm short of time."

Kyle offered his profound sympathies and expressed his full understanding. He hadn't taken his hands off the box as if she was about to snatch it. Now he turned it towards him "Ah, I see. What I need from you now is the unique access code and you can open your safety deposit drawer."

Olivia removed her wedding ring. "Surely I put in the code?"

"Ah, no, it must be a bank employee. Fear not, I input the code, the technology checks it is correct and this little button turns green. At that point I leave you and you have as long as you like to remove the contents. When you are done, please do not close the box. Simply sign this form confirming it is empty and press this buzzer. I will return to collect your form and escort you from the building. The code?"

"The code is engraved inside my wedding ring."

"Ah. Very well. May I?"

She hesitated a moment, but passed him the gold band with obvious reluctance. He tilted it this way and that, before opening a drawer for a jeweller's loupe.

"Eyes aren't what they used to be," he smiled. He used the magnifying device to check the numbers, typing them one at a time onto the keypad. Finally he replaced the loupe in his drawer and returned her ring.

"Ah, lovely, we have a green light. I shall leave you now. Just buzz when you are ready."

He exited the room with a respectful hush and Olivia opened the box. She was expecting the contents, but the sight of three gold bars glinting under the fluorescent lights made her catch her breath.

"Thank you, my love," she whispered and stuffed the bullion into her handbag.

The Isle of Dogs. Could a crime network have imagined a more obvious place to establish their headquarters? Overlooked by the vast money-making towers of Canary Wharf, surrounded by a U-bend of the Thames and bisected by the Docklands Light Railway, the area had the reputation for a gangland history until its gentrification. These days, all the warehouses had been converted into contemporary apartments and on every corner, automated mini-markets offered ready meals for weary commuters. If one couldn't be bothered to cook, harbour-side eateries catered for every imaginable culinary whim available as dine-in or take-out.

Meanwhile, in the streets overshadowed by the towering symbols of financial trading, it was business as usual. Trading in drugs and guns was less legal and more tangible than stocks or shares but relatively speaking, the profit margins were similar.

Some cosmetic elements had changed, Olivia noted, but the layout of the place was printed on her psyche. She'd not set foot there for over two years, yet she'd still wager hard cash she knew these streets better than any of the passers-by. *Good job I'm not a gambler.*

She snorted a dry laugh.

Being here was the biggest gamble of them all. This pocket of London used to be wholly controlled by the Osman-Vargas underworld. Until she and Thanh had burrowed into their network, got dangerously close to its black heart and gleaned enough intelligence to topple the whole cabal. Even thinking about those days caused her pulse to race. Everyone knew the importance of timing, because those closest to the key players were the most vulnerable. The second the Met's undercover officers delivered their final report, arrests would begin and recriminations would start. Olivia and Thanh had to be well out of harm's way.

So far, so according to the book. But, once they'd nailed the criminals and justice was served, legal proceedings would begin against Olivia for unethical policing practices. Maybe Thanh too, but she was the one who had slept with a suspect. She had to finish the job, of course she did, because she was a professional. The one thing she could not risk was warning Thanh. If she tried, she might blow both their covers.

That was why she had told no one where she was going or why she was leaving. Encrypted documentation arrived in Meredith Reed's inbox twelve hours after Olivia had fled the country. By exposing the underworld organisation and going AWOL from the Metropolitan Police, she had signed her own death warrant. The only question was who would find her first and how painful they would make it.

And now here she was back on the very same streets, tempting fate. On a brilliant autumn day, the sun enriched the grass of Millwall Park and bounced off the water in the Outer Dock, a charming if deceptive ambience. Only the wind was unchanged, hustling along the pavements, ill-mannered and coarse as if it had just come in from the sea.

She remembered his home address. Whether he was still there or had long since shipped out, she couldn't tell. As ever, phone number, electoral register and council tax were all under a fake name. Not that it mattered. If she wanted to talk to the old boy, she knew where to find him. She leaned forward to address the driver of her luxury city car.

"Barry? Could we take a detour along Chapel House Street?"

The discreet chauffeur looked into the rear-view mirror. "Yes, ma'am. Is that where you want to stop?"

"Only for a minute or two, then we're moving on to the pub. Would you mind waiting in the next street while I check something?"

"Not a problem. Take my card and call me to collect you when you're ready."

"Thanks." She gave it a quick glance. "Oh, I'm sorry. Your name is Brian, not Barry. I must have misheard. I apologise."

"Don't give it a second thought. Most people who hire me for the day call me James."

Olivia rolled her eyes. "As in 'Home, James, and don't spare the horses'?"

"That's the one." He smiled at her under the peak of his cap, his blue eyes crinkling.

"Well, I'm not one of those people, Brian. Please call me Olivia. I'll come find you in about five minutes." She flashed him a friendly grin and took her backpack into the street. This tactic was nothing more than a card up her sleeve, but she knew the importance of belt and braces.

The house was a classic two-storey terrace with far too many garden ornaments on a lawn the size of an oriental rug. A large white van was parked outside, exactly the kind which jangled her nerves. What was it concealing? Assault rifles? Cocaine? Semi-conscious East European teenage girls? Olivia strolled to the end of the street and back down the opposite pavement but could see nothing of the interior of the house. Net curtains. Who the hell still hung net curtains?

She was just about to risk knocking on a pretext when a

woman bounced past her, huffed up the path and rang the bell. The door opened immediately and his wife stepped out in leggings, trainers and a sweat band, all in shades of blue. They jogged off in the direction of the park, talking and laughing like typical non-serious runners.

Olivia cradled her hands around an imaginary phone as they passed and caught a snatch of their conversation.

"... delivery just thrown at the porch. Soaked, it was!"

"That's not on, Sheila, you should complain. I did and I got a voucher for twenty quid."

Sheila. *Of course.* She'd met her once or twice at the employees' summer barbecue or Christmas party, along with all the other wives and girlfriends. As far as Olivia could recall, they'd never spoken. Why would they?

She strolled around the corner and found Brian and his black Mercedes with tinted windows waiting under a sycamore tree.

"Ready?" he asked as she slid into the back seat.

"As I'll ever be. Thanks, Brian. To the pub."

The exterior of The Boar's Head, known informally as The Whore's Bed, looked the same as ever – run-down, hostile to strangers, littered with fag ends with a gloomy forbidding interior. The moment she opened the door, all heads turned and silence fell, as if she had wandered into The Slaughtered Lamb.

To Olivia, the intimidation acted as reassurance. Nothing had changed. Strangers were not welcome. But she was not a stranger. She stood in the doorway, surveying the room with a few nods, stating her authority. With her sunglasses on, she could see precious little, but she knew where to look. The barman was new, at least to her. The smell of hops, sour beer from overflowing drip trays and frying onions assaulted her nose.

A mongrel growled from under a table from where three men stared in her direction. All three were smoking, despite the ban. Olivia ignored them and stalked over to his table.

He was in the same corner, scowling over a carmine-coloured drink. One could imagine no time had passed since she'd fled. She strode across the dirty floor, crunching peanuts or pistachio shells underfoot. His hand slipped under the table.

She shook her head. "No need for that, Spence. Let me buy you a drink."

He tilted his head like a dog hard of hearing. "You're not ..."

"I am." She lifted her sunglasses and met his eyes.

"Stone the crows. You lost your mind, girl?"

"Looks like it, me ole mucker." If he wanted to ham up his East End lingo, she'd make him realise how ridiculous he sounded. She sat down at right angles to him, so that she could see the whole room, and beckoned the young guy gawping over the beer pumps. Most people ordered and collected their drinks at the bar, but if you sat at Spencer's table, you got personal service.

"Another port and lemon for him and I'll have a bottle of Budweiser. If you don't mind, I'll open it myself. Why don't you have a drink on me?"

The barman's eyes widened slightly and he shot a glance at Spencer.

"It's awright, Kelvin, she's kosher. Oi, I want ice and *fresh* lemon in mine, you hear me?"

Kelvin walked away and ostentatiously took a lemon from the fridge. Conversations in the dingy room resumed. Olivia turned to Spencer, who didn't take his eyes off the drink preparation behind the bar.

"Gotta watch him. He waters the gin, you know." Spencer's

eyes were cloudy with cataracts but his hawkish posture was unchanged.

"How the fuck would you know? You only drink port and how's he gonna water that? With Ribena?"

His laugh built like someone starting an engine; a cough, a stutter and a rhythmic rumble which made her wonder if she needed to administer the Heimlich manoeuvre. He dragged a neatly folded handkerchief from his pocket to blow his nose and dab his eyes. Tears, of course, were only acceptable if physiological. God forbid he'd show emotion.

"Didn't think I'd see you again, girl. At least not in one piece."

"Didn't think I'd see you again either. Things change. You doing all right?"

He coughed into his hanky twice. "I'm doing all right. Why the bleedin' 'ell you come round this manor? They got geezers all over Europe looking for you."

The barman placed the drinks on their table. "That'll be nine pound fifty."

"No fucking way, you cheating shithouse!" shouted Spencer.

Olivia noticed Kelvin's right hand was missing two fingers. Now she recalled his face, weeping and pleading on the floor of Milo's office. She placed a twenty-pound note on the table. "Keep the change, Kelvin. I never forget a name." She gave him a smile and saw the confusion on the young man's face. He didn't recognise her. So much the better.

"Ta very much." He pocketed the note and wandered across the room to chat to another miserable old sod who seemed less than steady on his bar stool.

"Cheers, Spence. To your very good health."

"Cheers ... well, now, what do I call you? See, I used to know you as Zoe when you was Milo's bird. But that ain't your real name, is it? Maybe I should call you the Old Bill?" His smile was sly.

"That wouldn't be accurate since I'm no longer on the force. You can call me Zoe, Joey or Minnie bloody Mouse, I don't give a toss." She cracked open her bottle and raised it to her companion.

He lifted his glass. "Cheers, Zoe. To your health an' all. Let's face it, you're gonna need it more than me."

The beer was cold and refreshing, reminding her of holidays on the Portuguese coast with Sal. She could almost smell grilled fish, hear Atlantic waves and taste salt on warm skin. She shook herself and focused on the job in hand.

"What's the story, Spence? How's tricks?"

"Never mind me. I got some questions for you. Like where you been, why you back and what do you want wi' me?" he asked.

"I've been in Australia. I'm back because I couldn't cope with the spiders. What I want with you is to know what happened to the family."

Spence shook his head in disbelief and addressed an imaginary audience. "She wants to know what happened to the family." He put down his glass and pointed a gnarled finger at her. "The family are banged up at Her Majesty's Pleasure. As you damn well know because you stitched 'em up. To think I used to like you." He shook his head sorrowfully. "When all the time you was one of the filth. How can you sleep at night?"

"If I ever have trouble sleeping, it's due to seeing the punishments you and the boys dished out to your innocent young employees." That was an honest response and he didn't like it. "Let's not get into all that, eh, Spence? I read the papers and I know what happened to the brothers. Alex is in Belmarsh, Milo is in Whitemoor and they put Dinis in ..."

"Wakefield. You know what they call that shithole? 'Monster Mansion'. He's banged up in there with some right psychos, poor sod." Spencer's tone was reproachful.

Couldn't have happened to a nicer guy. Olivia kept her opinions on Dinis to herself. "Right. So all three brothers in secure Category A prisons. What about their parents?"

"Why do you care? You planning a visit?" Spencer coughed as if outraged and Olivia detected the onset of emphysema. His lungs were wrecked.

"No, I'm not planning a visit to any of the family. My job was to break the network apart and take down the major players. Namely, the brothers. I'm talking about Vitor and ..."

"Oi! I'm having none of that. You, of all people, calling him by his first name! That's taking the piss, that is. His name is Don Vargas and don't you forget it." Spencer's nostrils flared and flecks of spittle flew across the table.

Olivia was glad she was drinking beer from the bottle. She clenched her toes and watched the old man dispassionately, giving herself time to think.

Allegiance and honour are often pledged with no merit. To ally oneself with a cause, there must be a belief in its mission. Even then every member should question that organisation's methods, regularly and rigorously. Otherwise people label themselves as loyal to the gang, the party, the religion or the movement with blind devotion, ignoring the fact it grows closer and closer to those it opposes. Identity is easy. Thinking is hard.

Finally she spoke, keeping her tone low and her diction precise. "Sorry, Spence, it'll be a cold day in Hell when I call that piece of shit anything other than his name. Vitor Vargas is not the head of a sexy mafia family with its own code of honour, but a dirty little gangster who built his tainted wealth on exploitation. You know far better than I do the misery he inflicted. Unless you need a reminder?"

Spencer swirled his drink in circles, refusing to meet her gaze. "You shouldn't speak ill of the dead."

Olivia raised her eyes to heaven and made no attempt to

hide it. "Don't mess me about, you silly old sod. Vitor is not dead."

"As good as. In a coma, he is, kept alive by machines. Massive stroke, probably caused by the shock, they reckon." He challenged her with a baleful stare. "The family have to decide when to let him slip away. What an 'orrible way to go for such a powerful ..." He fizzled out as Olivia placed an elbow on the table and glared him into silence.

"Talking of horrible ways to go, what was that kid's name? You remember, the one Dinis bludgeoned to a pulp with a claw hammer. Nasty business, wasn't it?"

"Keep your voice down." Spencer shifted in his seat. "Dunno anything about that."

"Maybe I can jog your memory. You and Aggie got rid of the mess. Spence and Aggie, specialist subject: body disposal. We used to call you Burke and Hare, you know."

Spencer hissed, his teeth clenched. "One more word and I'll come out of retirement."

Olivia emptied her beer in two swallows and slammed the bottle on the table. "Fair enough. But how about a bit less talk about horrible ways to go, OK? The Vargas boys are behind bars and their old man is in a coma. What about Mama Bear?"

To her surprise, he smiled, revealing a dental monstrosity worthy of Francis Bacon. "She hates your guts. Word is, she's offering a million quid as a reward to anyone who captures you alive." He looked around the room. "If I tell them who you are, half these punters will help me bundle you into a van and we'll split the dosh." He picked up his glass and used a cocktail stick to stir the slice of lemon, with a smug expression.

Olivia rested her left cheek on her hand, allowing her right arm to fall to her side. "You wouldn't do that, would you, Spence?" Beneath the table, she withdrew the knife, flicked it open and thrust the point into his groin, right beside his femoral artery. "No, you wouldn't. Once, because we're old mates. Two, because if I cut you, and it takes one quick slice, you'll bleed to death. Might lose that testicle too, which would be a shame as it's the only one left. Where is she?"

His impulse was to reach beneath the table, but she saw him weigh up his chances and his shoulders sagged. "I don't know, honest to God. She went underground. I've heard rumours, but no one knows for sure."

"Rumours?"

"It's just talk." His face had lost all its alcoholic ruddiness and his complexion looked like a bowl of porridge. "Word is she went to ground in India. Others swear she's gone home."

"By home, you're talking Portugal, right?"

Spencer shrugged. "That's what I heard." Sweat beaded at his temples.

"It was good to catch up." Olivia kept up her pressure on the blade. "I'll leave you now because my colleague is waiting at Chapter House Road. He's been spending the afternoon with Sheila. When I'm out of danger, so is she. Nice seeing you again."

She withdrew the blade and stared into his rheumy eyes.

"You go. I won't say a word, I swear. No need to mess about with my wife."

"Insurance, know what I mean? Unless you betray me, your wife and your last remaining bollock are safe." She folded her knife and shouldered her backpack. "How can you stay loyal to someone who cut your balls off?"

"Not balls. Ball. Vitor only took one."

Olivia gave him a sad smile. "Whatever. You were emasculated long before you lost your right nut. Best of luck, Spence, take care."

She nodded to Kelvin and the rest of the punters before striding out into the sunshine.

17

The fuse was lit at both ends and burning fast.

She ran outside and saw Brian's black Merc waiting opposite. She flung herself into the back, locked the doors and instructed him to drive her to Heathrow Airport.

He asked no questions, started the car and drove away.

Police officers were probably trawling the Calder River, urged on by the Met, looking for an excuse to arrest her as a murder suspect. The UK didn't have the death penalty because it didn't need to. The vagaries of its archaic legal system would leave her in limbo until she died of natural causes. That was precisely the reason she had run away.

She had no doubt the minute Spencer found his wife safe – or knowing that old bastard maybe even before – he'd alert what was left of the Osman-Vargas network to Olivia's presence in the city. Every sycophant hanger-on aiming to fill the Vargas boots would crawl out from under their stones and sniff the air. The longer she remained in Britain, the further she was chancing her luck. And sooner or later, a long run of good fortune was going to run out.

Her driver asked her flight time and destination.

"The 18.45 to New York. Sorry, Brian, I can't remember the terminal ... wait a second."

"I'll find it. You relax, ma'am. We have plenty of time."

She smiled into the mirror but couldn't tell if he'd noticed as he was wearing aviator shades. It crossed her mind to remind him that her name was Olivia, not ma'am, but she actually didn't care what he called her so long as he got her to Heathrow in one piece. *Just leave the guy alone to do his job*. She took the complimentary bottle of water from the recess by the door handle and drank deeply, washing away the taste of beer and watching London pass outside the windows. She gazed at the brickwork, the red buses, the quirky fashionistas, the black cabs and signs for Tube stations. This was goodbye. One way or another, she was never coming back. Either one of her pursuers would catch up or she'd get away and spend her life on the run, never to see her loved ones again. Her eyes swelled in self-pity for a second. Then she remembered. She hadn't said goodbye to Katie.

The phone she had programmed with her sister's number was sitting somewhere on top of a mattress storage facility in Dewsbury, but there was nothing wrong with Olivia's memory.

"Brian, next time we see a phone box, could we pull over for a minute?"

He seemed uncertain, scanning the traffic. "Might not be easy round here. Would you like to use my mobile?"

"Thanks but this is a personal call."

"OK. I'll try and find something as soon as I can."

He was as good as his word. Two kilometres later, he eased into a parking spot beside a bank of public telephones, just past The British Museum. Olivia hopped out, still clutching her rucksack and used a handful of coins to make the call. It was not yet half past two. Her sister would be in surgery, splinting wings, clipping talons or removing fishing line from some avian patient or other. She dialled the mobile number and as expected, it went to voicemail.

"Hi, Katie. Guess who? I suppose I should thank you. Any yearnings for home or family are now well and truly cauterised. It was a surprise, I'll be honest, to learn you'd betrayed me. But facts are facts; no one else could have alerted my pursuers that quickly. Only you. My little sister, always the scaredy-cat, turns out to have claws after all. How was dinner at The Malthouse? That long skirt suits you. I'm leaving now and all I can say is I hope what they paid you was worth it. You're now an only child. Goodbye."

Her head was hot and her vision cloudy as she returned to the car. "Thanks for stopping, Brian. All sorted. Now let's get to Heathrow."

He tipped a finger to his peaked cap and the Mercedes eased onto the A40, heading west. Olivia checked her crappy watch and saw she had plenty of time – over four hours to get to the airport and catch her flight. Her eyes closed against their will. She should force herself to stay alert and only relax and rest when cabin crew tucked into her First Class berth. A thought made her stiffen. Her body was heavy and exhausted, as if she'd been doped. Had Spencer managed to slip something into her beer? No, she had been careful, ensuring nobody could tamper with her bottle of Bud. This was simply the tension and emotion of the past few days hitting her like a tidal wave. With her rucksack acting as a pillow and her coat acting as a blanket, she lay down on the back seat to catch an hour's shut-eye.

A horn blasted her awake and she opened her eyes with a gasp. A truck barrelled past the car, its slipstream shaking the vehicle. Outside night had fallen but the area was floodlit and artificially bright. Olivia sat up, her eyes dry and her bladder full.

She was in the rear of the luxury car, but no one was in the driver's seat. She clutched for her rucksack as reassurance. Still there, still heavy. The vehicle was now parked near a two-storey building with a sign saying Port Authority. Quite clearly not Heathrow Airport. A neon sign ahead offered a confusing set of numbers and letters. She blinked and squinted and saw the temperature was 11° and the time was 20.10. Departure of the next ferry was due at 20.45.

A slam of the boot made her jerk in fright and she snatched up her knife. The door beside her opened and she saw Brian, her driver, silhouetted against the lights, holding her suitcase.

"Awake at last! About time. Come on, move your bones, OJ, you got a ferry to catch."

She shrank away from him, trying to comprehend how his voice had changed.

He took off his chauffeur's cap and stuffed his sunglasses into his breast pocket.

"Thanh?" she whispered, her pulse drumming in her ears. "What the ...?"

He crouched on the pavement in a yogic squat and pressed a finger to his lips. "I told you if I ever saw you again, it would be the last time. This is it, the last time. Will you please come out of there and get onto that ferry?" He stood, reached out and beckoned with all four fingers.

Olivia stuffed her knife into her waistband and took his proffered hand. His grip, as steady and reliable as a steel cable, pulled her out of the car to stand in front of him. Their eyes locked.

"You put something in that water, didn't you?"

"I needed you to relax. Didn't think you'd drink it like a camel."

"Meredith said ..." she began.

"Since when do we ever use names, OJ? You used to be security smart."

"Sorry, you're right." Her sleepy mind could not recall Meredith's codename. "Umm, the thing is, M said you were dead."

"M?" He laughed, that silent shake of his shoulders she knew so well. "That's pretty good. Wouldn't she just love to be M? Here's the deal. M is mistaken. The persona I was using is now defunct. A body carrying my ID washed up in Tai Van Bay and a certain convenience store is now looking for a new owner."

That information sank in and Olivia's mind hurried to keep pace. "I thought I'd dropped you in it. Again." The passing of another truck almost drowned out her voice.

He checked his watch and replaced his cap. "We need to get a shift on or you'll miss the boat. Let's walk and talk. I'll bring your cases. By the way, I helped myself to some of your cash. Call it a gratuity. I'm guessing that wodge of notes came from the casinos?"

"Old habits die hard." Olivia zipped up her coat and shrugged on her precious rucksack.

"Thought so. She swings by Macau to find someone under police protection and liberates several hundred grand from the Chinese mafia. Swear to God, OJ, you have a death wish. You were lucky to get out of there alive. You won't miss 30K because I doubt you'll live that long. Check-in is on the left."

Thanh led the way, his chauffeur's cap set low over his eyes. The ferry port was noisy with vehicles and machinery and brought back a sharp, poignant reminder of saying goodbye to another man to get on a boat.

"I don't deserve your help. I abandoned you once and led them to you a second time." Olivia had to shout over the noise although her words were meant as a contrite whisper.

"You didn't drop me in it so stop with the cat o' nine tails, will you? This time it was the other way round." Thanh wheeled her suitcases along the walkway. "You asked me to have a word with the management so you could get in and out of the UK without fear of arrest. I refused, felt bad about it and made a call. Thought I was doing you a favour until I twigged it was the opposite. Certain people, like 'M', might be able to keep their mouths shut, but when the news gets out, it becomes a kind of currency. Information, as I think we've established, is power. Shit, this wind is vicious." He stopped to zip up his collar.

Her head grew clearer with every step. "Wait, how did you find me? Where's Brian, my driver? Why the hell should I get on this ferry?"

"And she's back in the room, ladies and gentlemen! I found you the same way you found me – by knowing your habits. Brian did as he was asked, pocketed five hundred quid – yours, by the way – and went home on the Docklands Light Railway. The reason you're getting on the ferry is because if you get within sniffing distance of Heathrow Terminal 5, you're either dead or as good as. Listen to me, OJ, this is your last chance to sneak out of the UK and get a head start. We've got twenty minutes before this ship sails and if you miss it, you're on your own. I've got better things to do than babysit you. Here's your new passport, driving licence and vaccine certificate."

She read the writing on the manila envelope: Iris Simons. "How did you choose that name?" she asked.

He cupped his hands around his mouth and whispered into her ear. "Simons, in homage to Sal. And Iris after the Portuguese word for rainbow. Hope you find your pot of gold, OJ." He snapped into business-like mode once more as two latecomers came scurrying down the path.

"First Class cabin, as you requested, ma'am. Use the check-in on the left and my advice would be to make the most of Room Service for the first leg. *Bon voyage!*" He thrust the handles of her suitcases towards her and began walking away.

"Thanh!"

He looked over his shoulder. "What did I just say about names?" His eyes flashed in the floodlights, but not with anger.

"It wasn't a name. I said thanks. Thank you very much. I ..."

"You're welcome. I'm out of here." He tipped his hat and set off at a jog in the direction of the car.

Olivia watched him go until a bell sounded, followed by a recorded warning for latecomers. *All passengers, please board immediately if you wish to sail tonight.* As if jabbed by a prod, she speed-walked to the First Class check-in desk, handed over a brand new purple passport in the name of Iris Simons and offered the official her ticket. He scanned it with some impatience and waved her up the gangway. Due to her being one of the last to board, the reception area was not cluttered with fretful travellers stumbling over each other's luggage. She stood in the oval space, trying to put her brain in gear. An older woman behind a desk called out. "Over here, madam! *Aquí, señora.*"

Thirty minutes later, Olivia was in a suite, sitting on the bed and watching the lights of Portsmouth recede. Only when the view was nothing more than night sky and black sea did she check the ferry's destination on the room's TV.

Santander. Could be worse.

18

Thirty hours was not long enough to process the events of the previous week. Olivia didn't leave her cabin once in the first twenty-four hours, merely sitting on her balcony to watch either the enormous expanse of the Atlantic or the French/Spanish coast drifting past. She rarely dressed, spending most of the day in a cotton robe and bare feet. The confinement accompanied by isolation made her think of the word 'asylum'. Padded, protected and alone, she did little more than eat, sleep and gaze at the scenery. Her brain took the day off. Whatever Thanh had dropped into that water bottle took its time to get out of her system.

On Day Two of the crossing, she lacked the energy to confront the past, but roused herself enough to envisage the future. Over a breakfast omelette with spinach, a jug of coffee and some grapefruit juice on her balcony, she sketched a loose plan. A small voice floated a plaintive question, but she drowned it out by examining maps, browsing estate agents and reading local news. Her immediate curiosity led her east into Andorra, along the border between France and Spain towards the coast of Catalonia. Somewhere she had never been. For a second, she let her imagination run free, before the little voice caught up.

You don't speak Catalan. Why go to Catalonia?

She ignored it and pictured a hotel room in Perpignan, taking a trip to Figueiras or Barcelona and drinking a coffee beside the Mediterranean.

Nice. But what are you going to do there?

Settle down. Find a little place with a garden somewhere quiet, keep chickens, grow flowers, read and relax.

What's the point?

The point is ... there is no point. I'm alive and I want to live in peace.

Inner voices had no facial expressions but its silence was enough to make her turn inward. What *was* the point? To exist in solitude, forming no connections, rejecting everyone in her emotional orbit? Why not? She'd done it before. Alive with no life.

She would live off grid, just as she had done in Brazil, using a little of her money to purchase a home, a base where she could protect herself and appreciate her environment.

The inner voice snorted its disbelief. *Who with?*

With nobody at all. I am self-sufficient, travelling light. No family, no loved ones and therefore, no obligations. Everyone's dream existence.

She didn't need her inner voice to point out that was pure bullshit. She got dressed and went to the shopping deck in search of a straw hat.

At 05.00 classical music emanated from the speakers, the gentlest of alarm calls. Olivia opened the curtains and saw tiny lights penetrating the sooty sky. Houses, cars and street illumination guaranteed Spain was sparkling in its welcome. A certainty settled on her as she threw off her robe and stepped into the shower. She changed her plans and her mind. East was the wrong direction. She would head west along the north coast, from Cantabria to Galicia, choosing her moment to swing south to Portugal. Somewhere in the interior of that rural country, a little cottage with a patch of land, far from the beachside crowds, was waiting for her to call it home.

Breakfast was light – a croissant, fruit salad and a pot of coffee. She ate everything, her appetite back to full strength. The docking process was long and uninteresting, so Olivia used the time to plan her route across the Asturias and as far as La Coruña before taking the less-travelled road inland. Most people stuck to the coast when going south, but it was too painful for Olivia. The city of Porto held many happy memories of Sal, roaring at a football match and dancing in the street after a victory, wielding a plastic hammer at São João, driving along some remote road overlooking the sea and laughing. 'Why would a person live anywhere else?'

Why indeed? She and Sal had always dreamed of retiring to Portugal and living the simple life by the sea. Whether Porto or the country as a whole would chafe at her grief remained to be seen, but it was one of the few places she could remain anonymous. She spoke the language, knew the landscape and had enough money to live an unobtrusive existence as long as it lasted.

An intercom announcement advised all drivers to return to their cars. Foot passengers should assemble in the reception area. She threw on a linen dress, hooked her thumbs under the backpack straps and heaved it over her shoulders. A new country, a new name and the next stage of her adventure awaited. Olivia called for a porter to collect her suitcases and arranged a taxi to meet her at the dock. She waited until the last minute to leave her cabin. Crowds harboured all kinds of danger, even when she wasn't running for her life. Large groups of people inevitably pissed her off. After most passengers had streamed down the gangways, she emerged in her cheap summery dress with a wide-brimmed hat and asked the uniformed porter to deposit her luggage in the waiting cab.

She'd been to Britain and got out again. So far, so good. Now to erase her footprints

She told the driver to deposit her at the bus station, where she caught a large air-conditioned coach east to Bilbao. There she located a second-hand car dealership and after some protracted haggling in half-baked Spanish, bought a battered Seat Ibiza in cash. It had a few dents, but reasonable mileage on the clock, relatively new tyres and enough room for two hefty suitcases in the boot. 'Iris Simons' agreed on the final price, handed over a roll of Euros and flicked through the paperwork.

The garage owner couldn't hide his grin. "Gold. Nice colour for a lady."

According to the manual, the paintwork was described as 'mystic magenta', a combination which made her bilious.

"*Muchas gracias, señor.* To be honest, I don't see it as gold."

He squinted at the car. "No?"

"No. For me, it's champagne. An even better colour for a lady. Now, can you tell me the best way to get to San Sebastián?"

Bags in the boot, rucksack on the passenger seat and her hat shading her face, she drove out of the city, with no intention of heeding the man's directions. But should anyone be following her, it was one more red herring to throw them off her scent. She retraced her route west in the direction of Santander on a wide, well-kept motorway. Two hours elapsed before she stopped checking her mirror every thirty seconds.

Because she was not in a hurry and had no clear destination, Olivia-now-Iris took almost a week to travel along the coast, staying in *posadas* and *paradors* until she reached the city of A Coruña. From there, she turned inland and spent another two days zigzagging south until she crossed the border into Portugal between two national parks. After a detour up the Douro river to marvel at the vineyards layered over the hills, she continued south, with the vague destination of the Alentejo, a rural inland region south of Lisbon. It was another two to three days' drive, in her estimation, as she intended to take the scenic route. In some of the towns she stayed overnight or stopped for lunch, she browsed estate agents' windows, trying to gauge property prices. Run-down buildings known as 'do-ups' were in abundance, but she was no starry-eyed expat, dreaming of transforming a pigsty into a palace. She wanted a small, solid house in need of minimal renovations, with some land, a village or town within cycling distance and a sizeable city around an hour's drive away. Ideally, a view of some water, a lake or a river would be perfect. Each night, she repeated her affirmation: my name is Iris Simons. Over breakfast, she practised her new signature. Olivia Jones was no more.

Two weeks after she'd departed from Britain, Iris drove through an autumnal landscape of gold and green with undulating hills all around the valley. It was approaching two o'clock and she decided Viseu would be a good place to stop for some lunch. The city surprised her with its colourful flower displays, fountains, green spaces and imposing squares. She parked outside a pretty restaurant with pink umbrellas, as always hoping for a table where she could keep an eye on her car. The vehicle itself was replaceable. Its contents were not. She was wrestling with the parking meter when above her head, shutters flew open.

"*Olá! Bonjour! Hello! Bom dia! Willkommen!*"

The man was in his sixties with crazy hair and glasses so huge he resembled a startled owl.

With a quick assessment of which language was safest to use, she replied in Portuguese. "Good afternoon, I was wondering if you're still serving lunch?"

"Still open? Of course! The crowds don't get here till around three. Come in, *senhora*, come in, we have two specials today, both mere moments out of the ocean. You want to sit inside or out?"

She flicked her eyes to the terrace but before she could open her mouth, he continued. "Yes, good idea, the breeze is warm today and you can people-watch. Not that they ever do anything interesting but we live in hope. I'll bring you some bread with a fresh white wine. Find a table you like, make yourself comfortable and let me tell you all about the monkfish. Salad or soup to start?"

Olivia was unused to giving her order by craning her neck to look up at a window and hesitated. The man carried on as if he'd only stopped to draw breath. "And as for water, still or sparkling? If you're having *vinho verde*, you're safest with still. There's such a thing as too much fizz. Just a minute, *senhora*, I'm on my way." The shutters slammed shut.

Olivia walked to the entrance and chose a spot on the terrace with her back to the restaurant and a clear view of her champagne-coloured car. There were a few other diners seated around tables covered with checked tablecloths, including several couples and four men in hi-vis jackets, but most of the action, judging by the noise, seemed to be indoors. The menu, wedged between a salt cellar and a serviette dispenser, announced the restaurant's name: A Pantera Rosa. She shook her head with a smile. The Pink Panther? What kind of name was that for a seafood joint?

The owl man emerged from the interior with a tray the size of a cartwheel. It was laden with carafes of wine and water, bread baskets, a steaming tureen and half a dozen bottles of beer. He distributed the beers between the men and placed the tureen in the centre of their table, whipping off the lid with a flourish. "*Olha, os meus amigos*! Fresh mussels cooked in white wine and garlic. Plenty of bread to soak up the juices and a plate for the shells. Enjoy!" On Olivia's table, he placed a bowl of green soup, a carafe of water and another of wine along with a basket of bread.

"*Caldo verde*! When someone cannot decide between soup and salad, have a soup made of vegetables! Tell me where you're from, *senhora*, because I can't place your accent. At first I said to myself, Alonso, she's a *tripeira*. That's because of the politeness of your enquiry. Porto is nothing if not middle class. But then I thought again and noticed you said '*esta servindo*', which is how a Brazilian would express herself. Now excuse me making a personal comment, but you don't look very Brazilian. To look at you, I'd have guessed French, but the thing with the French is they can never hide their accents. To be honest, most don't even try." He raised his eyebrows and shoulders. "Now then, I can't stand here chatting to you all day, *senhora*, I have customers to serve. Today's special is monkfish is cooked with onions, peppers, tomatoes and parsley, served with potatoes and it goes beautifully with a half bottle of the local red. In case you are a foreigner, that means Dão. So I suggest monkfish and a glass of Dão and we'll see about desserts so long as you've cleaned your plate. Enjoy the *caldo verde*, it's my speciality." With that, he bustled off to collect plates and compliments from a couple by the door.

Olivia watched the most voluble man on the Iberian Peninsula deliver another monologue, shout a greeting to a passing cyclist and clear two tables simultaneously while barely pausing in his incessant barrage of words. She took a spoonful of soup and closed her eyes. Cabbage soup flavoured with chouriço tasted like home and this was as homely as it got.

As Alonso had predicted, the restaurant grew more and more crowded until barely a space was available inside or out. A different waiter brought Olivia's monkfish and wine with a brief smile. She was almost disappointed by the wordless exchange but certainly not by the main course. The delicious mixture of vegetables baked in the fish juices was enough. She cleared the plate and poured a second glass of wine from the half bottle. One of those rare meals when the food, wine, ambience and weather coalesced into perfection. The clientele thinned out and noise levels dropped. Viseu gave the impression of a pleasant city, worth an overnight stay. No more driving for her today. She made up her mind to have a coffee, pay the bill and wander nearby until she located a hotel with its own garage. After that, perhaps a siesta.

"I knew you would love it, *senhora!*" Alonso's voice came from the steps to the interior, turning all heads. But his pronouncement was aimed at her as he beamed his way across the terrace, carrying an espresso. "The wine too! Didn't I tell you they are made for each other?" He began gathering her crockery and cutlery onto his tray. "I can tell by the look on your face you are not interested in a *sobremesa*, so I just brought you a coffee to round off your meal. What was your opinion of the monkfish?"

Snatching an opportunity to speak, Olivia asked a question. "Senhor Alonso, it was all delicious, but I'm curious about the name. Why would you call an exceptional fish restaurant A Pantera Rosa? It really was exceptional, I'm not exaggerating. I'd say that was one of the finest meals I've enjoyed in Portugal."

He peered at her through his owlish glasses, placed the tray on the low wall encircling the barbecue and swung into the seat opposite. "In that case, I ask myself what kind of restaurants you have been frequenting. Don't get me wrong, this establishment is, as you say, exceptional. Not just in my biased opinion, ask anyone and they'll tell you the same thing. A Pantera Rosa uses the best ingredients and cooks them simply. Classic Portuguese cuisine. It's nothing special. There are beachside cafés in this country serving food to rival any Michelin-starred eatery, with less pretension and more heart. You never told me where you're from, *senhora*, which is your prerogative. My guess is from the Algarve and you only ever ate ..."

Despite her satiated and rather sleepy frame of mind, she tried out her new identity. "*Com licença*, Senhor Alonso, can I interrupt? I'm from Galicia. My name is Iris Simons and I used to work all over the world. My accent tends to change depending on where I am. Growing up, Portugal was right on my doorstep but as a typical teenager, I craved the big cities. Don't we all?"

He took a breath to respond so Olivia pressed on with her speech. She lowered her voice and leant forward in a confidential pose. "About two years ago, I had to leave my high-salaried job. Burnt out." She glanced up to make sure her audience of one was suitably attentive and shook her head. "Not something I want to talk about, too painful. Forced to retire at my age? Tragic. Why spend my life on the corporate hamster wheel when life is out here? I made a choice – live in the moment. This is what brought me here, to appreciate all the beauty the world has to offer. Can I buy you a glass of wine, Alonso?"

For once, her host was speechless. He clasped his hands together and pressed them to his lips, his head bobbing in tiny nods.

Olivia knew his emotions were soon to erupt in an epic speech and forestalled him. "That is why I seek a quiet little house where I can grow vegetables and keep chickens like my grandparents. From what I read, the Alentejo region is trying to attract newcomers due to its ageing population. Tonight I'm staying in Viseu and tomorrow, I'm heading south."

His head jerked upwards. "You want to buy a *quinta*?"

"God, no, not the whole cows and agriculture and vine-yards business. I don't have the energy or the faintest idea how to run a farm. Just a little place, near some water, far from other people where I can be as self-sufficient as it gets. I thought I'd base myself somewhere in the middle, like Evora, and start searching."

He jumped to his feet and held out a hand. "Come with me! I have some people I want you to meet." He glanced at the sky and placed his palms together in thanks. "This was meant to be! *Obrigado, O Senhor*! Iris, today is a fortunate day for us all. Bring your coffee and come inside. I will open a vintage port."

19

And so it was that Iris Simons purchased sixteen acres of land near the river Dão. The Alcafalche small-holding belonged to Nestor and Lana Gomes, who had worked it all their lives. Now in their late sixties with no children to take over the business, they were seeking a buyer.

Over a conversation at A Pantera Rosa, and another the next day at the property itself, Iris soon established that the couple didn't want to leave their home. It was a fertile, well-tended little farm protected by high brick walls around its borders. Once inside, there was a sweeping view down to a wide section of the river Dão. Three houses formed a triangle although none was visible from the other: a small lodge at the entrance gate where the Gomes couple now lived; a central squat farmhouse with three outbuildings closer to the river, and a shepherd's cottage up on the hill. The whole enterprise was much bigger and farther north than she'd planned, not to mention requiring a great deal of work. And yet, the second she heard the name, she knew. A Quinta Douro – the farm of gold – was the right place for her; she could sense that in her bones. It contained everything she wanted and it was enclosed by walls. Finally, she had found her safe place.

They negotiated a deal. Iris paid a reasonable sum to acquire A Quinta Douro on the understanding that Nestor remained as farm manager. He knew the land better than anyone after all. She asked Lana to continue as housekeeper and bookkeeper, because she'd managed the farm accounts all her life. The lodge was their home and there they should stay. Iris was prepared to hire labour, purchase farm equipment and plough a chunk of cash into modernising and renovating the buildings. The day they signed the contract, Iris invited them both to dinner at A Pantera Rosa and bought a bottle of champagne.

After some substantial repairs and a thorough cleaning, Iris moved into the main house. The weather grew autumnally cool and she tried to get as much done before the onset of winter, guided by Nestor's wisdom. He and the two new employees worked all day in the fields and forest, tilling, digging and hammering. Iris was a little vague on exactly what they were doing, but trusted that it fell under the umbrella of 'preparation'. She and Lana added several cosmetic touches, such as painting the bricks lining the driveway a brilliant white, replacing the entrance gates and commissioning an artist to replace the faded name of the farm on the outside wall with a classic colourful mural. She found the older woman pleasant, calming company and best of all, an excellent cook.

The amount of effort she threw at her new home occupied the majority of her physical and emotional energy. She slept well and blocked all waking thoughts of ex-lovers, ex-colleagues and what used to be family. Olivia Jones was a skin she'd shed. She was now a new woman called Iris Simons, content, safe and out of trouble, exactly who she wanted to be.

It took until springtime until she realised being content, safe and out of trouble did not make her happy.

. . .

Lana was washing root vegetables in the heavy ceramic sink, her skirt swishing as she moved from side to side. One of the best things about Lana was her silence. She never spoke for the sake of speaking, only if she had something to say. On the rare occasions she did have something to say, everyone listened; the farmhands, Iris, Nestor and even the chickens paused in their scratting. Today, it was just the two of them in the large cool kitchen, an April breeze ruffling the curtains through the open window.

Iris was peeling and coring a crate of cellar-stored apples for a batch of tarts, wondering if she could make an excuse, jump in the champagne-coloured Seat and run off to a city, any city, for just one day. She'd seen the same faces every day for over six months and while she appreciated their skills and personalities, everyone deserved a break. The farmhands, Paula and Rafi, went south for the winter. Why not, when there was hardly any work for them to do? At Carnaval, Nestor and Lana spent a long weekend with her nieces in Vigo. Only Iris stayed home alone, with the chickens.

Lana cleared her throat. "Tomorrow is Friday, the day Aveiro has a flea market. Second-hand furniture, crockery, garden tools, carpets; it's a good place to find what you need."

"I don't need anything," answered Iris, without stopping to think. She pulled out the pastry cases from the pantry and layered the apples in decorative circles. With a sprinkle of brown sugar and cinnamon, they looked oven-ready. Still, Iris had to check with the chef.

Lana focused her critical gaze on the baking tins and nodded her approval. A bluebottle buzzed through the open window, glinting green and black as it flew between patches of sunlight. Lana wafted it away with a wet hand, scattering droplets of water into the golden air. "It's only an hour's drive from here and you've never visited the city. There's a shop run by a man called Fabio and he sells mirrors at a fair price. Free-standing, framed and all decent quality. Go and haggle. You could do with a looking-glass." Lana shook the green turnip tops and placed them on a tea towel.

Iris laughed as she closed the oven on three apple tarts. "You mean to say I'm letting myself go? I've no urge to preen and prettify myself, Lana. I have everything I need."

They worked in silence for some time to the soundtrack of Nestor's tractor and the shrieks of swifts dashing through the spring morning. Lana heated olive oil in a blackened skillet and threw in some chopped onions and garlic.

"Everything you need, yes. What about the things you want? Once in a while, it's a good idea to look in the mirror. *Grelos cozidos* for lunch – with eggs or rice?"

"Eggs. One of my favourites." She wasn't lying. Turnip tops with oil and garlic were rich and earthy on their own, with eggs, fish or even mixed with pasta. "I'll call in the field workers."

She opened the kitchen door and tolled the little brass bell, alerting everyone their midday meal would be served in half an hour. When she returned inside, Lana was stirring the pot with a patient expression. Iris set the table for six and thought about Lana's words. The woman rarely made a suggestion without good reason. Only minutes before, Iris had been aching for a change of scenery and here was her opportunity.

"OK, if you think it's worthwhile, I'll drive to Aveiro tomorrow. Shall we make a shopping list?"

"No. You're not shopping for the farm, you're having a day off. Go exploring and have some fun. They call it the Portuguese Venice, you know." She pointed at the table. "We only need five places today."

"Five? Why?"

"Paula called in sick this morning. If she's not better tomorrow, I'll go and see her, make sure it's nothing serious. This is a busy time of year for Nestor."

"In that case, it makes no sense for me to go gallivanting off to Aveiro when I could be helping out on the farm." She put away the extra cutlery.

"We can manage just fine. Rafi and Diogo are hard workers, if a little fanciful. Rafi was trying to convince us he'd seen a UFO this morning." She rolled her eyes. "Are you keeping an eye on those apple tarts?"

Next morning, Iris left without eating breakfast, oddly nervous about her first foray into a new city. Ridiculous, considering she used to think nothing of jetting off to an international hub like Rio de Janeiro or Hong Kong. But the butterflies in her stomach were testament to the fact that in the last seven months she'd barely left the farm. Since the beginning of the year she only had eaten in a restaurant once and that was A Pantera Rosa. She was getting to be far too much of a homebody. Lana was right. A change is as good as a rest.

The first thing that struck her about Aveiro was the colour. So many façades of buildings were either painted or tiled in beautiful hues of duck-egg blue, fire-engine red or sunshine yellow. Even plainer edifices had vibrant shutters, awnings or multi-coloured umbrellas. Then there was the water. As Lana had mentioned, the city was situated on a lagoon and crisscrossed by canals. Narrow boats shaped like gondolas, but painted in harlequin shades bobbed up and down the banks and beneath the decorative bridges.

Iris was charmed as she wandered through the old town and along to the fisherman's quarter. Naturally, fish and seafood restaurants were in abundance, as were traditional Portuguese eateries, but she wanted to seize the chance of eating something different. Dismissing an American diner, various Italian pizzerias and a Brazilian churrasqueira, she opted for an upscale Japanese place called Zuma, because it vaguely reminded her of Jackson and his dance class. A server showed Iris to a table and explained the placemat was actually a computer screen, where she could read the menu and place her order directly. She could even choose the design of her table mat.

"Can I get you anything to drink while you decide what to eat?"

"Yes, please. I'd like a Japanese beer. Nothing too strong."

"I will bring you an Asahi. Oh, you can also use that to surf the Internet, if you like." The guy walked off, clearly unaware of the effect his words had on his customer.

Iris froze, staring at the screen as if it was a fire-breathing monster. Since leaving Britain in a frantic dash, she had steered well clear of the World Web Web, even to the extent of locking away her laptop to remove temptation. Now, with one tap of her finger, she could access any information she wanted. For example, why not check in with what was new at the Soure police website? Or *The Dewsbury Reporter* obituaries? Perhaps even the Metropolitan Police? She squeezed her eyes shut and reminded herself Iris Simons had no interest in any of those things.

She perused the menu and selected beef yakitori with soba noodles and a glass of red wine. The waiter returned with her beer and a smile at her choice of table mat – cartoon pandas.

She sipped her drink, appreciated her surroundings and watched the activity on the street outside, all the while having a raging internal argument.

Stop thinking about it or go somewhere else.

Why not browse the BBC, that's innocent enough?

Why not put a beacon on your head and shout come and get me?

I can surf anonymously, hiding my location with a VPN.

If you think that's sufficient protection against the top trackers who are desperate to earn the bounty on your head, not to mention the prestige, be my guest.

I won't look at anything which could connect them to me. I'd just like to know how Dad is.

Remember what happened the last time you checked on family? Your own sister blew the whistle. It is not worth the risk.

It's important to know what's going on in the world. I've lived like a hermit these last few months.

The point is you've lived. When the Osman-Vargas gang catch up with you, you'll wish you were dead.

"Skewered chunks of tender beef with slices of spring onion brushed with homemade yakitori on a bed of spicy noodles. With one glass of Bordeaux. *Bom apetite!*"

Iris ate, distracted for a moment by the richness of her meal, recalling a particularly appreciated meal of egg rolls with duck sauce in a Hong Kong hotel room. It seemed several life-times ago. This meal joined those egg rolls in the all-time top ten, a game she used to play with Katie. 'Nope, ten is the max. If you want to add spaghetti carbonara, the sardines have got to go'.

Katie. In one swift move, she moved the plate to one side, tapped the screen and opened a private window to browse the Internet. She went straight to Dewsbury Veterinary Practice and opened the Practice News page. A hurried scan showed no major announcements regarding staff members and the personnel page still showed Dr K. Lane as the ornithological expert.

Something had registered in Iris's consciousness. She flicked back one page and read the announcements again. Congratulations for an assistant on passing her exams, puppy training courses, photos of a cattery and lost/found pets. There it was.

FOUND: Brazilian bloodhound sniffing around Mirfield area.

Healthy young male with scar tissue on right ribcage. No chip, but name on collar says GIL. Please contact Dr Katie Lane for details.

Iris stared at the screen, incredulous. It simply wasn't possible. She looked at the date and saw the notice had been posted just before Christmas. Her brain ran so fast it overtook itself and seemed to seize up entirely. She closed the tab and shut down the Internet, unable to think over the bass drum in her ears.

"Madam, didn't you like the food?"

Iris gasped and jerked away from the waiter. "No, I mean yes, the food was lovely, I just had a reaction to the ... umm ... spices. I'm so sorry, but I must leave now. Can I have the bill?"

The waiter eyed her with concern. "Would you like some water?"

"No, I just want the bill as fast as possible."

"Ma'am, the bill is on your screen and we accept contactless or credit cards. Are you OK?"

"Completely fine. I don't have any cards, sorry." Iris got to her feet and threw fifty Euros on the table. "Thank you and keep the change." She blundered into the street, trying to remember where she had parked her car.

The city, hot and oppressive in the afternoon sunshine, seemed confusing and illogical. The parking garage was over the river, she recalled crossing a bridge, but which bridge? She strode in the direction of the water and saw a sign for the Forum shopping centre. That was where she'd left the car, of course it was, because the Roman allusion had stuck in her mind. Twenty minutes later, after a sweaty walk and frustrating search for her parking ticket, she located her Seat Ibiza and followed the signs to Viseu. From there, she could find her way home.

. . .

FOUND: Brazilian bloodhound sniffing around Mirfield area. Healthy young male with scar tissue on right ribcage. No chip, but name on collar says GIL. Please contact Dr Katie Lane for details.

The words were burnt onto Iris's brain like a cattle brand and hurt almost as much. She drove in silence, reading between the lines.

Brazilian bloodhound. As far as she knew, there was no such breed and she was better informed than most. As kids, she and Katie had made their own set of Top Trumps, with details of breed, weight, coat, colour and height. The theme was mostly for Katie as the animal obsessive, but the precision entertained them both. The bloodhound reference was obvious.

Healthy young male sniffing around Mirfield area. The affluent Dewsbury suburb where Katie lived with her husband and two children was known as Mirfield, a postcode of pride and the last place you'd encounter a stray dog. *Healthy young male sniffing around* – someone looking for information. Why emphasise healthy? Was the message meant to indicate he was unhurt, intact or what? *Scar tissue?* The kind you might get from dragging people out of a burning drug factory?

No chip, but name on collar says GIL. This was no coincidence. *No chip* could indicate no hard feelings and *name on collar* ... Iris pulled off the road and onto the hard shoulder. Gil Maduro had tracked her from Soure to the UK?

The last line delivered the vital point. *Please contact Dr Katie Lane for details.* In her professional role, Dr Lane used either her initial or full name – Katherine. Only close family or friends called her Katie. This was a message aimed directly at her sister, the only family she had left.

The gates of A Quinta Douro were open and Iris exhaled a huge sigh of relief as the Seat Ibiza crunched down the track to the house. In the distance, she could see three figures working in the fields. Inside the farmhouse, all was silent and Iris recalled Lana's words. 'Paula called in sick this morning. If she's not better tomorrow, I'll go and see her, make sure it's nothing serious.'

The empty house soothed Iris's fevered mind. She drank a full glass of water and lay on the flagstones, trying to process four lines of text. Katie was calling out to her, using Detective Gil Maduro as a flare. But Katie knew nothing about Gil Maduro or her life in Brazil. No one knew his importance in her life, apart from the two of them.

Two possibilities presented themselves. Gil Maduro had tracked down her family, met Katie and convinced her to send out a plea. What wonderful luck for Sister Snitch, another way to squeeze more cash from the Osman-Vargas payroll.

Or Gil had come in search of her, looking for the woman he loved, trusting family was the place to start. She had promised to do the same, to return to Brazil and find him, once she was safe. It wasn't a false promise, just an unrealistic dream.

She rolled onto her front, elbows on the floor and rested her chin on her hands, remembering the evening Gil Maduro appeared on her doorstep and ...

"*Está aqui!*" She wasn't sure whether the young voice belonged to Diogo or Rafi and the words could mean 'she's here', 'he's here' or 'it's here', depending on the context. Whatever the meaning, one thing was certain – her peace and quiet was over. Iris scrambled to her feet, half wishing she could lock the door and hide under the table. From the courtyard came the sound of the tractor approaching, male shouts and an unfamiliar electronic buzzing.

The next instant a gunshot boomed into the air. Iris dropped to a crouch, her pulse thudding in her ears. In the shocked silence that followed, she heard a woman's tones raised in anger and recognised the voice as Lana's. With extreme caution, Iris peered around the kitchen curtain. Nestor cradled his shotgun and the two boys stood over some broken bits of metal outside the chicken coop. Lana was marching down the track in their direction, clearly about to read the riot act.

Iris opened the kitchen door. "What on earth is going on?" she demanded.

Everyone spoke at once.

"That was flying over the farm ..." said Diogo, pointing at the twisted metal.

Rafi interrupted. "I saw it yesterday as well, but they didn't believe me."

"I've never seen one before," added Nestor. "I didn't know what it was."

Lana spoke, shutting everyone up. "Is that what you usually do when you can't identify something? Shoot first and then ask questions?"

The three males looked chastened for a moment, but Rafi could not suppress his excitement.

"I knew what it was, *senhora*. I told them about it yesterday, but they didn't believe me. I know what this is."

So did Iris. Her skin went cold.

"It's a drone, Senhora Gomes. They have a little camera on the front, look." Rafi crouched, pointing.

"Don't touch it!" hissed Lana.

"I wasn't going to touch it. Just showing you is all. There's a little camera and it takes pictures and sends them back to whoever is controlling it."

"So why on earth did you shoot it down?"

"It's a kind of spy!" Diogo yelled, making everyone jump. "Senhor Gomes had to shoot it. Someone is spying on the farm."

Lana's voice was tight with temper. "Do you realise how close it came to my chickens when you shot it out of the sky? It could have killed them. It could have damaged this car. What if Senhora Simons had come out of the kitchen a moment earlier? Did any of you trigger-happy imbeciles think of that?"

233

Iris's head grew light and Lana's voice seemed to get further away, even though she wasn't moving. The sky became impossibly bright and her legs were suddenly incapable of holding her upright.

"Iris!" Lana's worried gasp was the last thing she heard before she collapsed.

When she regained consciousness, she was once again on the kitchen floor, but now in the recovery position with her head pillowed on her arm. The throw from the armchair covered her body and she could smell chocolate. Lana knelt beside her.

"Iris? How are you feeling?"

"A bit weird. Dizzy. Did I faint?" She tried to sit up and immediately felt nauseous. "Oh dear."

"Take it slowly." Lana laid a hand on her forehead. "You don't have a fever, so that's something. Yes, you fainted. Good job Rafi is so quick, he caught you before you hit the ground. Rest your back against the cabinet and drink some hot chocolate. I put a dash of brandy in it to restore you. Have you eaten anything today?"

Iris thought about the few mouthfuls of beef yakitori she had managed and shook her head. "Not much. I drank a beer in Aveiro. It was Japanese."

Lana frowned. "Well, that explains it."

The hot chocolate was sweet and comforting, with a powerful whiff of brandy fumes. Iris clutched the mug to her chest, warming her hands.

Lana opened the fridge door and withdrew a casserole dish. "*Arroz de Pato.* I made it for everyone's lunch today and saved a portion for you before I went into town. I'll put it in the oven now and you can eat that for dinner. That'll give you some strength. Feeling better now or do you need more brandy? After the day I've had, I might just have one myself." She came to sit at the kitchen table, poured a tot of brandy into a shot glass and proffered the bottle.

Iris handed over her mug. "Just a tiny bit. Alcohol on an empty stomach, you know. I'm going to get up off the floor now." She manoeuvred herself onto her hands and knees then, gripping Lana's hand, eased herself into a chair. "Thank you. You had a bad day as well? Did you go and see Paula?"

Lana's expression darkened. "Yes, but I didn't see Paula. They sent her away. We need to find a new farmhand."

"Who sent her away? Why?"

"Her family. Well, her father." She sighed. "Paula's pregnant. Her father is very old-fashioned and thinks her condition shames the family. So he sent her away to live with an aunt, I don't know where exactly. Her mother said it's somewhere in the Açores."

"That's archaic! To send a sixteen-year-old halfway across the Atlantic because she's expecting a baby?" A thought occurred to Iris. "Oh God, you don't think Rafi ..."

"No. Paula and her boyfriend Samuel have been sweethearts since primary school. Poor boy. He'll be devastated when he finds out." She let out another huge sigh. "This afternoon we just lost one of our best workers and then I come home to find those idiots playing *The Good, The Bad and The Ugly*."

The drone. The implications hit Iris like a juggernaut and she covered her eyes with her hands. How had she forgotten the damned drone?

"Are you feeling dizzy again?" Lana's hand rested on her shoulder. "Or is it something to do with that machine?"

Her voice, so calm, so gentle, filled with a maternal understanding, came dangerously close to provoking tears. She wanted to throw herself into Lana's embrace and cry, sob out the whole story and allow the older woman pat her back and stroke her hair. But that was not an option. Not least for Lana's sake.

She took a deep, shaky breath. "Yes. A bit dizzy. You know, I think I'll lie down for a little while. Thank you for the hot chocolate and for looking after me."

"*De nada*. The duck rice is on a low heat, so it will be warm when you're ready."

Iris lay on top of her quilt, staring at the ceiling beams, facing facts. A remote smallholding in the Portuguese interior where they kept chickens, ducks and a few sheep, grew modest crops of potatoes, maize and grapes and employed a couple of local teenagers was not of any interest to anyone. It certainly didn't merit an expensive piece of technology filming and photographing its activities. The only reason a person would operate a drone over her land was because they were looking for someone.

Somehow, they had tracked her this far and were now seeking proof. Walls were no obstacle to the Osman-Vargas organisation. They had tentacles everywhere. Now Nestor had shot down a drone and someone, possibly in a nearby vehicle, was making a call to the boss, asking permission to take the next step. They might already be on the property, creeping up to the house.

She had a choice. Stay here and wait for them to snatch her, drag her back to Britain and serve whatever punishment they deemed she deserved; or run faster, hide better, evade the inevitable one more time. The problem was, she simply couldn't face it. The thought of packing up her rucksack and abandoning ship forced tears from her eyes, leaking into her hair. She'd had enough.

There was another angle. What if the person operating the drone was not the enemy? For a second, she entertained the ghost of a possibility that Gil Maduro really had made contact with her sister and encouraged her to place that notice on the website four months ago. Frustrated by the lack of response, or perhaps he too realised Katie could not be trusted, he made his own enquiries and tracked her to Viseu. A couple of casual enquires resulted in a lead. *A foreigner who spoke good Portuguese? Why yes, Senhora Simons at A Quinta Douro.* Rather than march up to the front door, he sent in a roving camera to make sure he'd found the right woman.

She pressed her fingers to her eyelids and brushed away the self-pitying tears. Nice fantasy, but clearly impossible. Contacting her sister was the equivalent of placing a noose around her neck.

The only way anyone could have tracked her as far as Alcafalche was that all this time, she'd been carrying a bug. For example, someone had been in her rucksack while she was out cold, helping himself to some of her money and planting a tracking device in a piece of kit she would be unlikely to lose. Such as her laptop. An insurance policy Thanh could use if he were ever caught – exchanging her whereabouts for his freedom.

She ground her teeth. To doubt Thanh after he risked his own life to get her safely out of the UK, what kind of hateful, suspicious, ungracious bitch was she? Even as she berated herself for such unworthy thoughts, she unlocked the drawer where she had stored her computer and checked it thoroughly. She took her suitcases from the wardrobe and rummaged through every pocket of her rucksack, even slicing open the padded straps in search of a tiny tracking device. Her clothes, her pockets, even her shoes yielded nothing. How could Thanh or any other hunter know what she would keep? She might well have replaced all her gear in the last seven months. Only one thing followed her everywhere.

She looked at her left hand and the gold band on her third

JJ MARSH

finger. That personal banker in London, studying the engraved number through his jeweller's loupe, tapping one number at a time onto the keypad, giving himself enough time to attach a miniscule bug to her wedding ring. Even at the time she resented handing over her jewellery and had serious concerns about that private bank. She didn't even know there were bugs that small, but technology moved faster than she could imagine.

Her instincts were right. The game was up. She could never outrun those savage bastards because they would eventually find her and make her suffer. The only thing she could do was deny them their prize.

Why not? What did she have to live for? She'd lost her husband, left her lover, her father barely recognised his eldest, her sister was a Jezebel and to the farm folk, Iris was little more than a cash cow. She could write a will, leaving them everything and cheat the Osman-Vargas thugs of their last act of sadism. The answer was staring her in the face – the beams.

The barn had ropes; she'd seen them only a couple of days ago while searching for a yard broom. She knew how to tie a noose and preferred not to remember why. Then all she'd have to do was climb onto the wardrobe, secure it to the highest beam, place it around her neck and jump. Over in a second. A flash of guilt crossed her mind in the knowledge Lana would find her body. Suicides were never pretty. But on the plus side, they'd have all her money and the farm. They would have their freedom. As would she.

The church bells from the village clanged six, which meant the farm workers would have gone home for the evening. She had fourteen hours to herself. Slipping on her shoes, Iris ran down the stairs and across the courtyard, heading to the river. The sky was ripples of tangerine and peach, an inconvenient reminder of how beautiful the world could be. The scent of spring flowers and afternoon sunshine twisted the knife, throwing a scattering of butterflies and bumblebees into the mix. At the riverbank, the Dão rushed past, bouncing off rocks and shimmering like silver in the final rays of light. The ambience seemed almost romantic, the ideal background to say goodbye. She tugged off her ring, kissed it and hurled it as far as she could across the water. It glinted once and was gone. She didn't even see it splash. *I love you, Sal.*

Crickets and frogs chorused through the meadow, in an ironic form of applause as she marched uphill. She ignored them and yanked open the barn door. The latch was getting stiffer, she'd have to mention it to Nestor tomorrow. *Ah.*

The shock of what she was about to do stopped her in her tracks. Something moved in the dusty shadows and every muscle in her body tensed. A brindle cat unwound herself from the woven pannier Lana used to collect eggs, sauntered past Iris and out into the sunset.

She shook herself and selected a length of medium rope the farmhands used for delineating vegetable patches. Footsteps sounded on gravel and Iris spun on her heel, reaching for her knife. Her pocket was empty.

"I came to see what you thought of the rice." Lana bent to stroke the cat. "And to check you switched the oven off."

"I'm not hungry, thank you, and you're finished for the day. Have a nice evening."

Lana's sharp eyes took in the rope. "Come, *filha*, let's go inside."

Some kind of embarrassment or politeness forbade Iris to argue. She allowed the older woman to usher her indoors, take the rope from her hands, shoo the cat out and serve a portion of *Arroz de Pato*. Iris ate as if she'd never seen food before, only pausing to blow her nose and wipe her constantly leaking eyes.

Lana sat opposite, constant as a lighthouse. "That machine, the one that scared you so much? It belongs to Alonso at A Pantera Rosa. Belonged, I should say, after Nestor's target practice. Some salesman flogged it to him for a stupid amount of money and he decided to use it for the community. His idea, and I suppose he meant it well, was to create a film of his friends and customers going about their business. Alonso is a good man who talks too much and thinks too little. Eat, Iris, I can see the colour in your cheeks for the first time today."

Iris obeyed, relishing every mouthful.

"I made Nestor pick up what was left of that machine and take it to the police station for a full confession. Alonso was already there, making a complaint about losing his property. That man," she shook her head, "paid over a thousand Euros for a flying camera. This is what men do when left unsupervised. After much debate, the police officer kicked them both out and they settled the dispute over several bottles of Super Bock. Nestor came home half an hour ago and I put him straight to bed. He's such a sentimental drunk."

"He's a very sweet man," said Iris, scooping up the last grains of rice. "That meal was exactly what I needed. Thank you, Lana."

Neither spoke for several minutes and as the sun set, the light threw shades of gold and grey across the table. The two women shifted in their seats to gaze at the dusk, peaceful in each other's silence.

"This is your home," said Lana, softly. "A place of security where you can always return. Nestor and I will nurture this land as we have always done. One day, A Quinta Douro is going to be enough for you and you will want to stay. But I don't believe that time is now. You are full of energy, drive, curiosity and have unfinished business. I can feel your restlessness, Iris."

"My name isn't really ..."

"I don't want to know. What I do know is that you have a strong sense of right and wrong. Promise me you will think hard about what a difference you can make. Don't waste your life on the past, because the past never changes. That gets very boring. I'm going home now before it's dark. Whatever you choose, I will never judge you. Goodnight."

"Goodnight, and thank you."

The older woman scooped up the rope as casually as if it was her coat. When she opened the door to leave, a goat bleated, the cat yowled and a scent of flowers filled the air.

"Lana?"

"Yes?"

"You remind me of my mother."

"There is no finer compliment. Sleep well, *filha*."

"You too. See you in the morning. Oh, and tell Nestor he needs to oil that barn door."

Dear Reader

Thank you for reading GOLD DRAGON. I hope you enjoyed Olivia's adventures in Southeast Asia and beyond. Her mental state after years on the run is now fragile. Will she heed Lana's words and look to the future instead of dwelling on the past? We'll soon find out in her next adventure, PEARL MOON, coming early 2023. Turn the page to read the first chapter.

PEARL MOON - CHAPTER 1

Dear Ms Simons

Thank you for your application. I am sorry to say it was unsuccessful on this occasion. The board acknowledges your enthusiasm for helping the disadvantaged girls and women of Angola. However, we seek individuals with immediately useful skills to offer. Self-defence training, fluency in Portuguese and being a native English speaker is not sufficient to become an instructor and/or teacher at our facility. Your combat experience appears little more than anecdotal, since you provide no official training records or references. Neither do you mention TEFL certificates or similar proof of your ability to teach languages. We strongly discourage charity tourism or 'voluntourism' as the long-term effects prove harmful to the work we are trying to do.

If you wish to support us in a practical sense, please find attached a blank invoice where you can donate to our charitable fund.

We thank you for your interest in our project.

The fourth rejection in as many weeks. For the first time in her life, Iris wasn't good enough. She threw the letter into the bin with a curse. It took a few minutes of wrestling with her ego before she retrieved it, smoothed it out and placed it on top of the others lying on her bedroom desk. She had to learn from these refusals and make her next application better.

She knew what an asset she could be to these NGOs, but to be fair, they didn't. Why should her truncated CV portray her as anything other than a hobbyist do-gooder, ticking items off a bucket list? Her difficulty was providing any kind of certificates for Iris Simons, an alias who had only come into existence at the end of last year. If only she were able to demonstrate the background, experience and qualifications of Olivia Jones, every one of these organisations would compete to employ her. She frowned at her tediously repetitive thought patterns. *You are Iris Simons. Olivia Jones no longer exists.*

The heat of the afternoon subsided and within the hour, the three farmhands would return from their lunch break and come buzzing down the lane on their mopeds. Nestor had already fired up the tractor and Lana was probably already in the orchard, getting on with the fruit picking. The agricultural calendar could not be postponed, not for anything or anyone. Irritable and disappointed, Iris planted her straw hat on her head and stomped across the farmyard with her baskets. Against her will, her dejection lifted. This was her favourite time of day. The heady mixture of fragrance from the farmhouse roses mingled with honeysuckle, lemon verbena and bright pots of sweet peas. Lilac and buddleia bushes lured a buzzing crowd of various bees and silent balletic butterflies. Iris inhaled the warm afternoon air and gazed down to the river. The sweeping meadow was shorn of its swaying grasses, now cropped, baled and ready to be stored in the barn as winter fodder. Trees along the riverbank were beginning to change colour, hinting that last year's autumnal display might well be outdone by this year's fireworks. Squeals and shrieks from upstream made Iris smile. Teenagers at 'The Beach', or in other words, one of the widest and most accessible sections of the River Dão, were making the most of the long, lazy days of late summer.

In the orchard, the stepladder she had used that morning was still resting against a plum tree and Lana was yet to arrive. She placed a cushion of grasses in the base of her basket, climbed the ladder and continued plucking plums, humming a half-remembered tune.

"Someone's in a good mood." Lana, sturdy and calm, swayed through the knee-length grasses, wearing an apron with her hair was tied up in a scarf. She reminded Iris of wartime photographs of land girls.

"Hard not to be when you're outside on a day like this. I've almost done this tree."

"A fine crop of plums we picked this year. Last year was even better but we had to let them fall and rot. Nestor and I couldn't manage the harvest alone. Since you took over the farm, everything's coming up roses." She smiled, shielding her eyes to look up at Iris.

"I hardly 'took over' the farm. You still have to tell me what to do and how to do it. Right, that's a basketful. Shall I give you a hand with the pears?"

"No, I can manage the pears and quince myself. I think we've got enough plums and our hedge fruits will last another week. Why don't you start on the peaches? You have a delicate touch so I trust you not to bruise them."

The two women worked in silence other than the odd alter-cation with a wasp. On the slopes above, Nestor and the farmhands moved up and down the vines, cropping enough A Quinta Douro grapes to fill the community containers. Tomor-row, a truck would come around to collect their harvest, check its weight and give them a receipt which could be exchanged for money or the equivalent in local wine.

The sun sank and the air cooled. Thin clouds on the horizon took on hues of nectarine, apricot, fig and blueberry, or perhaps Iris had been in the orchard too long. She and Lana lugged their baskets back to the house amongst the sounds of cicadas and into the chill of the pantry.

"Tonight, we eat fresh fruit," said Lana, her skin glowing from the sun. "Tomorrow, we make cakes, jam, *marmelada*, pickles and jars for the winter. That's assuming you will be here tomorrow? I saw the postman came this morning."

Iris collected a bowl of plums and peaches for breakfast, marvelling that she was not yet sick of the things. "Not only tomorrow, I'll still be here this time next year. Yet another NGO refused me. My skills are insufficient." The bitterness in her tone was audible.

Lana finished wrapping apples, quince and pears in brown paper then stretched with a sigh. "Do you have something to eat for this evening? I can whip up an omelette with ham and tomatoes before I leave."

"I'm not completely helpless, Lana. You're very kind, but I can feed myself." They emerged into the dusky light of the kitchen. "Go home, look after your husband. I'll see you in the morning."

Lana cleaned the sink and work surfaces, then switched on the kitchen lamp. "Iris, you have so much talent and intelligence. You are a hard worker and quick learner. These charity companies must be desperate for someone like you. If they are turning you down, you've approached them in the wrong way."

Iris was affronted. "What do you mean by that?"

"Let me ask you a question. When applying for a job, are you selling yourself or meeting the employer's needs?"

"I'm not selling anything. It's a volunteer position! They should ..." Iris bit her tongue.

"They should be grateful? Perhaps. You want to work in a Portuguese-speaking country in Africa, yes? How much do you know about Angola, Moçambique or Cabo Verde? How can you be sure you have what they need?" Lana's voice remained steady and she seemed to be waiting for an answer.

"My problem is ..."

"Your problems do not concern them. They have plenty of their own. You must understand how these non-governmental agencies operate, who they want and why. You cannot send off your resumé and hope they will beg you to come and save them. That's not how it works. Take out your little computer, dig into the company ethics, find out which skills they seek and tailor your letter exactly like a job application. You need someone to pick fruit? I am an expert. You want someone to raise chickens? Not a problem. Dig wells, patrol fences, drive to market, plant crops, I am your all-round handywoman. Look at it from their side, Iris, not yours." She pulled her shawl over her shoulders and went to the door. "Don't eat much more fruit tonight or you'll spend half the night on the toilet. *Até amanhã.*"

"*Até amanhã.*" Iris sat on her own in the kitchen for another hour, until the sky turned inky blue, considering Lana's words. Then she made herself an omelette, took a notepad from the office and started again.

ACKNOWLEDGMENTS

Abundant thanks Liam Klenk and his generous insights regarding Macau. Much gratitude to Gillian Hamer and Florian Bielmann for expert editorial and technical advice. To Paul Lewis and Rob Evans for their fascinating book 'Undercover', I am in your debt. As ever, I express my appreciation for superb cover designer JD Smith and attention to detail from Julia Gibbs.

ALSO BY JJ MARSH

Other titles in the Run and Hide series

WHITE HERON

BLACK RIVER

My Beatrice Stubbs series, European crime dramas

BEHIND CLOSED DOORS

RAW MATERIAL

TREAD SOFTLY

COLD PRESSED

HUMAN RITES

BAD APPLES

SNOW ANGEL

HONEY TRAP

BLACK WIDOW

WHITE NIGHT

THE WOMAN IN THE FRAME

ALL SOULS' DAY

My standalone novels

AN EMPTY VESSEL

ODD NUMBERS

WOLF TONES

And a short-story collection

APPEARANCES GREETING A POINT OF VIEW

For occasional updates, news, deals and a FREE exclusive novella, subscribe to my newsletter on www.jjmarshauthor.com

If you would recommend this book to a friend, please do so by writing a review. Your tip helps other readers discover their next favourite read. Your review can be short and only takes a minute.

Thank you.

Made in United States
Orlando, FL
10 December 2023

40326307R00155